RUNAWAY HEARTS

ALEXA ASTON

OLIVER
HEBER
BOOKS

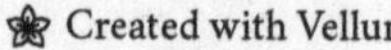

PROLOGUE
NEW YORK CITY—1865

Rye Callahan turned the corner from Anthony Street and found himself back in Paradise Square, the intersection of Five Points in New York. He glanced around at the area known for decades for its flourishing crime rate and houses of ill repute. The streets teemed with people this hot July day. He veered to his right and continued down Cross Street, knowing only two blocks remained until he reached home.

Home.

The crowded tenement would never be home again. Not with Bri dead. Nothing would ever be the same without his older brother's hearty laugh and gentle teasing. The sibling he'd idolized from birth and who'd kept him from a life in the gangs lay buried these past two years in an early grave. Guilt washed over him.

He held a hand up to shield the strong summer sun from his eyes as he stared down the familiar street, laundry hanging from windows and along railings. He'd left for the war a little more than two years ago, already over six feet at age fifteen. The recruiter didn't ask many questions, not with the draft riots rampant throughout the city. The Union needed soldiers— and not many volunteered two years into a bloody war that looked like it would go on longer than even the politicians predicted.

Rye continued down the street until he arrived at the tenement house. Dread filled him as he entered the darkened building and moved up rickety stairs that might give way any minute under his weight. The smells of old urine, spilled whiskey, and rat droppings assailed his senses.

He climbed to the top floor and hesitated before knocking. He anticipated the greeting he'd receive. His ma would be as cold as a blustery winter's day. And that was if she were in a good mood. She'd always favored her older son to the extreme. He knew she'd taken Bri's death hard. Da would be all smiles despite the fact the consumption had set in, rendering him unable to work.

Knocking once, he decided to plunge in and take whatever venom Ma might spew at him. He stepped through the entrance and closed the door behind him.

She looked up from her ironing, a sour look on her lined face. No greeting. No hugs. Just a shrug of a bony shoulder.

"You're expectin' to be fed, I'd imagine," she said brusquely. "Money's tight. Not much to be had around here. You'd best be on your way. We have no need of you."

Before he could speak, the door opened. His father shuffled into the single room from the hallway, a bucket of water in his hands. He broke out in a huge grin.

"Rye, me boyo!" He set the bucket down, sloshing water on the floor, ignoring his wife's rebuke as he folded his son into his arms.

"You're a sight for sore eyes, that you are."

Rye saw tears brimming in his da's eyes and knew they mirrored his own. He wrapped his arms around the old man, frightened by how thin he'd become and how sparse his white hair was.

His ma glared daggers at their reunion. Rye realized she wouldn't have mentioned her own son's return to her husband. She now trembled with rage and it exploded. She slammed the iron down.

"How dare you show him any affection, Seamus! He killed our boyo. *Our* boyo!" She bared her teeth at Rye as if she were a rabid dog. "I can't stand the sight of you. Get out! And don't come back."

Releasing his da, he faced her. "Don't you know I live with the guilt with every breath I take? That Bri is gone while I'm still here? You can't hate me anymore than I hate myself, Ma. I relive it over and over. The shot. The pain. Falling to the ground, helpless as a babe. Seeing that damned Johnny Reb charging me, his bayonet flashing in the sun."

He choked at the battlefield memory. "And Bri. Stepping in the way. Raising his gun to cut the bastard down."

"Now, now, Boyo," his father said, patting Rye's shoulder. "It was always Bri's way, to look after you. It's not your fault his gun jammed."

Rye turned to his da. "But death was meant for me that day. That bayonet should've cut *me* down. Not Bri. At least some lucky Billy Yank got to his gun in time and killed the Reb."

Harsh laughter bubbled from his ma. "Oh, now that's priceless, comin' from you."

"Sinead. Don't," Da begged.

"Don't? *Don't?* I blessed will say my piece, Seamus Callahan and you can't stop me. I'm tired of all the lies."

"Please. I beg you."

Rye saw the utter despair on his da's face as it crumpled in defeat. He turned back to his ma.

She waved a fist at him. "You, boyo, are the bastard!

The *real* bastard. You got my only son killed. All he ever did was take care of you. Bri wasn't your brother, you fool. He was your cousin. We're not your parents."

The pit of his belly turned cold. Stunned, he stared at the woman before him, her features twisted in rage and triumph.

"Your aunt Adeline is your mother. Your real da knocked her up and then raced off to California to get rich quick. She never heard from the blighter again. She waited and waited but no blighter with a fortune of gold ever showed up to claim you and sweep her away."

"Aunt Adeline... is my ma?"

The woman who'd raised him laughed like a hyena. "The one and only. Took off to look for him, she did, leaving us stuck with her mistake. She wrote one letter after she'd been gone a year and said you were better off without her. Then your da waltzed back and knocked up a few more fools in the neighborhood. Who knows how many bastard brothers you have, with those crazy golden eyes?"

"Enough, Sinead," said Da, who'd sunk to the floor in misery.

"Enough is right, Seamus. I've done more than enough for this bloody bastard and your selfish whore of a sister." She paused, her eyes narrowing. "When I get back, you better be gone, Zachariah Callahan. Good riddance!"

Sinead Callahan stormed from the room. Rye could hear her stomping down the stairs as he stood rooted to the ground, stunned at what he'd learned. He looked over to the man who'd always been a wonderful father to him.

"I can explain, Rye."

"No."

The silence fell heavily between them as Rye stared at the man who'd become a stranger in mere seconds.

At least he now understood why Sinead had treated him as she had all these years.

Because he was a bastard whose parents abandoned him.

He finally summoned his voice. "I trusted you all my life. Loved you. Thought no man could hold a candle to you. And all you did was lie to me. Over and over. Year after year." Rye shook his head. "I don't have a father. Especially not you."

Seamus Callahan looked at him in anguish. He started to speak, and then his hands flew to his chest. He gripped his shirtfront, clawing at it in desperation, then let out a soft moan as he fell over.

Dead.

Rye knew Sinead Callahan would put the blame of another death squarely on his shoulders. Though he longed to touch the man who'd been his da and give him a last kiss goodbye, Rye refused to honor a liar.

He slipped quietly from the room without a backward glance.

Emma Bradford thanked her father's valet for bringing in the breakfast tray and dismissed him with an assurance that Dwight Bradford would eat something. As the servant left, she turned to her father.

"Don't make a bald-faced liar of me, Papa. You must eat. You need to keep up your strength."

She held up a buttered toast point but he waved it away.

"I'm not hungry, Child."

Her old friend Guilt snuggled up next to her, her constant companion since the carriage accident five years earlier that cost her father the use of his legs.

"What will Cook say? You don't want to hurt her feelings."

He gave her a smile. "Cook doesn't care if I eat or not, as long as she gets paid."

"That's a dreadful thing to say, Papa." She set down the toast and picked up the cup from its saucer. "At least take some coffee. Dr. Kinder believes coffee gives you energy." She doctored it with sugar and a generous splash of cream.

"Dr. Kinder is an old fool, but I'll take a few sips to please you."

Emma helped him nurse the hot brew until the cup was emptied, glad at least to get something down him.

"We need to talk, Emma."

She smiled. "We talk all the time, Papa. About politics. Books. The mill. And I know you love listening to my stories."

Dwight Bradford closed his eyes, a trace of a smile on his lips. "Ah, my own Scheherazade. Who knows how many stories you've invented for me over the years? We've important things to discuss, though. I want to talk to you about my will."

Immediately, Emma lifted her chin. "We're not going to be morbid."

"No," her father assured her. "Merely practical. Louisa has been at me— again— to change my will." He looked sheepish. "In fact, I may have given her the wrong impression that I actually did."

She narrowed her eyes. "You know Louisa is not one of my favorite topics. I tried to warn you about that...nurse."

He sighed. "I know. You overheard her talking with her cousin John about marrying me."

"For your money! She doesn't love you, Papa."

His features softened. "Louisa cares for me. In her own way. It's only right she should be taken care of, the way she's devoted herself to me in my ill health."

"I could have continued to care for you as before," she pointed out.

"No, Dr. Kinder said with my heart problems on top of the paralysis, I needed constant professional care. Louisa has been attentive to me and my needs." He gave Emma a fond smile. "Besides, if not for her, how would John have come into your life?"

Emma smiled at the mention of John Fairburn. A distant cousin of her stepmother, she hadn't trusted

John at first, simply because she hadn't trusted Louisa from the moment they'd met. Moreover, John seemed far too handsome and sophisticated to be interested in someone like Emma.

But she'd had a change of heart in recent weeks, as John started courting her in earnest. Yesterday afternoon in the park, he'd even told her he loved her. The thought caused a thrill to wriggle along her spine.

"You're right, Papa, as always. It pleases me that John and I met and have grown close."

He raised his brows. "Close? Has he made certain feelings known to you?"

She nodded. "He says he loves me. And I may just love him."

Emma thought back to the young man she'd thought she loved five years ago, the one they'd been on their way to see when the horrific carriage accident occurred. It left Emma with a badly broken leg and months of recovery, while Dwight Bradford never walked again.

Had she really been falling in love with Howard, and he with her?

She couldn't remember her exact feelings, only that after visiting her twice in the weeks after the accident, Howard lost interest and stopped coming. Only a few months later, he became engaged to her good friend, Sarah, who'd known about Emma's feelings toward Howard.

But that was in her past.

"I know John will do the right thing and help you look after Louisa once I'm gone. She knows I've settled a monthly allowance upon her in my will, but the bulk of the estate goes to you, my darling girl. I'm only sorry that David is not here to take over at the mill and continue the Bradford name."

Her heart ached hearing her beloved brother's name. "David died an honorable death at Gettysburg, Papa. The Union was saved because of men such as David making the ultimate sacrifice."

"I know, but you must go and live *your* life, Emma. Don't be tied to me and this house any longer. Follow your heart, dear, whether that means pursuing your music or traveling far and wide."

He reached for her hand and squeezed it. "Promise me you'll spread your wings and fly to the moon, my sweet girl. If you wish for John Fairburn to be by your side, then I hope he is as faithful and loving a companion as your mother was to me."

Another flash of guilt ripped through her at the mention of her mother. After one son and several miscarriages spaced out over a dozen years, Darlena Bradford gave birth to Emma and promptly died two days later from complications after childbirth. Emma did everything she could over the years to make it up to her lonely father, finally silencing her protests when she saw he was dead set upon marrying his caregiver.

"If John proposes marriage— and I think he may— then I will hopefully capture what you and Mother had together."

He nodded. "I'd... like that."

She patted his hand, noting how sallow his skin appeared today. "I've tired you. You need to get some rest."

"Stay. For a little while," he asked.

"All right."

She sat as he shut his eyes, listening to his labored breathing. Louisa dominated his time in the sickroom, constantly by his side, so to share this rare, uninterrupted moment with him early in the morning was a treat.

Her thoughts scattered in all directions until a loud

gasp drew her back to reality. She leaned forward and took his hand, noting how he struggled with each breath. She decided it was time to call for Dr. Kinder when he gripped her hand tightly.

Then his grip loosened. He gave a heavy sigh— and breathed no more.

Tears sprang to her eyes but she felt gratitude in her heart that it was she and not Louisa with him at the end. She sat for several minutes, his hand in hers, allowing the grief to wash over her.

Finally, she composed herself and leaned over to kiss his brow one more time. She couldn't put it off any longer. She rose to find her stepmother and break the news to her.

Emma thought she might find Louisa at her desk in the library, since she often met with Cook at the beginning of each week to plan out the menus. She walked along the carpeted corridor, her heart heavy at the news she would share.

As Emma reached an alcove just off the main stairway, she heard whispers and smiled, despite her heavy heart. Last week, she'd caught her maid, Molly, kissing a footman in the small space, and it wasn't the chaste kiss John had bestowed upon Emma's lips yesterday. She hoped their butler, Moses, wouldn't find out about the stolen moments the two servants partook in while secreted in the alcove, and dismiss one or the both of them on the spot.

The low, throaty laugh caused her to stop dead in her tracks.

Louisa.

No one in the household had such a suggestive tone when amused.

Emma took a few steps back, grateful for the plush carpeting that muffled any noise from her shoes.

"I've tried. Over and over. But the fool refuses to

change his will. He assures me I'll want for nothing, but I'm not going to settle for a modest monthly sum that won't even cover the cost of a few new hats. I've put my time in. He owes me more."

"You don't have to worry, love. I'll simply marry Emma. Her money will become mine. *And then ours.*"

"What if she won't marry you? If she suspects us? She's no fool, John."

"All women are romantic fools, darling. Emma is no exception. And besides…accidents *do* happen."

Emma heard quiet laughter before a long pause. Then a moan. Disgusted, she reversed her direction and returned to her bedroom.

John and Louisa were lovers. The realization brought a sudden wave of nausea to her. She fought it, not wanting to give in to even a tiny bit of pity. She swallowed hard, forcing down the bile and her wounded pride.

She should have figured it out long ago. They probably weren't even cousins as they claimed.

Fear filled her. She had no one to turn to. Her father could no longer protect her. She knew John Fairburn would press his suit and try to marry her as soon as her mourning period ended.

If she allowed that to happen, he would kill her. As clever as John was, Emma knew it would appear to be an accident, especially as clumsy as she was. She was known for falling and tripping. All sorts of crazy things had occurred in the past, from breaking her collarbone to twisting her ankle. She'd even run smack into a tree once and chipped her front baby tooth.

She needed to escape. From John and Louisa. From this house. Her father had encouraged her to follow her heart. She intended to do so with the promised inheritance. By this time next week, she planned to be far from Connecticut.

A piercing scream invaded her thoughts. Louisa must have discovered Dwight Bradford's now cold body.

"Emmeline!"

CHAPTER TWO

$\mathcal{E}$mma helped shepherd the last visitor out the door. The whirlwind of the last few days was close to an end, with her father's funeral taking place this morning at ten, followed by a small reception in their Connecticut home.

With the final guest taking his leave, the inevitable reading of the will would take place. She reentered the drawing room and catching Daniel Mitchell's eye, signaled the lawyer with a nod.

He cleared his throat loudly and the servants scurrying around came to a standstill. Louisa looked up from where she languished on a green velvet settee, giving a pout as the attention turned from her. Emma turned away, finding it harder and harder to hide her true feelings about her stepmother.

"I would ask that I be joined in the library at this time for the reading of Mr. Bradford's will. Mrs. Bradford? Miss Emma? Mr. Stannis? And Moses and Dawson, as well. Would you please accompany me?

John rushed to her side. "Might I join you, Emma?" He gave her a tender look. "I'd like to give you whatever support I can."

She tamped down the repulsion his nearness brought and gave him a false smile.

"Would you be so kind as to see to Louisa? She hasn't fared well these past few days. Papa's death has upset her greatly. I fear she needs a steady hand to walk even a few steps without collapse."

He bowed. "I will see to Mrs. Bradford at once."

Emma watched John scurry to his lover's side. She stifled the anger that raged within her at their deceit. At least they would soon get their comeuppance.

The group assembled in what had been her father's favorite room until the accident left him bedridden and relegated to an upstairs suite. Filled with over a thousand books and comfortable seating throughout, the library grew to be Emma's refuge once Louisa's presence dominated their household. She'd spent many hours here— reading, knitting, and writing in her journal.

She took a place on a gold brocaded sofa as everyone gathered, annoyed when Louisa plopped next to her. John came to stand behind them, his left hand resting on her shoulder. Emma didn't bother to check if his other comforted Louisa. She was certain it did.

Mr. Mitchell said, "I've served as Dwight Bradford's attorney and business manager for as long as I can remember. We were both wet behind the ears when our business relationship began. I am honored to state that it turned into one of deep, abiding friendship, as well. I shall miss Dwight until my dying day.

"With that being said, let us proceed to the matter at hand."

Emma watched the firelight dance in the grate as the family attorney read the legal language in a slow, lugubrious tone. He droned on for several minutes before he paused.

"That, in effect, is the legality of the document, so

that all present know Dwight Bradford was of sound mind when he executed his will. I shan't read word for word now. Instead, I will simply state in everyday language his bequests. The document itself will be available for perusal at your request, should the need arise."

Mitchell adjusted his spectacles and smoothed the pages before him. "There are several gifts to local charities that Dwight supported, as well as his church. I won't go into detail regarding these bequeathals. For every servant in service at Bradford House five years or longer, a small cash amount will be awarded, with a stipulated bonus for each year beyond the five served."

He glanced at the butler and housekeeper. "To Moses, his butler for over two decades, and Dawson, his housekeeper for even longer, Mr. Bradford provided additional funds to be available upon your retirement from Bradford House so that your golden years will be untroubled by financial worries."

Both servants nodded. Emma was pleased when Moses shot her a grateful smile, while Dawson gave her a wink.

"As to his mill manager, Ralph Stannis, Mr. Bradford wished for him to continue in his present position and has gifted him with ten percent of the company's stock, in gratitude for his wise counsel and business acumen."

"*Ten percent?*" Louisa hissed under her breath. "What was he thinking?"

Emma sat rock still. She didn't want to respond to Louisa's rude whisperings, knowing all too well the outburst that would soon follow.

"Finally, to his beloved family. To his dear second wife, Louisa, Dwight wished her to live a life of comfort here at Bradford House for the rest of her natural days. She will not be held responsible for any of the maintenance and upkeep of the estate, nor the salaries of the various servants, which will be maintained by the estate itself.

"Mrs. Bradford will keep all her clothing, jewelry, and furs and be given an allowance of two hundred dollars per month to spend as she sees fit. This will continue until her death or remarriage, and then said allowance and residence at Bradford House will cease to be provided."

Louisa drew in a loud, quick breath. Emma saw her clutch her folded hands until they turned white. She didn't dare look at her stepmother.

Yet Emma thought her father's provision quite generous. Two hundred dollars would be considered a small fortune, far above what the average worker earned in an entire calendar year. For Louisa to receive that amount each month with no expenses to pay, she would be incredibly well off. Emma also thought it only fair that if Louisa did remarry, her new husband would assume financial responsibility for her.

Still, she could feel the waves of fury emanating from the former nurse. Her stepmother obviously felt more than slighted by the terms of her late husband's will.

"The remainder of the estate in its entirety shall go to Miss Emmeline Bradford, the only living child of Dwight and Darlena Bradford. This includes the mill and the land it sits upon, Bradford House and its grounds, along with various real estate holdings and stock, both within the company and through other investments Mr. Bradford made over the years."

John's hand tightened painfully on her shoulder before it relaxed and gave her a brief squeeze. She saw Louisa ball her fists in her lap and sensed the trembles coming from her.

Mr. Mitchell thanked each of them. The servants and Mr. Stannis made a quick exit, no doubt wishing to be absent from the emotional outburst that would erupt from Louisa's lips at any moment.

"Emma?"

She looked up and saw Mr. Mitchell motion her over. She went to speak privately with him.

"I hope you will consider retaining my services as both attorney and business manager and advisor. Your father's estate can be complicated at times and you don't have any practical experience in running a business solely on your own."

He bestowed a kind smile on her. "Despite that, I know you were your father's shadow for many years. I realize you know more about the mill and business in general than people might think, since you discussed financial decisions with your father over many years. I know you are on first-name terms with most of the workers and that they think highly of you."

"Rest assured, Mr. Mitchell. I will be making no changes in the near future and am delighted Papa has enticed Mr. Stannis to stay on at the mill. I expect both you and him to be in my employ for many years to come."

"That's your first wise business decision, Emma," he joked. "Your father did mention to me the last time we spoke that you might want to travel in the near future. Is that still the case?"

She nodded. Papa must have known she'd need to escape Bradford House and Louisa's wrath upon his death.

"There are certainly funds for you to access to do so." He glanced toward Louisa and John, their heads together as they spoke. "Having a little breathing space as you mourn his death might be a good idea."

"I plan on taking a trip almost immediately." She hesitated. "I'd rather Louisa— and John— not know my exact itinerary. Much less my final destination."

"Understood."

"I'd rather not be overheard at this point." She leaned in and whispered, "But if you'll have your carriage just outside Mama's garden in an hour, you can take me to the train station. I can explain on the way."

The attorney gave her a fatherly hug. "I'll be waiting," he said softly.

She parted from him and Louisa caught her eye. Emma made her way toward her stepmother, her heart racing as the plan was now set in motion.

"Oh, my dearest Emmeline." Louisa took Emma's hand. "I'm so glad we have each other for comfort in such a time of sorrow. Loving your papa was simply my entire world. I don't know where to begin without him."

Louisa brightened. "But we will be together, my sweet child." Her low laugh that followed seemed out of place to Emma. "Of course, we are more as sisters than a stepmama and child. There aren't so many years between us, you know. I plan to be at your side, every step of the way, helping you make whatever decisions you must regarding Dwight's estate and the mill."

Emma seethed at her words but put on a look of wonderment. "I'm so surprised Papa left everything to me, Louisa, but surely you can see how he loved you. He's left you very well off. You won't have to worry about dull business decisions. I know how talking business bores you."

Louisa widened her eyes at that statement.

"I, too, shall be here, Emma. You know you may always count on me." John sidled up to her more than Louisa had, like a purring tabby wishing to be stroked.

Emma wished she could give him a cold shoulder, but she didn't want the pair suspicious of her actions.

"I appreciate your kind words, John." She frowned and touched her temple. "This day has left me exhausted. I feel a headache coming on. I believe I'll go to my room for the remainder of the afternoon."

She smiled politely at them both. "Please feel free to dine without me. I'm not hungry, but Molly can always bring me a tray if I change my mind. I'm ready to fall into bed right this moment."

Louisa kissed her cheek, as did John, and both encouraged her to get her rest. Emma could just imagine what their talk at dinner might be. Or their pillow talk in Louisa's bed tonight.

She didn't care. When they awoke in the morning, she'd be long gone.

Hurrying to her room, she threw a few items of clothing into a small carpetbag which she hadn't wanted to pack earlier. She didn't want Louisa or any of the servants privy to her planned escape. Her knitting needles and yarn, jewelry, and treasured journal went into her reticule, which already contained close to eighty dollars. That would see her through for the moment. She would arrange with Daniel Mitchell on the way to the train station how to contact him in order to withdraw funds while she traveled.

Emma had thoroughly enjoyed the trip she took with her father throughout Italy and France several years ago. She longed to return to Europe and go to operas, plays, and museums— but that would be what Louisa might expect. Instead, she'd decided to head in the opposite direction.

To the American West.

She was ready for adventure and new experiences. She'd heard cities such as San Francisco and Denver were thriving cosmopolitan areas, already bursting with culture and business. She'd go to both cities and see what they held. Maybe she could continue her voice lessons there or even take up painting, something that interested her.

A slight tap on the door sounded and Molly slipped in.

"I'm here to pack your trunk, Miss Emma. I know to keep it well out of sight from the likes of *her*." The maid sniffed. "I'll bring it to New York with me to-morrow afternoon. Have you decided where you'll be?"

"Papa used to stay at Astor House when he went into the city for business. I'm sure he's mentioned it to Louisa, so she'd think of that. The Metropolitan and The Fifth Avenue Hotels are far too well known, so I've decided to stay at The Gilsey at Broadway and East Twenty-ninth."

She opened her lingerie drawer and withdrew a sealed envelope. "In this is money for your train ticket into the city and other incidentals. Be sure you pack your things in my trunk. That way we'll only have the one to deal with."

Molly took the envelope and slipped it inside her blouse. "I'm excited…but just a bit scared, Miss Emma."

She hugged the maid. "Truth be told, I am, too. Pack lightly. We can buy whatever we need once we arrive."

"Where are we off to?" Molly smiled. "I might need to let a certain footman know."

Emma shook her head. "All in good time, Molly. There's no sharing to be done now. You can write a letter to him once we've reached our destination."

She turned and retrieved her carpetbag. "Remember, bring up a tray for me when they dine so they'll think I'm still here. Do the same for breakfast. Tell anyone who asks in the morning that I'm still doing poorly. You can even mention that I need the time to grieve."

Checking the watch pinned to her blouse, Emma slipped her reticule over her wrist. "I've got to hurry in order to make my train. Check the hallway, Molly."

Her trusted servant opened the door and looked both ways. "All clear, Miss Emma."

The two women flew down the corridor. Emma thought her beating heart might leap from her chest. Its drumming almost pained her. They reached the back staircase and sailed silently down the carpeted stairs. When they reached the bottom, Emma shot across to the small parlor.

The room had belonged to her mother. She caught up on her correspondence there. Planned menus. Sent invitations to friends. But more importantly, French doors opened onto a small garden. Her mother had loved flowers and opened those doors often, allowing the scent of roses to waft through.

Without a backward glance, she opened the door leading outside, trusting Molly to close it behind her. Emma raced along the edge of the path to an almost hidden gate and pushed it open. She looked up and saw Daniel Mitchell's waiting carriage as expected. Fastening the gate, she hurried toward it. The coachman assisted her up the steps and closed the door.

As she fell into the seat and expelled a long breath, the lawyer chuckled.

"I do believe this is the second-best decision you've made today, Emma Bradford."

CHAPTER THREE

New York City—1878

RYE CALLAHAN BREATHED in the familiar smells of New York. He'd left the city behind thirteen years earlier and never looked back. That day, a tired boy of seventeen returning home from a bloody war discovered his parents were actually his aunt and uncle. What Rye learned from a cruel Sinead Callahan about his true origins one long-ago afternoon changed his life forever.

The war taught him to think fast on his feet. He'd left the only home he'd known without a backward glance, carrying with him guilt over causing his cousin's death and possibly being responsible for his uncle dropping dead before his eyes. The pain inside him remained raw, never healing. He'd decided from that moment on never to let himself get close to another soul.

But at least he'd found a purpose in life.

Rye headed to the Pinkerton National Detective Agency's New York branch, wondering what his next case might involve. The summons from The Eye himself led Rye to believe it must be important. Alan Pinkerton usually allowed his two superintendents, George Bangs and Francis Warner, to assign cases. The Eye still enjoyed being out in the field, supervising agents and bringing outlaws to justice. For him to wire Rye to hand off his current investigation to another agent in Wyoming and return at once to the New York office made him extremely curious.

He turned the corner and spied a familiar head of curly blond hair heading down the street from the opposite direction. They reached the office building at the same time.

"Well, son of a gun! If it isn't Zachariah Callahan in the flesh."

Rye broke into a wide grin and pumped the man's large hand. "Eddie McLeod. It's been ages. I see you've grown a beard."

McLeod slapped him on the back. "You've made quite a name for yourself, Rye. Last time I was in Chicago, George wouldn't stop raving about you. Sounds like you're the number one investigator in his book."

"Ah, Eddie, no one could ever take your place. You taught me everything I know about being a Pink."

They both paused and then chanted in unison.

"Accept no bribes. Never compromise with criminals. Partner with local law enforcement agencies. Refuse divorce cases or cases that initiate scandal."

Both men laughed as Rye continued, "Turn down reward money. Never raise fees without the client's pre-knowledge."

"And keep clients apprised on an on-going basis," finished Eddie. "The Pinkerton Code. Verbatim."

Rye gave his friend and mentor a hug and they entered the building and started up the staircase.

"Are you still working mostly out of Chicago?" Rye asked.

Eddie nodded. "Lately, I've been investigating a series of shipping thefts for Midwestern railways. The Rock Island. The Illinois Central. I hear you've been out West chasing bank and train robbers."

"For the last couple of years. That's why I was surprised to get a summons to come all the way to New York for briefing on a case assignment."

Eddie's brows arched. "Really? Same here. Sounds as if we'll work this case together."

They arrived at the offices and entered. Immediately greeted, they were taken to a large conference room and given coffee and pastries. Left alone, they reminisced for several minutes on how they'd met during the Great Fire of '71 and other cases they'd worked together before being sent their separate ways.

"Good morning, gentlemen. It's good to see the two of you."

Rye turned as Francis Warner entered the room. They greeted Warner, who invited them to sit.

"I'm sure you're speculating what your new case is about."

"We'll be working together?" asked Eddie.

"Yes," Warner replied. "You'll be bodyguards for an Italian opera singer, Renata Abetelli. She's scheduled to perform in Denver at a brand-new opera house. Once the Denver run ends, the touring company may hit a few other towns in Colorado, such as Pueblo or Georgetown, before heading to San Francisco. They'll return by way of Salt Lake."

"What are we protecting Miss Abetelli from?" Rye asked.

"The manager of the touring company is worried about the reputation of the Wild West. News of train robberies and bank robbers and cattle thieves has made its way to Europe. Ivar Larsen, the manager, is concerned with Miss Abetelli's safety. While he wishes to bring culture to the far West , he wants to be sure his star is protected at all times."

"I've actually been to the opera several times in both Colorado and California," Rye noted. "Several Italian and German companies have come through in the last few years. Opera's the rage these days. I haven't heard of Miss Abetelli, though."

Eddie grunted. "Opera has no appeal for me. Give me a good Shakespearean comedy or vaudeville any day."

"They have those, too," Rye assured him. "Just because it's called an opera house doesn't mean only opera is performed there. The venues host plays and a variety of entertainment. Some towns even hold community meetings in their local opera houses."

Warner leaned back and lit a cigar. "The Eye happens to be friends with the owner of the establishment. Mr. Devinde's place is new and in direction competition with both Forrester and Turner Halls. He's been able to get this foreign company in for a song, mostly because Larsen is practically broke."

He puffed on the cigar a moment before continuing. "Seems Renata Abetelli is the reason they're so down and out. She's incredibly temperamental. She claims to be sick often and cancels performances on a whim. But she and Larsen need the money, so they've booked this American tour. I don't know much about it, but it seems Americans gobble up anything cultural if it's European. Opera's no exception. She's finishing up a series of performances tonight at the Academy of Music Opera House. I have tickets for you both to attend. You'll meet Miss Abetelli and Mr. Larsen backstage afterward."

Warner laughed, a twinkle in his eyes. "I'm sure you'll form an opinion of Miss Abetelli... very quickly."

~

RENATA ABETELLI COULD CERTAINLY SING, thought Rye.

He watched the soprano as the close of Verdi's *Ernani* played out on the stage in front of him. Abetelli sang the role of the heroine, Elvira, and she had now fallen, grief-stricken, over Ernani's poisoned— and very dead— body.

He looked at a glazed-eyed Eddie McLeod seated on his right and leaned close.

"Have you perfected the art of sleeping without closing your eyelids?"

His friend gave a sheepish shrug as the audience erupted in applause and the orchestra music swelled.

"Three men all in love with one fickle female? Plus, all that quarreling and shouting in Italian? They seemed like damned idiots to me. At least, that's what I got from it. And look— she destroyed them all in the end."

"Or they destroyed each other," commented Rye as they rose and joined in the thunderous applause being showered upon Renata Abetelli and her fellow castmates.

For her part, Renata deigned to give the audience a small smile full of secrets. She blew kisses to the crowd as tossed flowers fell at her feet on the stage. The soprano leaned over and swept one up, waving it triumphantly above her head. Then she gave a smart nod and waltzed off the stage.

Two more curtain calls followed before he and Eddie could make their way backstage. He thought the madhouse behind the scenes made a Civil War battle seem tame.

Rye fought his way through the crowds, Eddie on his heels. After getting directions from a stagehand, they arrived at Renata Abetelli's dressing room.

He rapped his knuckles hard against the door so it could be heard over all the noise.

It opened a crack. Then a little wider. A short, plump woman with iron-gray hair and a slight moustache gave him a withering look.

"I'm Rye Callahan." He gestured to his companion. "This is Edward McLeod. We're with the Pinkerton National Detective Agency and have an appointment with Miss Abetelli."

The woman glared a full ten seconds before speaking. "You wait." She shut the door.

Rye leaned against the doorjamb. "Ivar Larsen thinks he needs us as bodyguards? That pit bull of a woman could keep Jesse James on the straight and narrow."

"You are correct, sir. Are you Mr. Callahan or Mr. McLeod?"

Rye turned and saw a rail-thin man with pale blue eyes and a white mustache that matched his equally white hair.

"Mr. Larsen, I presume?"

The man nodded.

"I'm Rye Callahan." He motioned to his companion. "This is Eddie McLeod. We've been assigned to accompany you and Miss Abetelli to Denver and beyond. We would like to discuss security for the trip, as well as the time your company will spend in Denver."

Larsen gave a curt nod. "Of course. The guard dog at the door will become very familiar to you. Rozalia Cattaneo is Miss Abetelli's dresser. Actually, her nursemaid from childhood, so they've been close for many years. And yes, she's a *cane da guardia*. Guard dog, you would say in English."

The door opened again, this time fully. Rozalia Cattaneo gave them a sour look but nodded and motioned them with a wave of her hand. Larsen stepped in first, followed by the Pinkerton agents. The dresser swiftly shut the door again.

Rye looked around, having never been in a backstage dressing room. Obviously, this one was intended for a star, due to its size and tasteful decor. A large camelback divan in rich brown velvet looked as inviting as two wingback chairs facing it. A small coffee table rested between the furniture. Atop it was a tray of fruit and small sandwiches. Next to it rested a teapot. Bouquets of fresh flowers filled the room. He scratched his nose at the overwhelming scent as he sensed a sneeze coming on as the men seated themselves.

"Roz! My tea! I mustn't parch my throat after such a draining performance."

Out from behind another door swept Renata Abetelli in a peach silk dressing gown that shimmered, her hair and stage makeup still intact from the performance. Rye thought up close it looked garish, but he understood that the singer would appear washed out under the extreme lighting if not made up heavily.

She paused in her tracks, her mouth opening into a perfect O-shape. Then it closed as she studied them. He and Eddie stood, as did Larsen.

"Renata, darling, these are the two men from the Pinkerton Agency. They will accompany us on the train to Denver and remain the length of your performances there for Mr. Devinde."

Her mouth pursed. Rye couldn't tell if it was showing disdain or disapproval but the soprano didn't seem happy.

"They are to protect me, yes? From the evils found in this backward country?"

Rye bristled at her remark. He'd fought and bled for

this nation. He didn't appreciate anyone disparaging it. Above all, however, Pinkertons were to treat their clients with the utmost respect.

He smoothly said, "We're here to serve as your eyes and ears, Miss Abetelli. We'll protect you from everyone— even overzealous fans— and assure you the privacy you need. Your performance should always come first, so you are to concentrate on that. Mr. Larsen will focus on the business end of things. We'll handle everything else."

"And you are...?" She eyed him with more interest as she came closer. Rye thought for a moment that she inspected him as a sweet she'd like to pop into her mouth.

"My name is Zachariah Callahan, but I go by Rye. This is Edward McLeod, known as Eddie. We are highly trained and accomplished at what we do, Miss Abetelli. We will not fail you. Failure is not in our vocabulary."

She shrugged. "Very well." She looked at Larsen with a question in her eyes. "Must I be concerned with details, Ivar?"

"I'll handle everything with these gentlemen. Both men will travel on the train with us, Renata, but only one will stay close by, there and when we arrive at our destination. The other is what Mr. Pinkerton has deemed our *ace up the sleeve.*"

She frowned. "I do not understand this *ace.*"

Rye cleared his throat. "It's a gambling term, Miss Abetelli. Sometimes gamblers cheat at cards and will conceal an ace— the best card to hold— up their sleeve. No other player knows it's there. If the gambler feels he needs to play it to come out ahead, he will. And hope he doesn't get caught cheating.

"What Mr. Pinkerton intends is for one of us to remain near you at all times. The other will be in the area or roam about, be it on the train or the theater itself, possibly working among the crew. No one will know that agent works for you. He might hear or see a threat and be able to act upon it accordingly since no one knows he's connected to your protection detail."

"Hmm. I like this sleeve ace." She brightened and pointed at him. "You shall be my ace, Mr. Callahan. I will enjoy this idea of a secret protector." She gave him a seductive smile and reached for a cup of hot tea the dresser had poured for her. She took a slow sip, her eyes large above the rim, never leaving his.

"I go now. I will see you tomorrow."

The trio of men waited as she and the dresser left the room then took their seats again.

Larsen gave them a thin smile. "So, Mr. Callahan, you shall be our ace." He withdrew an envelope from his inner jacket pocket. "Here are your tickets for to-morrow morning's train. I shall see you then. Mr. Pinkerton himself assured me that even I would not be encumbered with the details. You men have free rein as you see fit. We will comply with whatever you ask. Within reason, of course."

They shook hands and the agents left the dressing room.

Eddie looked at him. "So, you're the Sleeve Ace," he teased.

"That makes Renata Abetelli your official responsi-bility," Rye answered with a grin.

"No, my friend," Eddie corrected. "She's *our* official responsibility."

"More like our pain in the ass," Rye noted.

CHAPTER FOUR

$\mathcal{E}$mma sat impatiently in the tearoom as closing time approached, scanning it again for any sight of Daniel Mitchell. If he failed to show, she didn't know what she would do. Her nerves had already gotten the best of her. She'd spilled one cup of tea while waiting for the attorney, and had also knocked over the vase of flowers sitting on the table while trying to rescue the errant teacup, earning a foul look from the girl who served her.

What was keeping him?

She smoothed the napkin in her lap again, going over the last few hours in her mind.

Molly hadn't arrived on the train as scheduled. Emma knew which one the maid would take into the city, per her instructions, and thought to surprise her. When Molly failed to appear, Emma's sense of foreboding grew. She waited for the next train, certain her servant would step from it. Again, no Molly.

She didn't want to believe that Molly would let her down, but wondered if the girl experienced second thoughts of leaving Plainfield, not to mention that very handsome, attentive footman.

No, mutual trust ran between them after so many

shared years together. If Molly didn't appear, something prevented her from coming.

The question was *what*. Or— more likely— who.

She'd returned to The Gilsey to ponder the situation. Just before she exited the hansom cab, her heart froze.

Walking up to the entrance was none other than John Fairburn, his stride and manner confident. John could only know she was staying there if Molly had shared the information with him.

Molly would never have done that willingly.

She crouched in the cab and fiddled with her shoe so John wouldn't spy her. The move allowed time for her suitor to enter the lobby of the hotel, allowing Emma to order the cabbie to take her to the nearest telegraph office. She cabled a guarded message to Daniel Mitchell, asking him to meet her at the tearoom, begging him to get on the next train to New York.

So, she waited. Hoping he would come swiftly. Afraid to even think of returning to The Gilsey and the treacherous John Fairburn.

"Emma?"

Lost in her thoughts, she startled at her name, then looked gratefully into the attorney's kind face. She stood and clung to him a moment, afraid she would fall apart in public.

"Shall we sit?" he asked quietly, guiding her to her seat and taking the one opposite her.

She poured him a cup of tea from the kettle on the table, her shaking hands rattling the saucer she passed to him.

He thanked her and then blew out a long breath, the kind her father did when he had something unpleasant to say. She saw the sadness in his eyes and knew the news couldn't be good.

"I'll be straight with you, Emma. No sugar-coating.

Your telegram said Molly didn't meet you as scheduled and asked me to come to you in her stead. I have news, Emma. Terrible news."

He paused, staring down at his manicured hands before finally meeting her eyes. "Molly's dead."

She gasped, causing others to turn and give her an odd look. She faked a smile to the staring eyes focused her way before using both hands to lift her teacup to her lips, closing her eyes as she sipped the hot liquid for a moment. When she calmed, she set down the cup.

"What happened to her, Mr. Mitchell?" she asked quietly, her throat thickening with emotion.

He leaned forward, his voice low. "Molly's body was discovered near the river this morning. She... well, she... I don't know quite how to say something so distasteful. She was attacked. Her body was... bruised and battered. She was strangled, Emma. And... violated."

"You're saying she suffered," Emma said weakly, her stomach lurching.

"Yes. The news spread through Plainfield like wildfire."

"I know who did it." She bit her lip. "John."

His brows shot up. "John Fairburn?"

She nodded. "Molly was to pack my trunk and ride in on the nine-thirty train this morning. Last night, I shared with her which hotel she should come to."

A wave of nausea ran through her. "Instead, I decided to surprise her and meet her train. When she didn't get off, I thought she might have had a little trouble getting away from her duties and had to catch the next one. I waited. Again, she didn't get off. I decided to return to The Gilsey in case I had somehow missed her."

She shuddered. "I saw John Fairburn going into the hotel just as my hansom cab pulled up. He had no business being in the city, much less at that particular hotel.

He could only know I would be there if Molly told him. And she would never have done that willingly. She was far too loyal to betray my confidence."

Mitchell handed her his handkerchief and Emma realized she was crying. She mopped her tears and gripped the handkerchief.

"There's more I didn't share with you yesterday. I overheard a conversation between Louisa and John." She wrinkled her nose. "They are *involved*. John revealed he would court me for my fortune and then share it with Louisa. He said that accidents… happen."

The attorney's eyes widened at her words.

"I was so afraid, Mr. Mitchell. I had no proof of anything because they hadn't done anything. But I had to get away from that house after Papa's death." She choked up. "Molly was to help me with my great escape. I feel responsible for what happened to her."

The lawyer shook his head. "You aren't to blame yourself, Emma. Unfortunately, Fairburn is a clever man. If he is the one who persuaded Molly to share your location, he did so in private. It would be most difficult to tie him to her death. Your suspicions aren't the proof needed to convict him in her murder."

Mitchell looked at her with a pained expression. "I don't trust you returning to Plainfield, Emma. I'm afraid what might happen to you."

She nodded. "I can't go back to The Gilsey. I must leave New York. The sooner, the better."

"It's so late in the day, my dear. You would have a hard time finding a departing train." He thought a moment. "My sister lives in Brooklyn. I could escort you to her house. She would let you stay the night."

"No. I don't want anything that would tie me to you, Mr. Mitchell. I don't want John and Louisa to know I suspect them of being involved in Molly's death. I'll send a messenger to The Gilsey and say I was called away unexpectedly. I can settle the bill that way. I'll stay somewhere else tonight and leave first thing in the morning."

Emma looked at him steadily. "I won't tell you where I'm going because I don't know myself at this moment. I will write to you once I do arrive. Or send a telegram if it's urgent."

He looked at her with determination. "Then let us talk again about how you may access funds while on your trip. I want to be sure you have no questions regarding that issue. And how you can reach me if you need me."

She squeezed his hand in gratitude. "Thank you."

"Your father would want you to be safe at all costs, Emma. We'll do our best to keep you that way."

~

"WHAT DO you mean that she wasn't there? That stupid cow of a maid said she would be there. She *had* to be there!"

"Keep your voice down, Louisa," John warned.

His lover gave him a withering look. "This is *my* house. I'll do as I like, Johnny. You can't tell me what to do."

He gripped her elbows. "I can. And will. We're in this together, Louisa." He tightened his fingers and moved to within inches of her face. "A woman is dead now. We're bound by blood and sin."

John thought of those many sinful nights spent together. How her body even now called out to him. He worried, though, how Emma had slipped away without a trace.

"We have to keep up appearances," he insisted. "You are the grieving widow. I am the concerned cousin, especially since my sweet, almost-fiancée is missing. Or will be discovered to be missing soon. Everything," he hissed, "is to remain above board. You know as well as I that servants hover and linger in the shadows. We don't want anything untoward to be overheard or seen."

He released her. She stumbled back, glaring at him, but she held her tongue. He was right— and she knew it.

Worry filled him. He had done some evil things along the way but, for the first time, he had blood on his hands. More than a confidence game or swindle or blackmail from the past. He had actually killed that servant girl once he got out of her where Emma had run.

After he'd had a little fun with her, of course.

John told himself that Louisa was every bit as guilty as he. She'd questioned Molly along with him. Always one with a cruel streak, Louisa seemed to enjoy the slaps. The punches. And worse. Fear rippled through him. They had taken their games too far and now a woman lay dead in the morgue.

He sat and reached for a teacup. "Come, darling. Have a seat. We need to discuss things. Quietly."

She nodded and moved to sit next to him. Not too closely so that the servant coming to take the tea trolley away would question things. But close enough that he could inhale the wonderful musk of her perfume. She loved to dip her finger into a jar of cream and then run it down the valley between her breasts. And lower. He could feel himself hardening at the thought.

A soft knock sounded before the door opened slightly. "Mrs. Bradford? Two policemen are here."

Louisa nodded at the butler. "Send them in, Moses."

John's brow furrowed as the servant exited the room. "You told me they'd already been here this morning while I was in the city. Why would they be returning?"

"They wanted to speak to Emma about Molly," she

said in a rush. "After they interviewed the servants. I told them she had been ill after the funeral yesterday and was resting and that they should come back. This time, I'll send someone up to fetch her. She won't be there, so look surprised," she warned him.

At that moment, two men entered the drawing room, escorted by Moses, who then retreated to the far side of the room. John wished Louisa had had the brains to dismiss the servant. The less the wily butler knew, the better.

A portly man with a thinning hairline spoke first. "Mrs. Bradford? I'm Captain Morrow. I'm sure you remember Detective Gadskill from his earlier visit." He indicated the stocky man to his left, whose intense eyes swept about, studying the room.

"My cousin and I were having some tea, gentlemen. Would you care for any?"

Both men declined and it pleased John when Louisa dismissed Moses with a curt nod. Still, he remained on edge, even as he tried to relax and appear normal.

"Please, have a seat. I would like to introduce you to my cousin, John Fairburn. He is Miss Bradford's fian–" She stopped herself and laid a hand against her breast. "Oh, I've spoken out of turn. I do apologize, John."

He took over smoothly, noticing his promotion from almost-fiancé to actually engaged. It might play out better this way in the long run, possibly allowing him more information regarding Emma if the authorities thought there was an official attachment between them.

"It's all right, Louisa." He faced the policemen. "Emma had agreed to be my bride just before her father's death. With Mr. Bradford's recent passing and the mourning period upon us, we decided it best to keep the engagement to ourselves. We'll announce our betrothal at a more suitable time."

He patted Louisa's hand. "Don't be concerned, Cousin. I'm sure these fine men will keep the news to themselves."

Detective Gadskill looked at him with interest. "Did you know the dead servant girl, Mr. Fairburn?"

"Know her?" He shrugged. "Not really. I knew she worked in the house. I've seen her around, of course. Frankly, I can't say that I would have known her name. But the face, yes. She seemed a good girl. Eager to please."

Captain Morrow said, "Yes, everyone thought she was a lovely girl, but we've hit a dead end, Mrs. Bradford. We'd really like to speak with your stepdaughter since the dead girl spent so much time with her. She may have confided in Miss Bradford in some small way that could help us in solving her murder."

"Murder." Louisa shivered. "Such an ugly word. It's hard for me to understand how a crime of this magnitude could happen in a community such as Plainfield. Molly was such a hard worker. Even if..."

John enjoyed how she let her voice trail off, her gaze averted now from the men, toying with them, reeling them in to the scenario now being concocted in his lover's devious mind.

"Even if what, Mrs. Bradford?" Detective Gadskill prompted.

She bit her lip. "I hate being a gossip, gentlemen. I wouldn't wish to speak ill of the dead."

"Think of it more as providing information, ma'am."

Louisa hesitated a moment. John bit back a smile. She really could have gone on the stage. He decided to jump into the conversation since he had an idea where it was headed.

"You should tell them, Louisa," he encouraged. "I am surprised none of the other servants have mentioned it already."

That got both officers' attention.

He frowned as he looked at their guests. "Mrs. Bradford caught Molly with a footman last week. Kissing him rather lustily. For all her good qualities, it seems Molly was..." he rotated his wrist, creating a circle with his hand several times, as he pretended to search for the correct word, "shall we say... a bit *free* with her affections."

"You don't say." Captain Morrow's eyes lit with interest.

"Do you know which footman?" asked Gadskill.

Louisa chewed on her lip. "I couldn't say. I rarely deal with any footman. They are under Moses' supervision."

She fluttered her lashes prettily. "Frankly, they all seem quite young and look alike to me. The point is, I believe Molly dallied with more than one of them. And if she flirted with our staff members, she may have done the same in public. With other men. I really couldn't say for certain."

"But," John added, hoping the police would follow the trail of breadcrumbs being laid out, "she *might* have done the same with another man. If she then rejected his attentions?" He left the question hanging.

"It could have gotten ugly," the detective finished. "I've seen it before. A woman leads a man on and then pulls back— and the man's having none of it. This might be a case of that, gone too far." He frowned. "Still, we'd like to speak with Miss Bradford. If she knew of the girl meeting a particular fellow, for instance, or even his name or where, that would be helpful."

"Of course," Louisa said, a prim smile set upon her full lips. "Let me ring for a servant."

Dawson appeared almost instantly, making John wonder if she and Moses had their ears pressed against the door, trying to glean any of the conversation.

"Dawson, please have Emmeline come down to speak to the police about Molly."

"Yes, Mrs. Bradford."

The housekeeper left. Louisa pressed a cookie upon each man while they made small talk about the weather.

As expected, Dawson returned with a frantic look upon her face.

"It's Miss Emma. She's… gone!"

ye stood in the train station as Eddie entered with their clients, touring manager Ivar Larsen and the *bird*, the agency's name of the person to be protected. Renata Abetelli shone today in a navy ensemble, wearing the largest hat Rye had ever laid eyes upon. He figured she had to wear it since it would have taken up an entire trunk by itself. Fast on the opera singer's heels was her dresser, Rozalia Cattaneo. She wore a nondescript gray dress and a glum expression as she motioned to various porters, giving them instructions regarding the baggage.

The endless stream of trunks seemed comical to him. He wondered idly if some contained the elaborate costumes worn on stage, or if the luggage consisted entirely of Renata's personal items. He didn't envy Eddie's job of remaining close to the opera singer at all times. Rye divided women into two groups— and the soprano fell into the one he labeled *Trouble.*

Rye had yet to meet a woman in the *Not Trouble* category.

The entourage passed him, Eddie on one side of the diva while Larsen walked on the other, his arm linked through Renata's. Rye averted his gaze as they passed.

Although the company manager and singer weren't supposed to acknowledge his presence, Rye didn't trust them. Civilians reacted differently from trained Pinkerton agents, and he didn't want any observer associating him with the opera company.

The touring group would take up a good portion of the train's passengers. At the conclusion of their meeting, Larsen gave the Pinkerton agents a list of personnel involved with the company. Rye couldn't believe how long it ran. Besides the principals who had leading roles on stage, it included both supporting and chorus roles, as well as the group of musicians who played before and during the performance. Along with the cast was a large crew who created and managed the sets, the props, the lighting, and dozens of other roles, though many in the crew worked multiple jobs.

Francis Warner had seen to the travel itinerary, booking the company on a train from New York to Chicago, where they would switch to a line that would carry them through to Omaha. From Omaha, the troupe would travel straight to Denver. This would put them on a rail car close to six consecutive days before they reached their destination.

He wished Warner had simply bought out the entire train, but with limited seating available, there would be few strangers present, meaning less of an onboard danger to the bird. He would easily be able to spot non-company members once he became familiar with the traveling troupe. Thankfully, he had an excellent eye for faces and instant retention of names. Learning the members of the company would take little time. Larsen obliged him and came down to the station early today and identified company members as they came through the facility and boarded the train, before the manager left to escort the bird to her own private car.

His eyes swept over the crowd as he moved through

the depot and caught sight of a woman seated alone, reading from a thick book. He stopped a moment at a nearby pillar, leaning against it as he smiled at the sight. Reading had become both his pleasure and refuge during the years since the war. He rarely went anywhere without a book. The life of a Pinkerton could be lonely, as most detectives worked cases alone. Rye traveled from city to city, case to case, year after year. While he relished his work, he didn't make many friends or share conversations with many people, so books became his constant, steady companions.

The woman smiled at something on the page and it tugged hard on his heart, surprising him. He never made time for women and never gave a thought about having a family. But if he had? This beauty would have been the one for him.

Strawberry blonde hair twisted in some womanly knot rested against her nape, setting off flawless, milky skin. Her smile revealed even, white teeth as she shook her head and regarded the page with amusement. Then she pursed her lips as she continued to read, and an unexpected wave of desire washed over him.

He wanted to kiss that lush mouth.

Rye shook his head as if trying to clear cobwebs, wondering where such a fanciful notion sprang from. Kissing and romance went hand in hand, and he chose neither to be a part of his busy, solitary life.

She smiled again and marked her place in the book with a ribbon before closing it and slipping it into her reticule. As she looked up, their eyes met. Her azure blue were as clear as a summer's sky. Rye swallowed, suddenly as nervous as a schoolboy wet behind the ears.

He tipped his hat to her and decided to speak.

"Good day. Forgive me for seeming presumptuous, but I noticed you were reading to pass the time. I'm quite fond of books and look upon them as good friends."

The woman smiled sweetly. "That's a lovely thought. I myself read voraciously. Anything and everything I can place my hands upon." She indicated the novel inside the reticule resting on her lap. "I'm in the middle of *Bleak House* now. For at least the fifth or sixth time. I can't imagine anyone who doesn't adore Dickens."

He broke into his own smile. "I'm Zachariah Callahan. Mr. Dickens happens to be my favorite author. I've enjoyed *Bleak House* countless times. The case of *Jarndyce* vs. *Jarndyce* does go on and on."

"Not to mention secret marriages, murder, and betrayal. Absolutely everything one would want in a novel, I'd imagine."

She stood and offered him her hand. "My name is Emma Bradford. Fan of Mr. Dickens, as well as Sir Walter Scott and Miss Jane Austen."

He moved to clasp her gloved hand and bowed slightly, pleased that introducing himself to a female stranger hadn't caused her to have a case of the vapors or run screaming from the terminal.

But as their hands touched, he sensed a spark between them, as obvious as a match being struck. His jaw dropped in surprise as he released his grasp. He swallowed hard, trying to remember what comment she'd made to him so he could reply in a rational manner.

Finally, it hit him that they conversed about authors. He cleared his throat and replied, "I second your choices and would toss in Miss Alcott and Mr. Hawthorne as personal favorites myself. And Poe. I probably shouldn't admit to being a Poe fan in polite company."

She shivered. "Oh, Mr. Poe causes me nightmares."

She paused, a mischievous grin lighting her face. "Absolutely every time I read him."

Rye couldn't help but laugh. "Your secret of enjoying the macabre is safe with me." He paused. "Are you traveling far today?"

She nodded but paused, almost as if she gauged him. "I am. And you?"

He realized his questions had become too personal. No gentleman should address a lady in public unless she's known to him, much less inquire about her travel plans.

"An apology is in order, Miss Bradford. Forgive me for my much too inquisitive nature. Have a safe trip."

Rye touched his hat again and turned. Walking briskly away, he chastised himself for being so forward with a total stranger.

Even if she did resemble an angel.

As he made his way to the departing train, the image of those clear, blue eyes and strawberry blonde hair of Emma Bradford's remained with him.

EMMA WATCHED THE TALL, broad-shouldered man walk out of her life. He'd only been in it for a little over a minute yet she felt as if an old friend had slipped through her grasp.

She shook off the glum feeling as she leaned down and retrieved her new carpetbag. She was about to embark upon a true adventure to the West . No room for sadness belonged in her life— even if she wished she could learn more about the book lover with jet black hair and unusual eyes. Those eyes did throw her off for a moment when she first looked at him. They were an odd, golden hue, rimmed with flecks of green. She'd never seen a pair like them before.

He had seemed like such an interesting gentleman, talking knowledgeably about books. John had chastised her several times for reading so much, telling her she frittered away her time on something useless.

The thought of her former swain caused a bitterness to rise and she swallowed hard, pushing it down. John Fairburn hadn't a clue where she might be or where she headed.

Thank the Good Lord for that.

As Emma walked with her suitcase in hand, sadness crept in, despite her fervent wish to celebrate her freedom as the start of a new life on the horizon tantalized her.

Her beloved father had passed. With Molly's murder coupled with it, the deaths weighed heavily on her heart. The servant had been a good friend to her, and Emma placed responsibility for Molly's death squarely upon her own shoulders despite what Mr. Mitchell had said. She knew John— and probably Louisa— was involved in it. She didn't know how she would accomplish it but, at some point, she would find justice for Molly.

Strolling to the platform, she found her train had arrived and was now boarding. Good fortune smiled upon her. The ticket seller this morning told her this particular train was carrying a large group of people— a famous opera company— and Emma purchased one of the last tickets available. She wondered if the troupe would stop in Chicago to perform or continue on as she did, to the Great Plains and beyond.

With no trunk to see to, Emma allowed the conductor to assist her up the steep steps. She showed him her ticket and asked about seating arrangements. He directed her to the dark green seats of the Pullman sleeping car section. In this open section, pairs of seats faced one other. Since she had a tendency toward motion sickness, she chose a seat facing forward on the right side of the aisle. She hoped the conductor would be helpful when it came time to converting the seats into upper and lower berths. Looking at them, she hadn't the faintest idea how this task might be accomplished.

Mrs. Givens, a mother with two small children soon joined her, and Emma enjoyed chatting with her new acquaintance as the train pulled out of the station and headed west. She looked around and saw her section at full capacity. She caught bits of Italian and French and what she thought must be German scattered among English conversations. The opera company certainly seemed international in its flavor.

She soon helped Mrs. Givens with taking care of the girls, named Dolly and Polly. She thought it dreadful to call children rhyming names within the same family but kept her opinion to herself. Mrs. Givens seemed worn out as she spoke of joining her husband on the prairie just outside of Kansas City, little Dolly sucking a thumb in her arms as her mother spoke.

"Mr. Givens left over a year ago to make his fortune and find a place for us to settle. I've been a parent on my own ever since, with no family to help me." She patted Emma's hand. "That's why meeting you on the train has been such a blessing, my dear. Polly certainly has taken to you."

Emma glanced down at the small girl nestled against her.

"Would you tell me a story?" the child asked.

"Of course, Polly. I used to tell my own papa stories nearly every single day. I'd love to share one with you." She thought a moment and then began. "Once there was a fairy princess who lived in an ivory tower, with only a white dove to keep her company."

She spun the story to the small child much as she used to imagine stories in her head and tell them to her father, weaving in dialogue and descriptions. When she finished, Polly clamored for more.

Making eye contact with Mrs. Givens, the woman shook her head. "She's heard enough. We mustn't spoil the child."

Emma didn't see how telling a second fairy tale would necessarily spoil a little girl, but she wouldn't press the point with the parent.

"May I sing to her then?"

Mrs. Givens looked a bit surprised, but nodded her consent.

Emma sang often growing up, even taking voice and piano lessons for many years. When her father entertained, he often called upon her to sing and play for his guests. After their accident, those evenings became a thing of the past. She stopped the lessons and the piano sat idle in the drawing room. Other than singing verses in church, she might hum a little while she sewed or did her knitting or needlepoint. She often proved clumsy with a needle, though, and tried not to distract herself from that task. As she looked over the landscape rolling by, she thought a song might be a nice way to pass the time.

Instead of the lively pace the songwriter intended, she began singing *She'll Be Coming 'Round the Mountain* as more of a slow ballad. As Emma sang, she noticed the rail car quieten until everyone around her listened. She ran through as many of the verses as she could remember, and then glanced down and saw Polly fast asleep. She looked across and saw Dolly also asleep in her mother's arms. Even Mrs. Givens' eyes were closed, a faint snore emitting from her.

Suddenly, a voice behind her said into her ear, "I could've sworn she wore pink pajamas. Instead of red."

Emma looked over her shoulder and found Zachariah Callahan sitting behind her.

CHAPTER SIX

Rye moved through various compartments on the train as it chugged along, familiarizing himself with the number of cars and occupants in each. He already recognized a majority of passengers from Ivar Larsen's comments at the depot, glad that so many of the train's occupants wouldn't be a threat to the bird, since their livelihood depended upon the soprano.

Only a few travelers remained and Rye could count these outsiders to the opera company on both hands. He knocked on the bird's private compartment and Eddie opened the door. His partner ushered him inside.

He looked around and saw a wealth of clothing lying in piles everywhere. With raised brows, he looked at Eddie questioningly.

The detective shrugged. "The bird's been trying on costumes. I assume Her Grumpiness will pick all these up and tend to them in time."

"Her Grumpiness?"

Eddie chuckled. "My pet name for that woman. The dresser."

Rye nodded. "Ah, Miss Cattaneo. So, you two haven't hit it off?"

"She's as fierce as a lioness protecting her cub. I'll

give her that. Larsen said she's the childhood nursemaid who never left. She does the bird's makeup. Cares for her costumes. Makes sure all food and drink are up to snuff. Guards her from any pressure or stress."

"You're telling me that if the train is robbed, there'll be three watching out for the bird?" He grinned, thinking he had definitely gotten the better end of the job at this point.

"I'd say Larsen would make the fourth. He's got a lot invested in this company and wants it to succeed. I'm sure he'd stand between any threat that headed the bird's way." Eddie paused. "How's the train look?"

"Cozy. All but six passengers are involved with the touring company Four of the six are located in the sleeping car section. A mother with two little ones. A woman traveling alone sitting with them. The other two are a pastor and his blushing bride, headed for a posting in Kansas City."

Eddie nodded as he took in the information. "No apparent threats on the train. At least this leg of the trip. I doubt we'll see any problems before Chicago. And even to Omaha."

"I agree. The lines run through civilized towns. It'll only be when we get past Omaha that I'll worry about criminal activity outside the locomotive."

From the next compartment, a woman's shrill voice rose. Then another chimed in. The two men listened a moment. Rye thought they sounded like alley cats fighting over disputed territory.

Suddenly, the door flew open. Renata Abetelli stormed in, tears streaming down her face. She held a dress in her hands which she wadded up then tossed aside, her brown eyes blazing with fury. Rozalia Cattaneo appeared, shaking her fist as both women yelled at each other in what he assumed was Italian. Hands flew in wild gestures before Renata clamped her lips into a thin line and collapsed into a nearby chair.

Ivar Larsen appeared, walking calmly through the door from where the women had emerged. He gave an imperceptible nod to Rozalia and the dresser returned to the other room. Larsen proceeded to comfort Renata, murmuring to her in more than one language. He offered her his handkerchief and she dried her tears.

With a trembling smile, she gave the crumpled, damp cloth to him. He smiled and took it, and they returned without a word to the other compartment, Larsen quietly closing the door.

Rye let out a long breath and gave Eddie's shoulder a pat. "I'll leave you to your work. And if Francis asks, I'll tell him he owes you double for this assignment."

Eddie grimaced. "It's been like that ever since we pulled out of the station. Anger, raised voices, tears, then silence. Then the cycle repeats all over again." He consulted his pocket watch, cursing softly under his breath. "It's only been two hours. I have a feeling it's going to be a long week to Denver."

"At least the bird has agreed to stay on the train at all times," he noted. "That helps keeping her contained in one area and not out and about at every stop. I wish there was a dining car on this leg, though. Larsen said we'll have one for the Chicago to Omaha trek."

"Don't worry, Rye. Larsen agreed to bring food back for the four of us when the train stops for meals. He's already given it plenty of thought and cabled ahead to our stops with the bird's preferences."

"I can help him bring the meals aboard when we arrive." He thought a moment. "It should just be twice today and again tomorrow. We should have transferred to the new train by the evening meal."

"No, Rye. Remember, you're not to acknowledge Larsen or the bird. Keep your eyes open for any threats.

I just hope the bird eats. If she's eating, I don't have to listen to her hollering or crying."

Eddie escorted him to the door and saw him out. Rye decided to do one more sweep through the train for good measure before he settled down in the car with Miss Bradford. The beauty intrigued him. He wondered where she was traveling and why. Maybe she was a mail-order bride journeying to meet her new husband. Or she'd been back east visiting family and now returned to her own out West . He caught himself.

Why so many fanciful notions about a woman he'd spoken to for barely a minute?

Yet she stayed in his thoughts until he entered her rail car once again. He slipped into the seat behind her, nodding to the gentleman next to the window. He remembered the man as the lighting director.

Miss Emma Bradford was in the middle of a story, entertaining the young girls with a tale of an evil sorceress who held a beautiful princess captive and the bold knight who rode to her rescue. He noticed the entire group in this rail car enjoyed the story she wove. No conversation occurred. Everyone hung on her every word.

It surprised him when the mother refused to allow another story but it turned out even better since Miss Bradford asked to sing to the children.

Rye had never heard a voice like hers.

Not even the famed Renata Abetelli could lay claim to such sweet, rich tones. In fact, he'd bet the diva would be green with envy. He had attended many shows at opera houses during his years of working for the Pinkertons out West . None of the women who had performed in them held a candle to Emma Bradford's soft, melodious tones.

She turned a bouncing, carefree children's song into

a lovely, almost mournful ballad. When she finished, no one uttered a word.

Without thinking, he leaned up and said, "I could've sworn she wore pink pajamas. Instead of red."

~

EMMA TURNED and met Mr. Callahan's gaze. She could have sworn his eyes twinkled as she said quietly, "Sometimes, they're red. I only sing the phrase *pink pajamas* if I include the verse about killing the red rooster."

She glanced down at Polly curled peacefully beside her before she looked back at the handsome stranger. "I chose to omit the rooster's death and let '*We will all eat chicken and dumplings*' be the next verse instead. I remember clearly when I first made the connection that a live bird became a very dead one that was cooked and appeared upon our dinner table." She shuddered.

"Bad memories?" he asked, one corner of his mouth turning up.

"I refused to eat chicken for a good month. Or beef. Even pork. The thought of it seemed too dreadful."

"And after a month?" he asked.

"I missed my baked chicken and roast beef. Oh, and ham." She chuckled. "*Especially* ham. Cook served ham every Sunday after church. Papa convinced me that God formed a plan for each and every creature upon the face of the earth. That animals served man, be it as food, a pet, or for transportation."

He looked at her skeptically. "You believed him?"

"Well, I did miss my Sunday ham." She grinned. "I knew with certainty that Cook wouldn't be coming after my cat and cooking him up anytime soon. So, I relented."

Polly stirred and turned away, resting her head

against the window. Emma leaned the other way, swinging her feet into the aisle and twisting around to look at Zachariah Callahan more fully.

Her heart skipped a beat as she sized him up. He was even more handsome than she remembered from their brief encounter, the broad shoulders filling out his dark charcoal suit and crisp white dress shirt in a way she had never seen before. He radiated strength and power, from the thick black hair atop his head down to his polished boots. The boots surprised her. They were in a western vein and not a working man's boot. A keen intelligence lingered in those golden eyes, rimmed with the interesting green flecks.

Yet it troubled her that he'd spoken to her, both in the train station and now. She determined to quiz him. She had to be sure John hadn't set this man on her trail.

"Are you perhaps related to a Mr. John Fairburn of Connecticut?"

He frowned, puzzled by her abrupt question. Both his reaction to the name and her gut told Emma this man had no association with John. She began to relax.

"No. I can't say I've ever heard the name. Is Mr. Fairburn an acquaintance of yours?"

"He is. Was. I thought I noticed a slight resemblance between you but now I see that I'm mistaken. Other than you both are over six feet and have dark hair, that is." She studied him a moment. "You do possess the most unusual eyes, Mr. Callahan. I've never seen any like them before. Do either of your parents share that feature?"

He paused before answering. "I've never seen another man— or woman— with my eyes. My mother's were green like my uncle's, I'm told. I never knew my father. I... was raised by my aunt and uncle."

Her throat tightened at his words. "I never knew my mother. She died shortly after my birth. I wish I could have grown up with her by my side. Papa worshipped the ground she trod upon."

At that moment, the conductor came through, interrupting their conversation.

"Next stop is longer for a reason, folks," he announced. "You'll have fifty-five minutes to eat a meal. Restaurant's in the station. This one's not half bad. Plenty of food carts outside, too, in case you'd rather have that. Five minutes until we arrive."

Emma blinked, hoping no tears would fall. She rarely pitied herself for losing her mother while still an infant. Knowing Mr. Callahan also shared a similar story, she felt an odd kinship with him.

And an attraction.

He cleared his throat. "I know this seems a bit forward of me, Miss Bradford, but I was wondering. Would you care to share a meal with me?"

CHAPTER SEVEN

*E*mma beamed at Rye. "I would be delighted to dine with you, Mr. Callahan."

Her unbridled enthusiasm and immediate acceptance of his invitation took him by surprise. Most well-brought up ladies would more than likely have refused him. Or at least played coy and kept him dangling before consenting. He looked at her a moment, torn by his realization of how well-bred she appeared. He could hold his own with any man, rich or poor, but did he have the courage to try on the social niceties and enjoy the pleasure of Emma Bradford's company while they partook of a meal together?

"I must warn you that the fare won't be anything fancy. You seem... well, you seem to know about the finer things in life, Miss Bradford. I'm not sure dining in a train depot's restaurant will live up to your expectations."

Her laughter tinkled musically. "I'll admit my upbringing was a privileged one. Papa owned a woolen and cotton mill along the Moosup River in Connecticut. It's always been productive, even with the cotton mill boom in the south the last few years. I began going to work with him almost as soon as I could toddle about on my own."

"That's quite unusual for a female. To take such an interest in business, let alone at a young age."

She shrugged. "Papa didn't know the first thing about how to raise a girl. He did what came naturally to him. In any case, my brother was a dozen years older than me and didn't possess an iota of interest in the mill. David wanted to study law and try cases before the Supreme Court. His idea of fun was memorizing famous speeches by Daniel Webster or Henry Clay and reciting them aloud to a captive audience of one." She grinned. "Me."

Her openness and enthusiasm was infectious. Rye sensed the attraction growing between them as he asked, "What did you do for fun, especially being so much younger than your brother?"

"Besides going to the mill every day? Oh, that was always an adventure in and of itself. I still know every worker's name and can ask after their family members. I know all about harnessing water power and the process in creating cloth. I can explain why ring frames replaced mule frames, and debate the merits of a bay size and how to place machinery in it for optimum output. If you'd like, I'll reel off prices for cotton and even tell you the best stocks you should invest in."

He laughed. "I'm afraid I don't have the kind of income necessary to play the stock market. If I ever do, I'll know who to turn to for advice. Not many people understand the intricate workings of a mill. You sound like an expert to me."

She laughed in return. "I spent hours over the years with Mr. Stannis, the mill's manager. He taught me a good deal about how to run a mill and manage workers. I also learned about business itself from Papa. I poked and prodded and extracted everything I know about finances and business as a whole from him."

Rye reeled at the knowledge she effortlessly tossed out. This woman had a keen intelligence that matched her beauty. It only made her more appealing to him.

"You are more than meets the eye, Miss Bradford. You are dressed as fashionably as any woman in society and possess knowledge many men would envy. What about away from the mill? Did you make time for any amusements?"

The train began slowing. The small child next to Emma stirred and awoke. She turned from him and began talking to the little girl. The mother sitting across from them snorted loudly and awoke, as did her daughter seated in her lap.

He overheard the older woman tell Emma that her maiden aunt lived at this stop and was meeting them for a quick visit if she cared to join them. Emma politely declined and wished the woman well.

"I hope you have a lovely visit with your aunt, Mrs. Givens. I'll be eager to hear all about it when you board again."

The locomotive pulled into the station, slowing until it came to a halt. The rail car's occupants eagerly rose from their seats, stretching and talking as they spilled into the aisle and made their way toward the exit.

"Remember. Fifty-five minutes. That's all you'll get," the conductor reminded the passengers as they left the train and moved across the platform. "We leave on time. Not a minute later. Trains have a schedule to keep."

Rye let the crowd dwindle before he climbed down the stairs and held out a hand for Emma to take. As before, a small frisson of pleasure rushed through him at the touch. He hoped he wouldn't embarrass himself during the upcoming meal. As a Pinkerton agent, he rarely dealt with the opposite sex, much less shared conversation and food with a pretty society lady who seemed to know far more than he ever could. His life revolved around criminals and their crimes. Neither made for appropriate conversation between two people who'd just met.

Yet he found himself compelled to be around Emma Bradford.

As he escorted her across the platform, his eyes scanned the crowd. He wasn't a betting man, but the overwhelming odds told him no threats to the bird would make an appearance here. He knew the agency had been hired to protect her. But any threats, perceived or real, would most likely occur once they moved west of Omaha. Besides, the soprano couldn't be in better hands than Eddie's and she wasn't leaving the train at this stop.

He glanced over his shoulder and saw Ivar Larsen hurrying along, a porter beside him. Rye assumed the porter would help Larsen return the food to the bird, her dresser, and Eddie. Rye looked back at his new companion and decided once again that he'd received the far better end of the deal.

EMMA MARVELED at the changes to her life in such a short span as she and Mr. Callahan strolled across the platform. A week ago at this time, she might be returning from her daily visit to the mill, going up to see her father to give him the news of the day while badgering him to eat as she entertained him with stories. Now, her beloved parent lay cold in the ground. She had discovered her fawning beau and scheming stepmother conspired to steal her inheritance after plotting her death, while her closest ally in helping her escape lost her life in the effort. Emma still carried a heavy heart thinking of Molly. Knowing the girl had no family, she was glad she had instructed Daniel Mitchell to pay for the maid's funeral arrangements from estate funds.

Thankfully, she had flown the coop and now ventured west, already finding life very different from her small town in Connecticut.

Especially with a man such as Zachariah Callahan escorting her as if they were old friends.

Life in Plainfield rarely presented an opportunity to meet new people. She guessed it was why she eagerly encouraged John to stay in town when he came calling on his supposed cousin, Louisa. The handsome John Fairburn brought variety to her routine and different conversation to the drawing room and dining table. The fact that he expressed a definite interest in her added to his immeasurable charm.

Now, she embarked on an adventure, truly on her own for the first time in her twenty-five years. She wanted to learn about herself. What she liked and found interesting beyond the routine, ordinary life in Plainfield. She had no one to care for except herself. She'd promised herself to be open to new experiences along the way.

That had led her to speaking with Mr. Callahan in the station. Normally, she wouldn't dream of striking up a conversation with a stranger, especially a man. Yet to her delight, he appeared as interested in books as she did. Finding him on her same train hours later seemed as if providence intervened. She found him easy to talk with.

And very, very easy on the eye.

He led her inside the crowded terminal to the restaurant the conductor mentioned, and they were seated and presented with menus and a basket of rolls with a dish of butter. No restaurants existed in Plainfield. She had eaten at a few when in New York with her father. Their trip to Europe consisted of dining in tiny cafés or simply buying bread, cheese, olives, and wine from street vendors.

She actually looked forward to this experience as she scanned the single page with interest. Suddenly, her stomach gurgled loudly, and she felt her face flame.

Her dining partner stifled a smile. "I see I'm not the only one looking forward to dining."

They placed their order with the waiter, who promised them a short wait since the menu was limited and time was short.

Emma buttered a piping hot roll and ate it faster than usual in order to calm her grumbling stomach.

"Thank you for agreeing to join me, Miss Bradford. I'm traveling a good way, and it's nice to have a companion to share a meal to break up a long road trip."

That spurred her curiosity. "May I ask your final destination, Mr. Callahan? Or would that be a little too personal?" she teased, remembering how he'd cut their conversation short when he'd asked the same information of her.

He laughed. "I suppose we now know one another slightly better than before, despite not having been formally introduced by an appropriate third party." He took a last bite of the yeasty roll. "I'm heading to Denver. And you?"

She had planned on stopping in the Midwest and seeing a bit of Kansas City for a few days before continuing on to Denver and later San Francisco for a longer period. Those two cities interested her the most.

"Denver, as well."

It surprised her when she told him that. For some reason, she wanted to get to know Zachariah Callahan beyond a surface level. Maybe she could do so over the many hours on the train to Denver. She hoped she could change her ticket once they reached Kansas City.

"That's a long way to travel alone. Are you meeting up with family in Colorado?"

Their food arrived and she busied herself with seasoning her potatoes and slicing the beef before she replied, hoping the interlude would help her maintain her composure. Although Mr. Callahan was close to being a stranger, she didn't fear him having a connection with John or Louisa. And despite trailing her to The Gilsey in New York, her former beau and stepmother had no idea where she now was and couldn't possibly be on her trail.

She looked again at her dining companion and chose to be honest with him. "My father recently passed away. Since I spent a great deal of time with him in his sickroom, I decided a change of scenery would be in order."

His brow creased. "I'm sorry to hear that. Especially with your mother gone. Will your brother join you at some point? If he's not scheduled to address the Supreme Court in the near future, that is."

She chewed thoughtfully before replying. "David never had the chance to practice law. He fell in action during the war. The letter from his unit commander assured us he died instantly and didn't suffer." She paused. "I'm on my own. Except..."

His brows rose when she paused for too long. "For?"

Her words tumbled out without thinking. "Oh, I have a stepmother. Papa suffered severe injuries in a carriage accident and became an invalid during the last years of his life. Louisa was...his nurse. He married her over a year ago. She'll remain in the house for the rest of her days, unless she remarries. We're... not close. Except in age."

She stopped, mortified with how much she had revealed. Her intentions of being honest with him had backfired. Discussing her father and Louisa opened the floodgates of her emotions. At least she had kept her head and not revealed how foolish she'd been regarding John Fairburn and his supposed intentions toward her.

Yet even as she mentally berated herself, Rye Callahan looked at her with sympathy, causing her heart to turn over. "You've experienced hard times, Miss Bradford. Losing everyone in your family. It must be hard having a stepmother you can't confide in or find comfort with now that your father has passed."

She fought the tears but a few spilled down her cheeks. He offered her his handkerchief, which she gladly accepted.

As she dabbed her eyes, she wondered why she trusted a total stranger as much as she did this man. She had already divulged far more to him than polite society deemed appropriate. Yet he possessed a quiet strength and steadiness that made her believe she could trust him. With anything.

They finished their meal in silence. Emma hoped he wasn't embarrassed by everything she'd brought up. Part of her wished they could be old friends and she could share with him the whole story. How she was terrified of John and Louisa. How she fled her own home to prevent them from doing her harm. How she had no plan for her future other than putting as much distance as possible between her and them.

He took care of their bill before she realized it.

"I didn't mean for you to pay for my meal, Mr. Callahan. I'm afraid I became lost in my thoughts."

"I invited you, Miss Bradford. It's only fair I should do the gentlemanly thing. I rarely have an opportunity to dine with others, much less such a lovely lady. I've enjoyed the pleasure of your company."

He rose and helped her from her chair and led her back through the station.

"I'm sorry I turned out to be such poor company."

His golden eyes gleamed at her. "Not at all. I appreciated our conversation and getting to learn about you. You are a fascinating woman, Miss Bradford. I hope you never change."

Her cheeks heated at his compliment, making her wish had a fan handy. "I feel you know practically everything about me, while I know very little about you, sir. Other than you are bound for Denver. What will—"

Suddenly, she stood by herself. He'd dropped her arm and taken off running across the waiting room and out to the platform. She hurried along and watched as he caught up to a young boy and wrapped his arms about him, lifting the boy from the ground. The boy squirmed, his dangling feet kicking away.

Mr. Callahan immediately released the boy and spun him around, their noses practically touching as he spoke to him in earnest. The boy nodded a few times and said something before he was set free. Then Mr. Callahan pulled something from his pocket and handed it to the boy. With a sheepish look on his face, the child started back toward the waiting room.

Emma moved aside as he entered through the door and moved toward a portly man standing with a woman, three children, and a mound of luggage surrounding them.

She turned and saw Mr. Callahan sauntering toward her. He stopped at her side and they watched the boy tap the man on the arm. He said a few words to him and then held up his hand, palm opened. The man reached to his waist as he glanced down. Emma saw no pocket watch hung from the empty chain. He patted the boy on the head and they both broke into smiles as the man accepted the proffered watch and reattached it to his chain.

Then the man reached in his pocket and extracted something. She assumed it was a coin, a reward for the boy having found the pocket watch.

Laughter bubbled up and spilled from her.

"You think stealing is funny, Miss Bradford?"

She looked at her companion, masking her smile with a solemn expression. "Not at all, Mr. Callahan."

The boy looked in their direction and tipped his newsboy hat before he melted into the crowd.

"You could have turned that child over to the authorities, you know."

He nodded. "I could have. But the law's harsh. That little rascal has a sick mama and no one else. Besides, our train is about to pull out. I wouldn't want either of us to miss it."

"You believe it was easier to give the pickpocket a little money and teach him a lesson by having him return the stolen watch to its rightful owner? And still make our train on time, of course."

"Exactly." He gazed at her a moment. "I believe it's time we board that train, Miss Bradford."

Emma flashed him a smile. "Only if you promise to tell me a little more about yourself the minute we get on board," she replied, and linked her arm through his.

CHAPTER EIGHT

$\mathcal{R}$ ye didn't know how to beg off from the conversation Emma Bradford wanted to have. He didn't want to lie to her. Lying, in his mind, produced the worst sin of all. His aunt and uncle had lied to him his whole life growing up, claiming to be his parents. When he'd come home from the war and learned the truth in such a harsh way from the woman he'd thought of as his mother, he never recovered from the discovery.

Revealing he was a Pinkerton, though, was out of the question. His identity must remain a secret. With most of their rail car being occupied by members of the opera company, he couldn't afford for any of them to overhear his story. The majority of the rest of the train was the same. He had a cover story in place if needed while on the train but the thought of telling Emma Bradford a lie seemed dead wrong.

How could he avoid telling her why he was going to Denver?

He accompanied her to her seat, where Mrs. Givens and her two daughters already sat. Immediately, the woman stole Emma's attention as both girls joined Emma, one claiming each side. Mrs. Givens began talking up a blue storm about her relative and their visit.

Rye caught Emma's eyes and mouthed that he was going to stretch his legs. She gave an imperceptible nod and continued listening to the woman's chatter. He escaped the monologue and did another sweep of the cars ahead of them. After twenty minutes, he returned, passing by as Emma was in the midst of telling the children another story. As before, the nearby passengers listened to her tale, enchanted by her storytelling and melodic voice.

He paused a moment to listen, admiring how she captivated her audience. She changed voices and accents at will. He'd never heard the story before and guessed it was an original one. He thought he might suggest to her that she write them down. Rye knew from personal experience how loss hurt the soul. Maybe penning her tales would help Emma keep her mind off her recent woes.

Continuing on his mission, he investigated the remaining cars until he reached the end. Seeing no one in sight, he knocked on the bird's door, wanting to check in with Eddie and assure him all was well.

The door opened a crack and then wider when Eddie recognized him. Immediately, Rye saw something was wrong.

Eddie's usually ruddy complexion now seemed washed out. His pale face wore a look of pain. His friend motioned him in and fell back on a nearby sofa where Ivar Larsen sat. The company's manager clutched his belly.

Rye closed the door as the bird's dresser opened the one at the far end of the car. He saw that she, too, seemed in distress.

She began chattering in what had to be Italian, her hands flying as tears made their way down her cheeks.

She crossed to Larsen, who answered her in the same language, both of them moaning and wan. After a brief conversation, she gathered her skirts and disappeared to where the bird was.

"We're all sick as dogs," Eddie told him with things now quiet. "You saw even Her Grumpiness is affected. I didn't think anything would get to that one." He grimaced. "All I can think of is the food that was brought aboard. We all shared in that."

"What did you eat?" Rye had seen dysentery throughout the war. Usually, the onset occurred a few days after being exposed. He assumed this had to be some kind of tainted food instead.

Eddie shrugged. "Something with noodles. A rich cream sauce. Wasn't familiar with anything I ate. It tasted fine at the time."

"With it acting as quickly as it has, all I can think of is some kind of food poisoning." He paused. "It won't be good."

"I think I already had that figured out, Dr. Callahan. What do we do with this cramping?" The Pinkerton agent groaned and wrapped both arms around his body and bent forward.

Larsen stood and stumbled to the table where the leftovers of the meal sat. He dumped the contents from a bowl onto the table and then vomited into the emptied dish.

Rye hadn't a clue what to do since he always found himself in excellent health. In the army, soldiers kept marching until they couldn't. He didn't know what had been done for the sick men with dysentery left behind since he was one of the lucky few to escape its path. He only knew dysentery killed more men than bullets during the war.

Whatever they'd been exposed to seemed even worse.

"I'll be right back."

He rushed through compartments until he arrived at the one Emma Bradford rode in.

"I'm sorry to interrupt," he apologized to Mrs. Givens. "Miss Bradford's presence is needed somewhere else. Now."

He latched on to Emma's elbow and helped her rise to her feet.

"Follow me."

He hurriedly retraced his steps back to the bird's personal car. He stopped and turned, grateful Emma had followed him without question.

"I couldn't say anything back there. This is a complicated situation. I didn't know what to do but I knew you had experience nursing your father. And you are by far one of the most intelligent women I've ever met."

He raked a hand through his hair. "There are four very sick people on the other side of this door. They all ate the same meal less than two hours ago. I assume it's the food that's made them all sick. It is extremely important that they are all right. I'm a Pinkerton agent charged with their welfare.

"Can you help me?"

~

EMMA'S CURIOSITY danced wildly with his words. She wouldn't have guessed in a million years what Zachariah Callahan had just uttered to her, but she knew she could help him.

"I actually have some experience with this. Who's in there and what did they eat?"

"Another Pinkerton named Eddie McLeod. Our clients. An Italian opera singer. Her manager who's head of the touring company. An older woman who serves as her dresser. Eddie couldn't tell me exactly what they ate. The bird's manager had telegraphed ahead with her dining specifications. The meal was at the station, ready when we arrived, and brought aboard for them."

She nodded. "Let's go inside."

He knocked. She heard the latch thrown. The man she assumed was the Pinkerton detective opened the door and backed up unsteadily as he admitted them.

Emma went to the table and looked at the remains of the meal. She breathed through her mouth, as the car already stank of vomit and worse. A thin man appeared from behind a partition, his eyes sunk into his wan face, his clothing disheveled.

She went to his side and helped him sit on the sofa. She looked at him and the Pinkerton who let them in.

"You definitely have some form of food poisoning. It could be from the eggs or the milk in the cream sauce ladled over the pasta. Maybe even both. You'll have nausea and vomiting, as well as abdominal cramping and some loose bowels. You'll also experience fever and possible chills."

"For how long?" the older man asked, grimacing.

"It depends upon how much you ate and how severe the contamination was. I would say a day or two but it could be even longer. Once it runs its course and you can keep bland food down, you will need to drink plenty of clear liquids to keep from becoming dehydrated."

"Like tea?" Mr. Callahan asked.

"Yes. Tea with lemon or ginger, which quells nausea, is especially good. And broth. That will help build up your strength. As it is, you'll be fatigued for a week or more."

She glanced at the two ill men. "Once you begin to recover and can keep solid foods down, eat only plain items— rice, potatoes— then you can work up to lean meats or chicken. But rest is paramount. Food poisoning can be exhausting."

Emma heard the groans coming through the closed door. "Are the two ladies in there? I'd like to speak with them if I could. Please send for a porter. I need to give him instructions soon."

Mr. Callahan went to the door and knocked. It opened after some moments. She saw an older woman clutching a handkerchief to her mouth standing there.

"*Chi e?*"

"*Lo sono qui per aiutare,*" Emma said, hoping her rusty Italian told the woman she was here to help.

"*Grazie!*" the woman proclaimed and motioned her in.

Emma stepped through the door and saw a younger, incredibly beautiful woman sprawled across an unmade bed. She cried softly into her pillow as she held her hand against her stomach.

Hurrying to the bed, she perched upon it and took the woman's hand.

"*Lo sono Emma. Lo ti aiutero.*"

She looked at the dresser. "Do you speak English?"

"Yes. We both do," she said. "This is *Signorina Abetelli.* I am Rozalia."

The dresser's words were heavily accented but it *was* English. Emma was grateful she wouldn't have to try to translate as she helped the women. She explained what was wrong and how long they would probably be ill, as well as what to do as they recuperated.

She insisted to Rozalia that she also lie down and placed wet cloths on both women's brows. She heard voices in the other room.

"I believe the porter is here. We need to see about getting you off this train. I know the motion doesn't help any."

"Don't go, *il mil amico.*"

"I will be back, Miss Abetelli," she assured the opera singer. "I know it seems as if you will die. I, too, have had food poisoning. In Italy, in fact. I recovered. You will do the same."

"*Giusto. Grazie.*"

Emma went back to the room where the men were. She was happy to see the porter had arrived.

"We have four very ill passengers," she told him. "They need to disembark at the next stop and will need care for a few days. Can you let the conductor and engineer know about the situation?"

The porter nodded and asked her a few questions before leaving.

"Are they all right?"

She looked at the healthy Pinkerton agent that she had dined with, a worried look still on his handsome features. It seemed hours ago since their enjoyable conversation.

"They will be but they will need plenty of the fluids I mentioned, as well as total bed rest."

The manager said, "The remainder of the company must travel on to Denver. It would be too complicated to change all of their tickets. Besides, they can be assembling the sets and preparing everything as usual. They won't need Renata for several days. She can work on regaining her strength before rehearsals begin."

"You should go with them, Rye," Eddie said. "They still don't know you're part of the protection detail. I think we'll be fine in whatever small town we pull up in."

"No. I don't want to abandon you in the middle of nowhere. I can always show up later and get a job with the company once we've all arrived in Denver. Besides, if there was a threat, you're in no shape to thwart it, Eddie, and there is still the rest of the train ride to Denver. You never know what might happen."

"It looks as if you don't need me while you're discussing your business," Emma interjected. "I should return to my seat."

"No."

Everyone turned to see Renata Abetelli swaying in the doorway.

"Please, *Signorina*. Emma. I wish you to come with me. I will pay you whatever you ask. Just don't leave me now."

CHAPTER NINE

$\mathcal{E}$mma looked at the frail opera singer and took pity on her. She glanced around the room and saw the others looked in even worse shape than Miss Abetelli. With no set schedule, she was free to get off the train at any town.

Meaning John and Louisa would never be able to find her now.

She doubted even if they put their own set of Pinkertons on her trail that any detective would have a clue where she had gone. If by some miracle they could trace her ticket purchased in New York, it would show her final destination as Omaha. By getting off at the next stop and then eventually taking a train to Denver, she would have dropped off the face of the earth. Besides, she remained a nurturer by heart. These people needed her. She wanted to feel useful at this point, with her life up in the air.

The bonus would be that Zachariah Callahan would also disembark with the party of sick people. She found herself strangely drawn to the tall Pinkerton agent and curious to learn more about him and his unusual occupation.

"Yes, Miss Abetelli. I shall leave the train with you."

Tears flowed down the porcelain cheeks of the dark-haired beauty. "*Grazie, Emma. Grazie.*"

Emma moved closer to the singer. "You need to lie down until we arrive at the next depot." She patted Miss Abetelli's shoulder lightly. "Go, now. I need to speak to the Pinkerton agents but I'll be with you shortly."

The singer nodded and turned away, closing the door to the bedroom compartment.

"What do you need, Miss Bradford?"

She collected her thoughts before she replied to Mr. Callahan. "I need to return and get my things. I have a small valise that contains my *Appleton's National Railway Guide*. Once everyone feels well enough to travel again, we can search it for the various rail maps and time-tables in order to plan our departure. I bought the latest edition when we left New York so it will still be up-to-date for another ten days or so. Barring any complications, we can easily leave for Denver before then."

"Anything else?"

She stared into the Pinkerton's unusual, compelling eyes. "The next stop will be a brief one. No matter how important or famous Miss Abetelli is, trains wait for no man or woman. We'll need to get everyone off as quickly as possible and escorted into the depot. Since the conductor has been apprised of the situation, I am sure he'll be more than willing to help in the process.

"I'll make those ailing as comfortable as I can while you find the nearest hotel. It will be easier to care for them all if we place the two women and two men in rooms next to each other."

The tour manager interrupted. "No," he said weakly. "Renata will insist upon—"

Emma cut him off. "She'll cooperate, sir. She and Rozalia will stay in one room. I'll sleep on a pallet nearby. Mr. Callahan can do the same for you men. I'm sorry but we haven't been formally introduced."

"Mr. Larsen is Miss Abetelli's manager and owner of the touring company. The fellow behind that panel puking his guts out is my good friend and fellow agent, Edward McLeod."

Eddie emerged from behind the partition, wiping his mouth with his sleeve. "Pleased to meet you, Miss Bradford. Sorry it's not under better circumstances."

"I quite agree, Mr. McLeod. If you'll excuse me, I'll fetch my things."

Zachariah Callahan opened the door for her and stepped out into the hall with her.

"I can't thank you enough for agreeing to stay. Miss Abetelli is a little… temperamental. I suppose all opera divas are."

"I'm sure you've served as a bodyguard for a plethora of opera stars in your time as a Pinkerton agent."

He chuckled at her teasing tone. "I think you're pulling my leg, Miss Bradford."

"Perhaps, Mr. Callahan."

"If we're going to spend time together nursing our group of invalids, the least you can do is call me Rye. Those who reside in the West stand on less ceremony than their hoity-toity cousins in the east."

She found herself smiling up at him. "I like hearing that, Rye. Please call me Emma."

～

RYE LEFT the ailing group in the small waiting room of the train station and hurried to speak with the ticket seller on duty. In his years of travels, he had found most of them a wealth of knowledge, especially those in smaller towns.

78

He approached the window, finding a man in his fifties with light blue eyes and a ready smile.

"Excuse me, sir, but I need some quick information. Four people in my traveling party have fallen ill with food poisoning. They aren't contagious in any way but they need a quiet place to rest and recover over the next few days. Would you have any suggestions as to what hotel we might check into?"

The man guffawed. "We don't have a hotel here, Mister. A general store? Yes. A church? Yes. But that's about it."

Rye shot back, "Then tell me what citizen in town would have a space large enough to house six people. I'm willing to pay a very fair price."

The seller's eyes lit up. "Very fair, you say?"

"Oh, yes. But besides rooms, we would need access to kitchen facilities. They'll need broth and weak tea and, eventually, soft foods. Either my traveling companion or I can prepare this or the lady of the house."

The man scratched his chin. "In addition to the very fair price?"

Rye saw where this was going. "Yes. I assume we'll be boarding at your place?"

Laughter filled the air. "Why, of course. Mrs. Peters and I have plenty of room to spare after raising seven children. Don't worry. They're all gone now. The loudest thing around is our rooster's call every morning. The rest of the time things are mighty quiet."

Rye offered a price, which Mr. Peters quickly accepted. He stepped from the booth and found a local boy outside, telling him to run to his place and have his wife hitch up the horse and bring their wagon to the station.

"Make sure there are plenty of blankets in back. Tell her I said so!"

Within half an hour Mrs. Peters arrived, and her

husband informed her of the situation. Rye spread the blankets in the back of the wagon and then escorted Renata and Rozalia to it. Both women, still pale and shivering now, lay down in the wagon's bed.

He instructed Emma, "Go with Mrs. Peters and get them settled, then have her return for Mr. Larsen and Eddie. I'll stay with them. By the time we arrive at the Peters' place, hopefully you'll have the ladies tucked in and a place designated for the gentlemen to collapse."

Another three-quarters of an hour passed before Mrs. Peters poked her head into the station. Mr. Peters stepped away from his booth to get Ivar Larsen situated in the wagon while Rye saw to Eddie. The men then retrieved the baggage.

On the way to their destination, Mrs. Peters told him they were about sixty miles from the Ohio border.

"We're still in Pennsylvania?" he asked.

"Yes, young man. Miss Bradford tells me you're with an opera company? That she's an understudy to Miss Aba-whatever and you're the agent in charge of all the touring. She said you handle the personnel and traveling arrangements."

He suppressed a smile, thinking of Emma spinning stories. She would never want this woman, who seemed as much a gossip as her husband, to know that she had hopped off a train with a group of strangers. Giving herself a role as a company member made perfect sense. He also thought it smart on her part to keep his and Eddie's true identities concealed.

"Yes. I'm actually Mr. Larsen's assistant, Zachariah Callahan. Mr. Larsen is the owner of the troupe and manager to Miss Abetelli." He nodded in Eddie's direction. "Mr. McLeod works on our sets. Painting. Construction. That kind of thing. And you met— or at least saw— Rozalia, Miss Abetelli's dresser. She cares for her costumes and wardrobe and attends to her personal needs. Much like a lady's maid."

"I see."

Rye bit back his laughter as he saw Mrs. Peters squirrel away all the nuggets of information he'd tossed out for her to collect.

They arrived at a large, two-story farmhouse with a wraparound porch. As he helped the men into the house, he spied the famously loud rooster prancing about the yard.

"Up here, Rye," Emma called from the top of the stairs.

"I can make it on my own," Eddie told him. "See to Larsen."

They ventured up the steps and Emma directed him to a large, airy room with two sets of bunk beds. Eddie collapsed on one lower bunk. Rye eased Ivar Larsen onto the one opposite.

Mrs. Peters hovered in the doorway. "This is where our boys slept. Four of them, all a year apart. The girls each had their own room across the hall. They came along a few years after the boys, thank the Good Lord. Those boys about wore me out, but my two girls were real gems."

"Thank you, Mrs. Peters. We appreciate you allowing us to stay in your home. Remaining on the train with this many being so sick was next to impossible."

"Happy to oblige, Mr. Callahan." She turned to Emma. "What else can I do, dear?"

"If you have fresh well water available, I'd like them to start sipping it. Or weak tea. Either is fine. They won't need anything else in their stomachs for quite a while. I've got their slop jars set up. Hopefully, the worst of that is over."

"I'll fetch the water for you and start the tea," the older woman said, leaving to head downstairs.

"I'll retrieve our bags," he said.

"Mrs. Peters said you can stay in here with the men. I'll be back and forth between all the rooms and probably sleep with Rozalia so that Miss Abetelli can have some privacy."

"Emma?" a weak voice called out.

"Sounds like our leading lady needs you. I'll be right back with the luggage."

He soon had the few bags brought to the appropriate rooms, grateful that Renata had been too ill to notice they left the majority of her trunks on the train. He led the horse back to the barn and saw to it before returning to the house. Entering, he heard the crackle of chicken frying and couldn't resist sticking his head in the kitchen to fill his lungs with the aroma.

Mrs. Peters smiled at him. "Just because your friends can't eat doesn't mean you and Miss Bradford should starve. Mr. Peters will be home soon and we can sit down to a quick supper. I don't have to ask if you like fried chicken, judging by the look on your face."

"It's one of my favorites, ma'am." He looked over his shoulder. "I need to see if Emma needs any help."

He bounded up the stairs and checked on the men first. Both lay slack-jawed and sound asleep. He stepped quietly into the hall and saw Rozalia in the bedroom directly across, lying on her side, her eyes closed.

The sound of a low voice caught his attention so he ventured to the next doorway and saw Emma sitting on the bed. She held Renata's hand as she told her a story. He caught enough to realize she was sharing *Great Expectations*.

"Oh, this Pip must have been so scared," Renata said, her eyes round. "He's such a little boy."

"Yes. To think one minute he is mourning at his parents' graves on Christmas Eve, and the next minute, he's confronted by an escaped convict in chains. That's only the start, Renata. I'll have much more to tell you over the next few days. For now, you need to get some rest."

"Must I?" the soprano complained. "I feel better already. I didn't eat very much of the tainted lunch. Rozalia is always pestering me. She says I eat like a bird."

The singer gave Emma a pretty pout. "I'd rather hear about what happens to Pip when he steals the food. Do you think the convict will take Pip with him? Does Pip have a family? Would he be missed?"

"I'm sure that pout works on everyone else but I have a heart of steel when I'm in charge of a sickroom. Close your eyes, Renata. I promise you'll feel even better when you awaken."

"To hear more about Pip."

"Of course." Emma stood and adjusted the quilt covering Renata, who obediently closed her eyes.

She turned and tiptoed across the room, stepping into the hall as Rye moved back a few paces.

"I'll bet no one ever tells Renata Abetelli what to do," she said, smiling. "I'm surprised she listened to me."

He noticed the dimple in her cheek. "You're probably the first person in her life that ordered her to do something that she actually did."

"I can be quite persuasive when I choose."

"So can I."

Without hesitation, Rye pulled Emma close and kissed her.

*E*mma found her head swimming as Rye kissed her. She thought she had forgotten to breathe, but realized she still did when a clean, masculine scent made her knees go weak. She clutched his shoulders to keep from swooning.

And gave in to the kiss.

Her heart drummed wildly in her breast as Rye's hands cupped her face before sliding down her neck to her shoulders. She'd never been kissed like this. Years ago, when Howard courted her before the carriage accident, she never dreamed of him touching her in such an intimate manner. Even John's recent attentions only involved pressing his cool lips to her cheek and once upon her lips. But what Rye Callahan was doing to her was delicious.

Sinfully delicious.

His lips brushed slowly against hers, lingering, playfully nipping at the corner of her mouth and then along her bottom lip. The tingling in her own lips traveled through her like lightning as his tongue eased open her mouth and sought refuge inside hers. He stroked her tongue with his in a dance that showed no hesitation. She quickly learned its moves and answered his call with one of her own. He responded, pulling her close, so close she felt the hammering of his heart.

The kiss deepened, quickly sparking like dry embers, exploding into heat and fire and need. Emma clung to Rye as if she were a ship tossed about in a perfect storm on a wild ride at sea. Instead of fighting against it, she went with the flow, ripples of desire coursing through her. She felt protected and yet challenged, giving and receiving, caught up in a maelstrom of need and want.

Then the beating waves stopped abruptly when he tore his mouth from hers.

She stared into golden eyes that simmered with a passion which stirred a deep longing within her.

"My utmost apologies, Miss Bradford. Emma." He released her and took a step back, leaving her swaying on unsteady legs. She locked her knees to try to stay adrift in the swirling emotions enveloping her.

"Why did you kiss me if you were only going to apologize?" she asked. She bit her lower lip in amusement and saw his eyes darken. "Or do you operate under the lesson a spoiled child learns, that it's better to act first and seek forgiveness afterward?"

She saw the blush rise on the chiseled planes of his face and stifled a laugh. She was recovering from the unexpected experience rapidly— and trying to provoke him into kissing her again.

Rye shook his head almost in disbelief. "I did act without thinking. I've... well, I don't think I've ever done that before." He looked at her in wonder, as if staring at her would help him understand his actions.

"I've never done that before. Kiss a man. Like *that*." She found her own cheeks heating. "You certainly are full of surprises, Rye. A detective. A book lover. And a spectacular kisser. Although I'm certain I shouldn't point out something of that nature. However, you did tell me the West stood on less formality." She eyed him appraisingly. "I do believe I'm looking forward to learning more about the West. And about you, Rye Callahan."

She turned and hurried down the stairs.

Rye watched Emma retreat, her skirts swaying temptingly as she descended to the ground floor. If those last words had been spoken by any other woman, he would've thought her a brazen hussy. But coming from an angel with strawberry blonde hair and twinkling blue eyes?

"I hope I'm the one who'll teach you more about the West," he called down the stairs. "And about other things," he said under his breath.

EMMA INHALED the dinner Mrs. Peters had prepared. She didn't realize how hungry she'd grown until the first bite of chicken passed her lips. She asked the couple all about life in their small town as she polished off second helpings of everything on the table.

She was aware of Rye's eyes on her throughout the meal. He said little beyond thanking Mrs. Peters for passing the platter of chicken or the basket full of flaky biscuits his way, concentrating on the meal at hand.

But she knew she had his attention. And she liked having it. It was a heady feeling, knowing an attractive man couldn't take his eyes from you. She licked her lips and caught him staring at her longingly. When their gazes met, he quickly became interested in the candied carrots on his plate.

She chatted happily with Mrs. Peters about the problems that could occur in quilting and learned all about the couple's grown children, now scattered throughout the state and beyond. Rye continued eating his meal in silence.

After Mrs. Peters served them apple pie with a dollop of cream, Emma didn't think she could move.

"Everything was delicious, ma'am," Rye said as he rested his fork on the empty dessert plate in front of him. "May I help you with the dishes?"

It touched her heart to hear him offer to take part in such a mundane task, one that women always seemed to be stuck performing.

"No, Mr. Callahan, Miss Bradford and I are perfectly capable of washing up."

Rye looked across the table at her. "I thought if I helped that it would free Miss Bradford to go check on her patients."

"Why, how thoughtful," proclaimed Mrs. Peters. "Did you hear that, Mr. Peters? Such a gentleman."

Her husband grunted. "Clear the table, dear. Mr. Callahan is a guest. He shouldn't have to do any dishes. He and I will go have a smoke on the porch instead and Miss Bradford can tend to the ill."

The look Mr. Peters gave let Emma know that, despite his joviality, his word served as law in his household.

Feeling like a rebel at heart, she said to Mrs. Peters, "I'll help you clear before I go up."

Minutes later, she carried a tray of lukewarm broth to those upstairs. She checked in first on the men. Both were awake and talking quietly.

She looked them over. "You both have some color in your cheeks. Do you think either of you can get down a little broth?"

"My insides are so empty and my mouth so dry, I'd sure like to give it a try," Eddie told her. "I haven't needed the slop jar in a while."

"I'll pass," Mr. Larsen told her. "The smell of grease

wafting up those stairs lets me know I'm still a bit queasy. Maybe by tomorrow. For now, I'll stick with water."

She made sure both men were comfortable and then crossed the hall to Rozalia's room. The older woman rested on two pillows, her olive complexion still pale. Emma left a bowl of broth with her and promised to look in on her later.

After that, her last stop was Renata's room. The soprano's eyes were closed but Emma knew she was awake because Renata's fingers drummed against the sheet.

"How are you feeling?"

Renata's eyes opened lazily. She gave Emma a mischievous smile. "I am weak and a bit tired, but my stomach has calmed. Is that broth?"

"Yes. Chicken broth. Your first step on the road to recovery is keeping this down and letting it help rehydrate you."

The singer's stomach gurgled in anticipation. "I would like some. Bread if you have it."

Emma shook her head. "Not yet. No solid food until tomorrow. I know you feel better than the others do at this point, but I want to be certain that the food poisoning has run its course."

She handed the bowl to her patient, who began daintily spooning the liquid into her mouth.

"Take it slowly," she warned. "You don't want to rush it or overload your stomach."

"*Si, Signorina Infermiera.*" Renata took her time and finished a few minutes later, returning the bowl. Emma set it aside and lifted her hand to Renata's forehead.

"You're cool as a cucumber. Have you had any more chills?"

"No. None since the train."

Smiling, she said, "Then my diagnosis is you'll be

the first to regain your appetite and your strength. If the others follow suit, you can all rest tomorrow, and then we might be able to continue our journey to Denver by the day after. I'll let Rye know."

She turned to leave and stopped in her tracks at the giggling. "Did I say something amusing?"

"You and the Pinkerton are now on a first-name basis?"

Emma bit her lower lip and nodded. "Yes. The unusual circumstances we've found ourselves in have allowed us to drop a few formalities. Remember, you've also asked me to address you by your first name."

Renata's eyes sparkled. "Yes, I did. But I did not ask you to kiss me like you did Mr. Callahan."

A hot blush flooded her face. "You saw that?"

"Oh, yes. It was quite entertaining. He is an interesting man, no?" She smiled at Emma. "I would like to be entertained by one such as he. *E bello, si?* Oh, don't be embarrassed, Emma."

She couldn't help it. What she thought was a private moment now seemed spoiled. The knowing glimmer in Renata Abetelli's eyes cheapened the experience. Regret filled her. How could she explain that she had never acted out of character in this way before?

What made it worse was she had enjoyed every minute of it.

Resolve stiffened her spine and helped her determine not to be alone with Rye Callahan again. After all, they were close to being strangers. She'd made a rash decision to help him when she chose to get off the train with the group of sick people. It made her wonder if her bold actions had led him to think he could kiss her in the first place. It certainly occurred out of the blue. Shame now colored the entire situation.

"I'll check on you later. I'll be sleeping next door with Rozalia. You may tap on the wall if you have need of me. I'm a light sleeper. I plan to look in on all of you several times during the night."

She spun around and marched from the room, anger building in her as Renata's laughter echoed behind her. She went down the stairs and out to the porch, determined to make things right.

Rye sat next to Mr. Peters, who smoked a pipe. Mrs. Peters sat in a rocker on the other side of her husband.

"May I speak to you a minute, Mr. Callahan?"

"Of course." He rose and followed her inside the house.

Emma moved to the kitchen, far enough away so that they wouldn't be overheard. She harnessed the embarrassment raging inside her. She didn't want him to see her emotions getting out of hand.

"I wanted you to know, Mr. Callahan, that all four patients are much improved. Taking them off the train was the right decision. They should all be able to drink and eat soft solids tomorrow. By the day after or in two days' time, I believe they can travel with no problems. They shouldn't exert themselves, but simply riding on a train for several more days shouldn't overtax them."

Rye stared at her, his brow furrowing. "I'm glad to hear that, Emma, but why so formal? Your speech and manner lets me know something's amiss." He smiled. "I am a detective, you know. I have a tendency to pick up on things."

She glared at him. "Because for all intents and purposes, we *are* strangers, Mr. Callahan. I plan to keep it that way. I'll be departing on the first available train in the morning."

CHAPTER ELEVEN

Rye awoke each morning still thinking Emma was in the house. For a moment, he knew peace and satisfaction. Within seconds, he realized she was gone.

What had changed?

It couldn't have been the kiss they shared. Although clearly a novice, Emma caught on quickly and returned his kiss with fervor. He'd seen the passion rising between them and had broken it off, as a gentleman should.

Yet even her saucy reply about learning more about the West— and him— let him know she would entertain the thought of exploring more time together.

And possibly an attachment.

That thought had surprised the hell out of him. Rye had never believed he was the type to settle down. As he moved from case to case and town to town, he'd scratched his occasional itch with local whores and then returned to his hotel room alone. Ideas of courtship and love and marriage had never crossed his mind.

Until meeting Emma. She had a sweetness about her, coupled with a bit of sass and a dash of mischief thrown in. She was beyond beautiful and probably the smartest person he'd ever met. When she was talking about her father's mill, he hadn't understood half of what she said but her knowledge impressed him all the same.

It had led to him daydreaming throughout dinner of creating a life with Emma. Finally settling down. Making babies and sharing the good times and bad.

Then out of the blue, his idea of pursuing a relationship with her came crashing down. Without warning, she had grown as frosty as ice floating in the Hudson on a wintry day, coldly informed him they were no more than strangers and that she would be leaving the following day.

She did. Without a backward glance.

He didn't realize how much a heart could hurt until he watched her riding away in the cart seated next to Mr. Peters as she returned to the train station to continue her journey west. As Emma rode out of his life, her posture ramrod straight, he knew his sudden, foolish dream of a life with someone he loved would never happen.

Oh, he didn't love her. Yet. At least he didn't think he did. But the connection they'd forged during their brief acquaintance signaled to him that she was the only woman he'd been interested in pursuing. Ever. Not that he knew the first thing about courting a woman. Even if she had stuck around.

Then she'd fled. The two days without seeing her sunny smile or hearing that tinkling laughter seemed an eternity. Rye had no idea where she'd gone. Although she had mentioned Denver, he doubted she traveled there now, knowing he and the opera company made that city their final destination.

A third day without Emma bringing joy into his life now unfolded. At least today, they would continue on their journey, with those afflicted by the food poisoning now strong enough to travel.

He eyed Renata Abetelli, seated on the bench of the wagon next to him, her smooth features in a mask he couldn't read. She turned and studied him a long moment. The satisfied look in her eyes, along with the smile that looked as if she were a cat who'd finished licking the cream bowl, felt like a punch in the gut. He'd seen that look before, when his so-called mother thought she'd pulled one over on an unsuspecting neighbor. His detective's gut told him something the diva said or did had caused Emma to bolt unexpectedly. What, he couldn't fathom, but he'd get to the bottom of the mystery.

They arrived at the train depot. Eddie jumped from the back of the wagon and helped Ivar Larsen down before he came around and assisted Renata and Rozalia to the ground. Rye tapped lightly on the reins and maneuvered Mr. Peters' horse to the side of the building. The hitching post was in the shade of an oak tree. He secured the cart and joined the others inside the station. Their luggage, brought by their host earlier that morning, awaited them.

He made his way to the ticket booth. Mr. Peters greeted Rye with a smile and handed him their tickets. When Rye started to push the money for their fares toward him, Mr. Peters stopped him.

"The tickets are on me, Rye. Best I could get for all involved. Your more than generous compensation will keep me and the missus in fine spirits for a long time to come, not to mention how much we enjoyed having your company these last few days."

A shadow crossed the ticket seller's face. "I'm just sorry Miss Bradford had to travel on ahead of you. We really think a lot of that fine young lady. Will you give her our best when you reach Denver?"

Gritting his teeth, he nodded. "The next time I see Miss Bradford, I'll be sure and convey your good wishes."

Rye gathered up the tickets and headed back to his traveling party, glancing at them as he went. He cursed under his breath, knowing that Renata was about to get her nose out of joint with the travel arrangements.

He handed the tickets to everyone and said, "Mr. Peters was able to secure sleeping car berths for the ladies. We gentlemen will—"

"Impossible! *Che e inaccettabile!*"

He turned to the diva, holding his temper in check at her outburst. "I'm sorry you find it unacceptable, Miss Abetelli, but private coaches are few and far between. The Pinkerton Agency has charged us with getting you to Denver as soon as possible. We will be taking this train and using the available seats. We will also avail ourselves of the food in the dining car since this Pullman is fortunate enough to have one. We will eat the meals provided there. I don't want any outside food brought in because of what happened before."

"Are you saying someone deliberately tainted our food?" asked Ivar.

"Not at all," Rye replied, "but I wasn't able to control that outside source. I will be able to speak with the workers in the dining car. When we transfer in Kansas City, if no dining car is available, we'll eat our remaining meals from the food vendors in the depots or the restaurant located inside the train station. No one knows Miss Abetelli's schedule as of this moment. Eddie and I would like to keep it that way."

He stared hard at the opera singer. "That means no cabling ahead for special favors, other than letting Mr. Devinde know when we'll arrive. I guarantee we'll get you safely to Denver, Miss Abetelli, and keep you safe during your performances there. I appreciate your full cooperation."

Renata sniffed, which sounded more like a disdainful snort to him. "So surly. Ever since Emma left, you have lost all your good manners, Mr. Callahan." She turned to Rozalia. "Accompany me to the necessary before we board the train. My hair is a mess after riding in that flimsy cart."

The two women flounced off. Rye wasn't sure which one appeared snootier. He gave a nod to Eddie, who shadowed them from a distance.

Ivar met his eye. "Renata is used to having all the attention lavished on her, Rye." He held a hand up as Rye started to protest. "I know she is your client and you and Eddie are providing a service to her." The manager shrugged. "But she is a woman, a hot-blooded Italian one, at that. I'm sure the slight attention you paid to Miss Bradford was enough to rile Renata."

"You think she said something to Emma to make her leave ahead of schedule?"

Larsen's tight smile was all the answer Rye needed. He didn't know when— or how— but he would confront the soprano. Normally, he would never get so personal with a client but she had interfered with something special. Something Rye might never have a chance to get back.

He aimed to find out exactly what the opera diva had said.

~

EMMA OFFICIALLY CONSIDERED herself the most miserable soul on the planet as she opened her eyes and stared at the ceiling above her bed.

"Why did I let Renata make me leave?" she asked herself aloud for the umpteenth time.

She sat up and fluffed the pillows behind her, crossing her arms as she thought about the last few days. She'd rashly gotten off the train to help Rye Callahan's fellow Pinkerton detective and their ill clients. In part. The bigger part had been because she was interested in— and fascinated by— Rye Callahan himself.

Emma knew she had intelligence. She had always done well at lessons, catching on quickly to whatever she learned, whether it was languages or understanding the machines at her father's factory. She was creative because she could make up elaborate stories on the spot.

Yet as far as her social life was concerned, she'd been very sheltered. She didn't know much about the opposite sex because she'd spent her prime years not on the marriage mart. Instead, she'd chosen to take care of business at the mill and nurse her father at home. That's why John Fairburn's arrival in town seemed like such a breath of fresh air and the attention he lavished upon her was so welcomed.

Regrettably, she had been gullible where John was concerned. Emma didn't want to make that mistake again. When Renata teased her about kissing Rye, she should have been mature enough to take it in stride. Instead, she had panicked and been mortified at her behavior, thinking perhaps she'd been too trusting— or forward— with Rye.

Just as she'd thrown all caution to the wind and followed her heart when she kissed him, she again reacted without thinking... and fled the Peters' homestead. Whatever relationship she might have built with the devastatingly handsome Pinkerton detective now stood at a dead end.

Oh, she wasn't that naïve. She knew relationship might be too strong a word, but she would have enjoyed getting to know him better, perhaps while she explored what Denver had to offer. If their budding friendship grew into something more, she would have welcomed the experience.

Instead, she'd run from that bully Renata and lost all chance of ever getting to know Rye better. She'd thought about it at length this past week— in her hotel room, while walking through Omaha, even while bathing in the claw foot tub— and she'd come to the realization that she'd behaved as a spoiled child.

She should have stood up to the soprano and called her out. Renata was no more than a greedy, pampered woman who enjoyed all attention being focused on her. She believed Renata might have been slightly jealous of the friendship that had developed between Rye and Emma and decided wounding Emma with words would be most effective.

In the long run, the diva won because Emma chose to leave. Most likely, she would never see Rye again.

"This is a life lesson I've hopefully learned," she proclaimed to the empty hotel room. "I will stand up for myself in the future and not blindly react without thinking things through. I will not let others judging me affect my feelings. I shall learn to keep my head and listen to my heart and be true to myself. If I seek advice from others, that's a different matter. But if someone disapproves of my behavior, I will answer only to myself."

She tossed the covers back and got out of bed, continuing her monologue. "There's nothing left to see in Omaha. I'll continue this journey to see the West. The real West. Not this middle patch of hilly ground where the stink of the stockyards penetrates every street in town."

Slipping into her dressing gown, she belted it. "Denver will be my next stop. It's a large city. I doubt I'll run into Mr. Callahan, but if our paths *should* stumble across each other, I will be cordial…and hope for the best."

Emma busied herself, packing her carpetbag and dressing for the day. As she twisted her long hair into a chignon, she wished again not only for Molly's skills at arranging hair but for the maid's companionship. Molly had earned Emma's trust and friendship over the years, and she still couldn't believe the servant had met her end in such a harsh manner. She knew John Fairburn must behind the girl's murder and determined to bring that cad to justice.

Maybe Rye could help.

She sighed and pushed all notions of Rye Callahan into a far recess of her mind. First things first. She'd make her way to Denver, which from all accounts was a bustling city, if not quite as spectacular as San Francisco claimed to be. She would fully explore Denver before she moved on to California.

Her first order of business once she arrived in Denver would be to see to a new wardrobe. She hadn't found much to her liking in Omaha, and the trunk Molly packed for their travels was likely still sitting in Emma's bedroom back in Plainfield.

After she saw to some new clothes, perhaps she'd sample the cultural life. Once suitably attired, she could take in an evening at the opera to see Renata Abetelli's performance. If she ran into Rye Callahan, she'd cross that bridge with her head held high.

Since she'd left behind her *Appleton's National Railway Guide*, she consulted the new one she'd purchased yesterday when itchy feet struck her. She opened the rival *Travelers' Official Railway Guide*, which told her she could make the slightly over five hundred miles trip from Omaha to Denver for about twenty-five dollars if she chose to ride first-class.

She studied the stops along the way— Silver Creek,

Wood River, Plum Creek, Antelope— which all sounded so picturesque. Determined now to move forward with her plans, she glanced at the watch pinned to her dress. If a ticket were available on this afternoon's 12:45 Union Pacific, then she would be in Denver by 6:45 tomorrow evening.

Arriving at the station, she managed to purchase a sleeping car berth all the way to Denver. Satisfied with those arrangements, she decided to buy a sandwich or something she could take with her on the train since she hadn't taken time for breakfast. It wouldn't do to have her stomach rumbling and offend those seated around her.

She found a food cart and purchased several items since she'd forgotten to check when the supper stop might occur. Her train pulled into the station on time and Emma boarded, finding her seat easily.

Just before it pulled out, a young woman a few years younger than she opened the door to the compartment, holding her hat with one hand, her face flushed with an excited grin.

"This is it, Ethel," she called over her shoulder. "I'll be fine. Be sure the luggage is loaded. You can check on me later."

With a sigh, the young woman marched down the aisle until she stopped at Emma's elbow.

"May I take the seat opposite you?" She flashed a smile. "I'm Bettina Devinde."

Emma nodded and the girl slipped into the seat. Emma guessed her age to be just under twenty.

"How do you do? I'm Emma Bradford."

"Quite well. My father will be opening a new opera house in Denver that hopefully will rival all his competitors and I'm traveling to visit him."

Emma's ears perked up with Bettina's statement. Renata was slated to perform at a new opera house opening in Denver. Surely, there couldn't be more than one new opening, even if Denver was a growing city?

"I'm also traveling to Denver," she shared. "It will be nice to have a companion to talk with on the way. I've never visited Colorado before. Perhaps I'll take in the production at your father's establishment."

Bettina's eyes grew round. "You're traveling by *yourself*? Oh, that's rich. Mama made me bring my maid, Ethel, as my chaperone from Chicago to Omaha. We stopped in Omaha to see my Aunt Dorothy, Papa's sister."

Bettina made a face like a child who had tasted cod liver oil for the first time. "Notice that Mama didn't accompany me on this visit. She's never liked Dorothy. Says she's too bossy and thinks she wears the pants in the family. Believe me, the two weeks I just spent there, I wouldn't wish it on my worst enemy. Not that I think I have any enemies, that is."

Emma unsuccessfully tried to hide a smile. Bettina certainly was a chatty whirlwind. As she looked at the young woman more closely, she wondered how young her new companion truly was.

The girl took off her hat and smoothed her hair before resting the bonnet back atop the ringlet of dark curls that framed her porcelain features. She fanned herself as the train began to pull away from the station.

Leaning toward Emma, she whispered, "Freedom," in a conspiratorial tone. "Aunt Dorothy is tight with her money. She knew it was proper that Ethel accompany me, but she stuck her with a third-class ticket. It's so liberating to be on my own."

"Have you ever been to Denver, Miss Devinde?"

"No, Miss Bradford. Emma. May I call you Emma? Papa's letters say the West is not so formal. As we are to be seat companions for hundreds of miles, perhaps we will become friends. Maybe even best friends. Call me

Bettina. It's a shortened form of Elizabeth. Mama came up with it. She despises nicknames such as Betty or Betsy or Eliza. But she saw the name Bettina in a book and decided that would be what she called me for life."

"It is rather original. And please, call me Emma. We seem to be close in age, you and I."

"I am nineteen. Soon to be twenty. I thought I would be married by now and have a child by twenty or twenty-one at the latest but my fiancé was lost at sea."

"How…dreadful." Emma didn't know quite how to reply beyond a few words, as Bettina rifled through her reticule now, matter-of-factly, no apparent sadness in evidence as she searched for some object.

"It is sad, I suppose. I was affianced to Charles at fifteen. He was a business acquaintance of Papa's and eager to make his fortune. He was involved in some business down in the Caribbean, wherever that is, and a tropical storm struck. The ship, its cargo, and poor Charles went down with it. Charles was almost twenty years older than me. We didn't know each other very well. We were to marry after I turned eighteen but he perished a month before the wedding. He missed my wonderful birthday party and our wedding. Through no fault of his own, of course."

"I'm so sorry for your loss." Emma shook her head at the rapid story emerging. Here she thought her tales could be wild at times.

"Ah, there it is." Bettina pulled out a small looking glass and touched her hand to her hair. "I do look presentable, after all. That wind was fierce outside the station. I don't see how my aunt manages to live on the Great Plains.

"Anyway, I know I should have been sad but I barely knew Charles. We hadn't spent but one afternoon tea alone together. It was as if hearing someone of brief acquaintance had passed." She wrinkled her nose. "Mama insisted upon a full year of mourning. All that black. If I never see black again, it will be too soon. That ended a year ago and Mama took me on a European tour to cheer me up. We were gone months and months and only recently returned."

"Your father has been in Denver all this time?"

"Denver. Chicago. New York. Business takes Papa all over." Her voice dropped. "He and Mama live *separate* lives, which means they each do as they please and are the happier for it. Mama enjoys her friends and a full life in Chicago, which is where I was brought up. Papa goes here and there but he's always been loving and kind to me."

Emma's curiosity was stronger than that which killed the cat. She prodded, "So you're visiting him in Denver. At his new opera house."

"Yes. The building itself has just been completed. His letters say it will rival all the great opera houses, especially Goodnight's in Pueblo and Forrester's in Denver itself. He's landed some impressive soprano from Europe to open the season."

"Renata Abetelli?"

Bettina's eyes grew large. "Yes. How did you know?"

"I, too, have traveled in Europe. Although I didn't have the pleasure of hearing Miss Abetelli sing while I was there, I did meet her on a train coming out of New York. She was on her way to her engagement in Denver."

"Oh, I wish I could sing as sweetly as a songbird. That's what Miss Abetelli sounds like. Mama and I heard her twice, once in Rome and again while we visited Munich. What's she like, beyond the stage, I mean?"

Emma considered the question. She didn't want to color Bettina's view of the singer. For the most part,

Renata had been very kind to her, despite the abrupt ending of their time together.

"For such a petite woman, she has a commanding presence. Very self-assured and quite beautiful. I'm sure she is an immense talent. Your father is lucky to have landed her for the first engagement of his establishment."

"You'll have to come with us on opening night. Papa has a box and I know any friend of mine will be welcomed." The young woman looked at her beseechingly and took Emma's gloved hand in her own.

"Please say you'll come to opening night, Emma." Bettina smiled winningly. "And the gala afterward. Simply everyone who's anyone in Denver is going to be there. Even the governor and his wife will attend."

Emma wondered if Rye Callahan would be at the festivities. Since it was his and Eddie's job to protect Renata, she assumed he would be present.

She looked at Bettina and smiled. "Thank you for your gracious invitation. I would love to attend both events."

CHAPTER TWELVE

Rye came into the train compartment and seated himself next to Eddie. "We should be in Denver in the next few minutes. Walt Devinde is personally meeting us at the station. We should be able to go straight to the hotel and get our diva settled."

Eddie looked thoughtful at the news. "Miss Abetelli told me earlier that the trip has exhausted her and that she'll want to retire for the remainder of the day. Larsen wants to get her to the theater first thing in the morning for rehearsals and costume fittings. Have you decided on your cover story?"

He nodded. "I will have met Larsen on the train. He's hired me to assist with carpentry for the set design. Later, I'm to switch to being a stagehand. I'd like to meet with Mr. Devinde in private after we get Renata parked at the hotel and make sure he's in the loop regarding our strategy."

"I'd like to gag Renata and dump her in a wagon headed for parts unknown. Preferably where buffalo might trample her. Then the buzzards could pick at her bones."

"Has our diva been giving you trouble, Eddie?"

His partner rubbed his eyes. "She doesn't seem to

complain much when you're around. I think maybe our little soprano's a bit intimidated by you. The moment you leave the area, she's all piss and vinegar. It almost would have been worth it to wait and book a private compartment on the next available train than to have to listen to her discontented ramblings the last couple of days."

"With the delay due to illness, we didn't have a choice." He grinned. "Maybe she's just comfortable with you, Eddie, and finds it easy to talk to you."

The agent grunted. "I wish you were the shadow and I was the ace in this case, Rye. Give me train robbers, corporate swindlers, or even cheating husbands any day over a woman with a mouth on her that never lets up."

Minutes later, they pulled into the Denver depot. Eddie retrieved their party while Rye stepped outside and scanned the crowd. Only one person stood out as he spotted what had to be Walt Devinde, a well-dressed man in an expensive suit and a gold pince-nez perched upon the bridge of his nose. His salt-and-pepper hair and dark mustache were neat as a pin, as if he'd just come from a visit to his barber.

He stepped forward. "Mr. Devinde?"

"I am, indeed. Are you Mr. McLeod or Mr. Callahan?"

He offered his hand. "Rye Callahan, sir. Eddie McLeod will be here momentarily with Mr. Larsen and Miss Abetelli and her dresser, a Miss Cattaneo. We'd like to get them settled at their hotel and then have a word in private with you."

Devinde said, "There's been a slight change in plans. My daughter, Bettina, has come from Chicago for an extended visit. When she heard I was putting Miss Abetelli up in the finest hotel in Denver, she claimed I was an insensitive oaf and insisted that the singer stay at our house. We've plenty of room for her, Mr. Larsen, and her dresser. For you and Mr. McLeod, as well." He laughed. "I've never done things halfway in my life and my Denver house is no exception. Bettina's already been lost in it, trying to find her way around with the friend she brought."

Rye quickly reflected on the change in plans. "It would be more secure than a public hotel, although I must warn you that Miss Abetelli has the fiery temper that most Italians exhibit. You might be bargaining for more than you or your staff can handle by asking her to stay in your home."

Devinde guffawed. "Sounds exactly like my wife. She's temperamental and quite the perfectionist. No, don't look alarmed, Mr. Callahan. The two women won't have a chance to clash. The missus and I have found marriage suits us— as long as we reside in different cities, preferably a few states apart. She makes Chicago her home. That leaves the rest of the world as my domain."

Rye took the news in stride. Over his years with the Pinkertons, he'd learned one simple fact. The rich made their own rules. It was none of his business where Mrs. Devinde stayed. As long as Renata could be coaxed into the change, it would help security measures immensely.

He turned and saw Eddie escorting the others toward them. After making quick introductions, he delicately broached the new housing arrangements.

"Miss Abetelli, Mr. Devinde knows how you value your privacy above all else. While he's booked you into the largest suite available at the finest hotel in Denver, he believes you would be more comfortable residing at his mansion for the duration of the run. His staff would see to your every need."

The diva eyed their handsome host with speculation. "Is this so, Mr. Devinde? I have a tendency to require...pampering."

Devinde smiled broadly. "My house is the largest in Denver, Miss Abetelli. You'll have ample rooms provided for you and your party, and my staff is second to none in meeting the needs of our guests. My coach and driver will be at your disposal, day or night. Whatever you desire, I'll see to it. Please say you'll reside in my home during your engagement."

Rye saw Renata mull over the decision. Everyone waited expectantly until she gave a curt nod. "I accept your kind offer, Mr. Devinde."

"Call me Walt." His eyes gave her an appreciative gleam, which Renata returned. Rye was thankful that no Mrs. Devinde would be present. He supposed a few nocturnal visits might be on the agenda for these two.

"Shall we make our way to my carriage?" Devinde took Renata's hand and pulled it through the crook of his arm. "We'll need to stop and pick up your trunks. I've had them held in your suite ever since they arrived on the train with the rest of your company."

"Oh, I can't wait to shed these rags I'm wearing. We had so little time to pack before we left the train when we all fell ill."

The couple strolled away, Rozalia shuffling along behind them like some avenging angel on the warpath. Ivar turned to Rye.

"She'll be happier with these arrangements. I don't know how you managed to have Mr. Devinde agree to this, Rye, but I'm grateful." The manager took off after them.

Rye and Eddie brought up the rear. Eddie noted, "That woman is like night and day. A hellcat one minute, and then a purring tabby the next."

"Let's hope it's smooth sailing from here on."

~

THEY ARRIVED at Devinde's imposing house after a stop at the hotel to cancel the previous arrangements. As Rye jumped down from the carriage, his eyes caught a woman turning the corner at the end of the block. For a moment, his heart pounded wildly because he thought it might be Emma. He shook his head, banishing her from his mind. No good would come from fantasizing that he saw her on every corner in Denver. He needed to stay focused on the job at hand. Keeping Renata Abetelli safe was what The Eye was paying Rye to do. When this case ended, though, he was tempted to ask for time off.

To find Emma.

The front door flew open. A young woman hurried down the porch stairs. He assumed Bettina Devinde was greeting them in person. She looked to be about twenty, barely over five feet, and had a mischievous gleam in her eyes that told him she could be trouble if given the chance.

"Hello, Papa," she called as her father stepped from the carriage and handed Renata down. Larsen and Eddie disembarked after the prima donna.

"Ah, my darling, as you can see, your wish has been granted. Miss Abetelli and her group will all be staying with us."

Rye noted the opera singer taking in the worshipful glance in the young woman's eyes and suppressed a smile.

"Hello, my dear Miss Devinde. I am delighted to make your acquaintance."

Bettina held out her hand. Rye wasn't sure if Renata would refuse, wanting the younger Devinde to bow to her or kiss her gloved hand as if the singer were the pope. Instead, Renata surprised him, clasping the

Devinde girl's shoulders and then drew Bettina to her, kissing her on both cheeks in the European fashion.

Flushed with excitement, Bettina drew Renata up the sidewalk, chattering away. He met Eddie's eyes and they both shrugged. If Renata took to Bettina, all the better. Maybe she'd watch herself while a guest in the Devinde home and behave in the regal manner she first did when they'd been introduced to her back in New York.

By the time the men entered the house, the two women mounted the stupendous staircase that served as the focus of the entrance, their heads together, already as thick as thieves.

Walt slapped him on the back. "That's my girl. She can charm anyone from their surliest mood. Never met a stranger. Why, she even met her best friend on a train. Bettina swears they'll be life-long companions."

"I'm sure she captures everyone with her winsome ways," noted Ivar. "Renata is a bit hard to please so I hope they will become friendly, if not friends."

"Shall we go into my study and discuss a little business?" Walt asked.

As they followed their host, Rye looked back and noted Rozalia already ordering the staff about as their luggage and Renata's trunks were brought in.

They settled into deep leather chairs of burgundy, and Devinde insisted on cigars and brandy to celebrate their arrival. Rye and Eddie took turns asking about the layout of the opera house and the Devinde mansion and explaining their roles in the protection detail for Renata.

"We'll walk your home and adjoining land later, but Mr. Larsen is eager to get to the opera house and see the status of things. We'd like to accompany him there. He'll introduce me as an additional hire to the company and I'll begin to learn about the group."

"I still hope you plan to stay here, Mr. Callahan, despite working within the company."

"Eddie and I agree that it would be best to have two pairs of eyes here at the house. I can say that I'm staying with my sister in case anyone in the touring company offers to put me up with them. She can be the reason I've come to Denver in the first place."

Larsen rose. "If you're ready then, shall we visit your grand opera house, Walt? I'm eager to see where our Verdi production will take place."

"I can escort you there but I've got a business appointment at the bank that I need to attend."

"That's perfectly fine, Father," Bettina said as she breezed into the study. "Miss Abetelli is lying down for a bit of a rest. I'd enjoy showing these gentlemen around if they'd allow me."

"Splendid idea, my dear. Then you can drop me at my bank and continue on to the few blocks to the opera house with Bettina."

In the carriage, Rye explained to Bettina Devinde how he was to be employed within the company while Eddie was the more visible bodyguard.

"It's very important that you don't acknowledge my connection to Mr. McLeod or the Pinkerton organization in any way," he emphasized to the young woman. "I'm simply hired labor so don't give me the time of day."

"Pish-posh, Mr. Callahan. I can keep a secret when need be."

Larsen told him, "I shall introduce you to Giovanni and tell him you are to have a job."

"Giovanni is the head of set design and building, correct?"

"Yes. He'll also be responsible for the lighting of the production. We've worked together for several years now. He's a good man. Steady as a rock. Not nearly as moody as most of the Italians employed in the company."

"Most of the members of your troupe are from Italy?" asked Bettina.

"Yes," Eddie answered. "At least from the roster Mr. Larsen shared with us. A few Germans and Frenchmen sprinkled in. One Belgian that I recall."

"Mr. Devinde will need to hire more to run the place," Larsen added. "We have enough people to get the sets built and the costumes completed but he'll need to employ a business manager, ticket sellers, ushers, and orchestra members. We have a few musicians that came with us from Europe and others we picked up in New York, but I need to make sure we round out the orchestra pit. That will be my first order of business once I've seen the house itself."

They arrived at their destination after stopping to let out Devinde at his bank, and then entered the opulent structure, rich in hunter greens and mellowed golds. Larsen called a brief meeting of the crew and cast members that were on site, assuring them that Renata was now in perfect health and would be present tomorrow for costume fittings in the morning and rehearsal in the afternoon.

"We don't open for another two weeks so we have plenty of time to finish the sets and props and rehearse. Miss Abetelli has sung this Verdi opera many times before so she won't need as much rehearsal as some of you," he shared. "I'll be working with individuals and groups on numbers that don't involve her in the mornings. She'll arrange to be here every afternoon. We'll have the kinks worked out in no time."

He gestured to those seated to his left. "Some of you may know Mr. Devinde's daughter. She'll be giving me a tour of the facilities, along with Mr. McLeod, who is from the Pinkerton Detective Agency."

Those assembled began murmuring at the mention of a Pinkerton being involved and Larsen quieted them. "We don't expect anything to be amiss but Miss Abetelli is a very famous star. Mr. McLeod is here to protect her from her more exuberant fans. Mr. Devinde is close friends with Allan Pinkerton, founder of the agency, and both men want the opening of Denver's newest opera house to go off without a hitch. Please cooperate with Mr. McLeod fully."

Larsen looked at Rye. "I met Mr. Callahan on the train coming out. He has experience in carpentry and painting. Giovanni, if you'll take him under your wing, I'm sure you have plenty for him to do. Antonio, he'll also work with you on props and as a stagehand once the production begins."

Both men nodded at Rye and he could tell they sized him up. He returned their assessment. He remembered them from the station and the train itself. Both men possessed a confident air that told him they knew their jobs and would expect him to know his. Larsen assured them back in New York that he'd carefully screened all employees of the opera company so Rye didn't expect any internal problems— but his eyes and ears would be alert at all times, in case Ivar Larsen had missed something.

The manager dismissed the troupe. Eddie and Bettina joined him for their tour of the facility. Rye headed in Giovanni's direction and introduced himself. The set designer gave him a brief overview of what had been accomplished so far and what would need to be completed within the next week. The Italian put him to work painting, where Antonio, the prop master, joined him.

Brush in hand, he helped Rye paint a large backdrop while filling him in on the type of work that he'd be involved in when the set design was completed and full-blown rehearsals and then performances began. Antonio was organized and obviously knew his stuff. Rye felt the physical labor of his job wouldn't be a problem.

Close to two hours passed before the trio returned from touring the entire building. He asked Giovanni if he could take a five-minute smoke break.

"Not a problem, Rye. You are a hard worker. You take ten minutes and be back, okay?"

He nodded in agreement and caught Eddie's eye. They met up out front.

"I'll arrange with Walt to walk you through tonight after everyone's gone," Eddie told him. "It's a large place, Rye. Lots of nooks and crannies backstage. The offices are on the upper level where the boxes are."

The door opened and Bettina Devinde stepped out. "I told Mr. Larsen you and I would be leaving, Mr. McLeod. He asked that the carriage be sent back for him at six. Dinner is served promptly at eight. I can drop you off at home, but I have an appointment at my new dressmaker's." She checked the watch pinned to her blouse. "I'm meeting my dear friend there and don't want to be late."

"Then we'll be on our way. Wouldn't want to keep anyone waiting. See you tonight, Rye," Eddie said. He motioned in front of him. "After you, Miss Devinde."

As they moved toward the carriage, Rye heard her say, "I can't wait to surprise Emma with all the new company staying with us."

Emma?

No, it couldn't be. It had to be a coincidence. Emma was a common enough name. No need in getting his hopes up. Rye turned and headed back inside the theater.

CHAPTER THIRTEEN

$\mathcal{E}$mma allowed Madame Drummond to fuss over her as an assistant pinned the last dress to be hemmed for now. She wondered if every dress shop owner was pretentious enough to take the title *Madame* in order to sound French. Did that really convince women to patronize a certain shop? Emma supposed it did, thinking of Louisa and her champagne tastes where clothing and accessories were involved. Everything from hats to gloves to gowns and their accompanying undergarments had to be made from the finest, most expensive materials. Louisa would be seen in nothing but the best, usually wearing it only once. She considered it a *faux pas* to appear in public in an ensemble previously worn.

She wondered how her stepmother fared, living on her generous allowance in the house where she had become a widow, with no husband to occupy her day and no stepdaughter to pretend to like. Emma figured John had either moved into a guest bedroom at this point or visited frequently. She laughed to herself, thinking he might actually have to entertain the idea of working for a living since she had escaped without a trace, drying up the source of revenue he'd counted upon once they wed.

That reminded her that she needed to telegram Daniel Mitchell. She had let the attorney know of her stop in Omaha but hadn't been in touch with him since her arrival in Denver. She still felt a little uneasy showing up on the Devinde doorstep and moving in, but Bettina wouldn't take no for an answer. Emma found her friend to be as generous as she was persuasive.

Mr. Devinde acted as if it were the most normal thing in the world for his daughter to bring a permanent houseguest with her. Emma thought it slightly pathetic, that she was like a stray dog Bettina had decided to bring home and fawn over.

Yet the two got along as if they'd known each other from the cradle. Even though the younger girl could appear a bit immature at times, she had a quick wit and easy charm about her. They fit together as well as peas in a pod. Mr. Devinde had even pulled Emma aside and told her how grateful he was for her bestowing her friendship upon Bettina, and suggested she would be a good role model for his daughter. He encouraged her to stay with them as long as she remained in Denver.

Fortunately, the city was everything she'd hoped for. In the short time since her arrival, she and Bettina had explored to their hearts' content, and she had recorded all the new places in her journal. They had discovered the perfect tea shop, a bookstore that rivaled any back in New York City, and numerous places to shop. Emma had decided to replace her entire wardrobe. She realized that between spending a large chunk of time at the mill and then in the company of her invalid father, she hadn't paid much attention to her attire, as she rarely mixed in polite society other than attending church every Sunday. Fashions changed rapidly and she was in her mid-twenties now. She wanted to dress in the latest styles and enjoy the freedom she now possessed. She even looked forward to the gala celebrating the opening of Mr. Devinde's opera house.

And tried not to think about possibly encountering Rye there.

Bettina was only too happy to accompany Emma to the various establishments around town as she replenished her wardrobe from head to toe. Both had ordered many dresses and new boots and shoes. Some of the gowns had been rushed and they already hung in a cupboard in her room at the Devinde mansion. Many more would be completed in the next week or so. She still needed several new hats, for that had always been her favorite part of any ensemble. She would need to mention that when Bettina arrived.

The tinkling bell sounded, and she heard Bettina's voice call out, "Hello?" and Madame Drummond left to summon Bettina to the back.

As always, Bettina swept into the room at full speed. Emma thought Bettina only slowed down in her sleep, and even then had her doubts. Her new companion was a whirlwind and a breath of much-needed fresh air.

Bettina cocked her head to one side and studied the gown Emma wore. The assistant stepped aside, her pinning completed.

"Green certainly suits you, Emma. I don't care whether it's a dark shade of hunter green or a lighter one as this mint gown, but that strawberry blonde hair of yours shines and your skin simply glows."

"You chose this color for me, Bettina. You have a good eye for color, as well as patterns and fabrics," Emma praised. Aware of the shop owner hovering at her elbow, she added, "Of course, Madame did the rest. She can work wonders with anything."

The dress proprietor nodded in acknowledgement. "We are through for the day, Miss Bradford. You may come for a final fitting of your dresses next Thursday at three. You, too, Miss Devinde. The rest of your gowns will need your approval before delivery."

"What of our ball gowns for the gala? They'll also be completed?" asked Bettina eagerly.

"But of course, *ma cherie*. You will both be *les belles de la balle* at your papa's gala."

Emma saw that statement brightened Bettina's face. Although she thought both their ball gowns stunning, she might need to advise her friend on the fine art of flattery and just how much could be believed, whether from an interested dancing partner or a shop owner who hoped for continued patronage.

"Let me change back into what I originally wore and then we can head home, Bettina. I've had an exhausting day."

"I have the carriage with me. We've walked enough of the city this last week. I've had a long day, too. I'm ready to get home."

She saw the twinkle in Bettina's eyes as she returned to the front of the shop and knew her friend must be up to something. Emma removed the dress and handed it to the assistant for the final touches before dressing quickly and rejoining her friend. They entered the carriage. She knew she wouldn't have to wait long. It wasn't in Bettina's nature to keep a secret.

"We'll have guests joining us for dinner. Tonight and every night. They're staying with us. Can you guess who, Emma?"

She swallowed, trying to maintain an outward appearance of calm. With Mr. Devinde being the owner of the opera house where Renata's company would soon be playing, Emma knew at some point she would encounter the soprano and her manager even before the opening night performance and gala. She'd visited the opera house once with Bettina and her father the day after they arrived in town, but had excused herself to other errands when Bettina returned twice more. Something told her the surprise guests would be her former acquaintances. At least the mansion was large enough that she likely would only see Renata and Ivar Larsen during meals.

"Don't you want to know who it is?" Bettina prodded when Emma was slow in responding.

She smiled. "I'm assuming you've convinced your father to have Miss Abetelli and Mr. Larsen stay. I know they will be much more comfortable in a private home than at an impersonal hotel."

Bettina laughed. "That's exactly what I told Papa. I said no matter how opulent Miss Abetelli's suite might be, anytime she left it would be like living in a glass fishbowl. Now, our staff can cater to her every whim as she enjoys the utmost privacy."

Emma almost snorted, thinking just how many whims Renata would feel needed to be addressed, but she refrained from speaking ill of the woman. Instead, she pitied the staff that would be at the singer's beck and call.

"I think it's incredibly thoughtful of you to consider Miss Abetelli's needs and take such good care of her and Mr. Larsen."

"See, Emma, you are a good influence on me. Oh, don't appear to be surprised by that remark. I know by now Papa has already pulled you aside and told you how wonderful you are. You really are. I'm ever so grateful that we wound up seated next to each other on that train."

The carriage slowed and the coachman assisted them from it. He promised to have the packages brought up to her room.

"I'm all for a brief nap before dinner," Bettina proclaimed as they entered the foyer. "I'll stop by your room at a quarter of eight. When we have guests, Papa likes to have everyone gather for a drink in the salon before dinner."

They parted when they reached Emma's room.

"Wear the lilac tonight, Emma. We'll need to look our best. Miss Abetelli will be expecting it. Europeans are known for their sense of fashion."

If only Bettina knew. Emma thought Renata wouldn't want anyone to outshine her, especially on her first night at the Devinde mansion but she kept silent.

Yet knowing of Renata's presence, Emma decided that she *would* wear the new lilac satin. With her pearl earrings and necklace, a gift from her father on her sixteenth birthday. She would treat it as her battle armor, because she feared once Renata knew she was there, they were in for a war.

TRUE TO HER WORD, Bettina tapped on Emma's door at the arranged time.

"You look wonderful, Bettina. I love how Ethel dressed your hair tonight. That shade of green makes your eyes even greener."

"No, Emma, you are the one who looks so beautiful. Oh, I wish my hair would stay in a chignon as yours does. It's much too unruly. You're fortunate yours is so straight and cooperates all the time."

They went downstairs and found Mr. Larsen chatting with their host. Both men looked up as they entered the room.

"Bettina. Emma. My, how lovely you ladies look this evening. Please, come greet Mr. Larsen."

Ivar Larsen kissed Bettina's hand and then took hers.

"My dear Miss Bradford. What a delightful surprise!"

"You are acquainted?" asked a puzzled Devinde. "Emma wasn't at home when you arrived today."

Larsen gave his host a smile. "Miss Bradford happened to be on the same train as we were coming from New York. She became our angel of mercy and disembarked with our party when we all fell ill with food poisoning."

Larsen smiled at her. "She graciously stayed on a bit to nurse us along and make certain we were on the road to recovery before she continued her own travels. I'll be forever in her debt." He kissed her hand, lingering longer than she thought appropriate.

"Emma! *Mio dolce amico!*"

"*Buona sera, Signorina Abetelli.*"

Renata crossed the room and kissed her on both cheeks. She turned to Bettina.

"Why did you not tell me my sweet Emma was here?"

"I'm sorry, Miss Abetelli. I was so thrilled to meet you earlier today. I forgot that Emma mentioned that you were slightly acquainted."

"*Nessun problema.* Think nothing of it." The singer turned back to Emma. "How do you like this Denver? Have you seen the opera house where I will perform Verdi? Will it suit me?"

"Yes, Bettina and I both visited it, Miss Abetelli. It is as grand— if not grander— than anything I've seen in New York. Or in Europe, for that matter."

"What is this *Miss Abetelli?* We are friends, dear Emma. You must call me Renata. You, too, little one," she told Bettina, who beamed at the thought of addressing the soprano by her Christian name.

"Would you care for a glass of wine, Miss Abetelli?" Walt Devinde asked.

Renata took one from the tray the butler offered and turned to Devinde. "I always take wine when offered," she said as she gleamed at him. "And please. I am Renata to you, as well. If we are to be living together, we must be comfortable with one another."

Emma looked at the way Renata appraised Walt Devinde and stifled a giggle. She thought the opera singer looked like a very hungry cat about to pounce upon a trapped mouse. Until she looked at Bettina's father and saw he returned the very same look. Emma sensed the blush creeping up her neck at the thought. She knew Bettina's parents led very separate lives, but this was far from her world of small town Connecticut.

She turned and accepted a glass of wine from the butler, sipping it slowly. Even though it made her stomach a bit giddy, she knew it would eventually calm her.

The group chatted for a few minutes about the upcoming production before Eddie McLeod slipped in the room. He came over to her as she stood listening to the conversation.

"Good evening, Miss Bradford. It's a pleasant surprise seeing you here."

"Hello, Mr. McLeod. Are you staying—"

"There's my protector," Renata proclaimed. "Have you gone over every inch of the opera house? And Walt's beautiful home? I know your goal is to keep me safe. And happy. Very, very happy."

Emma choked as she swallowed. Mr. McLeod patted her on the back until she recovered.

"I'm sorry. It went down the wrong way." She glanced and saw she had spilled some wine down the front of her dress. "Will you please excuse me? I need to change my gown."

She left the salon shaking her head. Renata not only had eyes for Walt Devinde but it looked as if she wanted to add Eddie McLeod to her collection of play-things. Emma should be shocked, but she remembered from her time in Europe that many people living there held a different standard of values than the ones Dwight and Darlena Bradford shared with their children.

As she climbed the stairs, Emma glanced down at her new dress, fairly sure the dribbles of red wine would refuse to come out of the delicate silk. She reached the landing and collided with someone quickly turning the corner of the staircase, falling back into nothing but air.

Before a scream could pass her lips, strong hands latched on to her, pulling her forward. She bumped against a solid mass of chest, grateful someone had saved her from a nasty tumble down the stairs. Her heart pounding rapidly, she looked up to thank her rescuer.

Rye Callahan stared back at her.

CHAPTER FOURTEEN

Rye stared into Emma's azure eyes, lost in them for a moment. Then he realized how closely he held her, her breasts against his chest as he clutched her arms and held her from falling down the carpeted staircase. He took a step back, bringing her with him and then released her, taking another step away from her for good measure.

Still, her perfume lingered in the air between them. His throat tightened as he looked at her oval face, now stained with a hot blush. Never one to shy away in any given situation, he took the bull by the horns.

"What are *you* doing here?" he demanded.

He saw hurt, then anger, spark in her eyes and wanted to kick himself for being so gruff and ill-mannered with her.

Her eyebrows arched. "I could ask the same of you but I suppose we are both guests in the Devinde home. Or rather, I'm an invited guest— and you are the hired help."

Her words stung him. Emma had never acted petty or cruel in their short time together.

Before he could reply, she said, "Forgive me. That was uncalled for." She paused and took a deep breath before continuing. "I realize we didn't part on the best of terms, Mr. Callahan. I apologize for my rudeness. Since it looks as if we both will be staying here, I hope that we can be cordial toward one another. Now, if you'll excuse me, I need to change."

He glimpsed a dark stain on the form-fitting lilac gown she wore. Despite the minor flaw, he knew he'd never seen a more beautiful woman. Emma Bradford could wear sackcloth and ashes and always be the most stunning woman in any room.

As she passed him, he took her elbow to stop her.

"Why?" he asked softly.

She looked up at him, her lush mouth trembling. His own legs wobbled as he studied her, her eyes filling with tears. His heart raced as if he retreated across a battlefield, the enemy's shots firing all about him.

"You left so abruptly. I didn't know... I didn't know what I'd done wrong," he admitted. "Whatever it was, Emma, I'll make it up to you. If you'll let me."

She bit her lip to stop it from quivering and the simple gesture undid him. Without thinking, he pulled her to him, his arms enveloping her, holding her close, her head tucked under his chin. He could feel her heart beating next to his chest. Smell the wonderful floral scent wafting up. Every nerve in his body stood at attention— and told him having this woman in his arms was where she belonged.

"Rye?"

He looked down at her and knew he had to taste her. His lips met hers in a searing kiss that warmed him down to his very toes. He ran his tongue along the seam of her lips. They opened like a budding flower welcoming the morning sun. He tasted the wine she'd drunk, along with a richness that words couldn't describe. He drank greedily from her, teasing her, his tongue mating with hers in an age-old ritual born at the beginning of time.

She brought her palm to touch his face, her thumb slowly caressing his cheek. He wanted this moment to last forever but reality called. Anyone could come across them, from servant to houseguest. Rye didn't want to compromise her in such a way. And Emma would be expected back downstairs soon. He broke the kiss and framed her face in his hands.

"I hope I'm forgiven, Emma." He stared at her longingly. "I hope you'll give me a second chance to get to know you better. You need to change now. You'll be missed."

She nodded, dazed, and turned from him to ascend the stairs. He watched each step she took, the only sound the swishing of her satin gown. At the top, she looked over her shoulder.

And gave him the most brilliant smile.

He felt like a schoolboy as he grinned back at her and then hustled down the stairs, trying his best to harness the maelstrom within him.

Entering the drawing room, he spotted Eddie and headed straight for him.

"How was your work with the crew?" his friend asked.

"Everything was pretty straightforward. How about your tour with Larsen and Bettina?"

Eddie briefly described some key points of the opera house before adding, "We've been given access to the building tonight while no one's there. We can thoroughly go over it so you're familiar with every inch of the place since your job won't necessarily allow you to be seen in certain areas."

"What about this house?"

"I've gone over it with a fine-tooth comb but I know

you'll want to do the same." Eddie paused. "There's an unexpected guest, Rye."

"I know. I ran into Emma as I was coming downstairs."

"It seems she's become friendly with Miss Devinde. She's the close friend Walt Devinde mentioned earlier when we arrived."

A butler offered him a drink, which he declined. "I want to take that up with Mr. Devinde now."

He made his way over to their host, noting that Renata Abetelli hung not only on every word Walt Devinde uttered but had smoothly slipped her hand through the crook of his arm.

"Ah, Mr. Callahan. I assume you've finished up your day of work on the opera crew," Ivar Larsen commented. "I hope Giovanni didn't overtax you."

"Giovanni is a pleasure to work with, as is Antonio. From what I observed, you have a group of hard workers, Mr. Larsen. Whatever timetable you've put them on, I'm sure they'll be ready." He turned to Walt Devinde. "Sorry I'm a bit late. I needed to clean up after my day of carpentry and painting."

"All that hard labor, Mr. Callahan?" Renata teased. "Mr. McLeod simply walked around looking important."

"We both have our jobs to do, Miss Abetelli. Don't worry. They'll get done." He looked at Devinde. "I hear we'll be given access tonight. I'm eager to see all parts of your opera house."

"I've provided Mr. McLeod with keys to everything. You both may go wherever you see fit. My only concern, as is yours, is that Renata is happy and safe during her time in Denver."

"Speaking of that, sir." Rye paused, trying to think how to be diplomatic. "You neglected to share with us that you had a houseguest. We want to be thorough in our protection detail so in the future, we'll need to know about any new additions to the house, be it staff or otherwise."

Bettina spoke up. "But everyone here already knows Emma. Why would that be a problem?"

Rye nodded. "You're correct, Miss Devinde, in that we did meet Miss Bradford before our arrival here. I understand that you two met on a train. Was it the one bringing you both to Denver?"

"It was, and we did. We have quite a few things in common. Since I am new to Denver, as is Emma, I convinced her— well, I actually begged her— to stay with me here." She fluttered her eyelashes at him. "I hope that wasn't wrong, Mr. Callahan."

He kept a straight face, despite her amateurish attempt at flirting with him. "There's no problem with Miss Bradford remaining here, I assure you. She is of good character and will be a charming companion to you. In the future, however, please alert Mr. McLeod or me if you choose to invite anyone else into your home while Miss Abetelli is residing here."

Bettina beamed at him. "Of course."

Rye sensed Emma's presence before she entered the drawing room. He turned and saw she stood in the doorway, assessing the room. He wondered how— and why— he was already so in tune with her. She crossed to where they were gathered, apologizing for having to change and delay dinner. She avoided looking directly at him.

"Oh, my. I thought the lilac gown was to die for, Emma, but this cerulean becomes you so," Bettina exclaimed.

"Yes, Emma. The lighter blue is a wonderful contrast to your darker blue eyes," Renata added.

"Since Miss Bradford has returned, we should go

into dinner," Devinde proclaimed, guiding his treasured guest toward the hallway.

They all paired up, with Rye being the odd man out. He followed Larsen and Bettina, with Eddie and Emma right behind him. Devinde led them to what he termed the small dining room, though it would fit a party of twenty comfortably. The millionaire took a seat at the head of the table, with Renata on his right and Larsen on his left. Eddie and Emma sat next to Renata, while Bettina landed next to Larsen, with Rye on her left.

That meant he was seated directly across from Emma. He caught her eyes as the soup course arrived and gave her a wink. She gazed at him blankly and then focused on her soup, but he noticed the corners of her mouth turned up as she did. He told himself everything would be fine. He would get to the bottom of whatever had caused her to flee. Rye also planned on a much more thorough investigation of her very tempting mouth. Soon. Very soon.

"What made you choose to build an opera house in Denver?" Emma asked, looking to their host.

"Because I've done everything else?" Devinde laughed. "I find I bore easily, Emma. I've built and leased buildings in several major cities. Bought and merged banks along the eastern seaboard. Invested in railroads and the budding cattle industry. I became curious as to where some of my rail lines went and decided I would come West and see for myself."

Devinde paused while the next course was served before he continued. "The rail finally linked Denver in 1870, which made it a stopping point for opera touring companies as they made their way out to San Francisco from Chicago or St. Louis. I enjoy the arts immensely and I've fallen in love with Denver. I wanted to bring a better quality opera house to the city than what now exists."

"There are other performance halls here?" asked Renata. "The train ride to Colorado was so long, with nothing but open spaces for miles." She patted Devinde's hand. "I was shocked to see this city rise up. I must say, I found being in the middle of nowhere an interesting place to build an opera house, much less a city."

"I'm not the first but I aim to be the best. My competition is Turner Hall and Forrester Opera House at the moment. Jack Langrishe's Denver Theatre burned to the ground last year, which left a huge void that I plan to fill. Langrishe left town to open up a theater in some godforsaken place called Deadwood, according to my sources."

"I've been to opera houses in Central City and Georgetown while traveling in Colorado," added Rye. "More houses are going up in Leadville and Golden."

"Don't forget Pueblo," said Devinde. "Theirs should be completed by next year." He turned back to Emma. "So, my dear, I hope I'm on the forefront in bringing quality entertainment to Denver. We'll host operas, naturally, but also touring plays or vaudeville shows and the occasional town meeting."

"Miners actually want to hear opera, Papa?"

"It sounds odd, Bettina, but they do. Of course, they work long hours and are interested in any kind of entertainment— dancing girls, bear fights, minstrel shows, to name a few. But it's almost uncanny how, at least in Colorado, communities want not just entertainment, but specifically opera."

"Shakespeare, in his day, wrote for the masses," noted Rye, "and opera is no different. It simply tells a story, as does a play, but all the lines are sung instead of being spoken. Bring in a great story and audiences will flock to see it."

"One person called the librettist writes the story. His text is called the *libretto*, Italian for *little book*,"

Larsen interjected. "Usually another, the composer, will set the words to music."

"I wish someone would write an opera in English," Bettina complained. "I never seem to understand what's going on."

"Tsk-tsk," Renata said, shaking her head. "You have seen the wrong performers, *il mio amico*. Opera comes from Latin— *opus*, which means *work of art*. It combines many art forms, from singing and dancing and orchestral music, to tell a powerful story. You should be able to follow the story from everything you see and hear. Funny. Scary. Sad. Mysterious. The *right* singer can convey all these feelings and moods."

Devinde smiled at the prima donna. "You are not only the right singer, but the best one, to help open the magical world of opera to Bettina."

"*Tu sei gentile, Signore*," purred the diva.

"I'll help you, Bettina," Emma promised. "I took voice lessons for many years, and my papa and I traveled extensively in Europe, where we attended over twenty different productions. I know the stories to many operas and can tell you about what you'll see when Miss Abetelli and the company perform."

"You sing?" Renata's brows arched. Rye couldn't tell if it was in interest or whether an undercurrent of jealousy ran through the singer's words.

He decided to jump to Emma's defense. "I've heard Miss Bradford sing and she sounds like an angel."

Emma blushed, touching a hand to her face. "Mr. Callahan heard me singing to a child I met while on the train," she explained. "I fear he is exaggerating my talent."

Bettina clapped her hands. "Oh, that's wonderful, Emma. Besides teaching me about the stories that Renata will tell on stage, perhaps you could teach me to sing an aria. Isn't that what it's called?"

"I'd be happy to work with you, Bettina, but I'm no professional. It takes years and years of training to truly do justice to opera." Emma smiled at Renata. "I'm so looking forward to hearing you perform. It's been quite a while since I attended the opera. I'm eager to lose myself in your songs."

Renata's pursed lips relaxed into a smile at the compliment. "Of course you are, Emma, and I guarantee I will not disappoint you. Everyone loves to hear me perform, don't they, Ivar?"

"Yes, my dear. You will be the toast of the town and far beyond."

The talk turned to various productions Renata had starred in throughout Europe, and the time passed quickly. When the meal ended, Rye and Eddie excused themselves in order to visit the opera house and allow Rye to thoroughly examine the building.

"I need to get the key ring, Rye. I left it in my room. It's massive and would never have fit in my dinner jacket. I'll be right back."

Eddie left Rye standing in the entryway, nodding to the women as they left. While Emma and Bettina wished him a good night and went upstairs, Renata came over to him.

"I am happy you are looking over me, Rye. I will feel safe with your eyes on me at all times."

He caught her underlying meaning and answered her stiffly. "That's what Mr. Pinkerton is paying Mr. McLeod and me to do, Miss Abetelli. We are professionals. In every aspect."

Her laughter tinkled musically as she eyed him. "But even professionals should enjoy their life. After hours, *si?*"

"A Pinkerton is on the clock, around the clock. We can't afford to let our guard down."

"Even in a small house in a little prairie town?" she asked, her voice laced with innuendo.

At that moment, Rye understood why Emma had taken flight from him back in Pennsylvania. Renata must have seen them kissing and confronted her. It would have been like a tomcat toying with a frightened little mouse.

"You are our client, Miss Abetelli. I will protect you from any known or unknown danger." He paused and looked her in the eyes. "But ours is— and always will be — a professional relationship. Even after my services are no longer required."

CHAPTER FIFTEEN

*E*mma breakfasted in her room, wanting to avoid seeing anyone.

Especially Rye Callahan.

"Why do I lose all sense of propriety when that man is near?" she asked herself.

She had arrived at many a decision by simply talking things out with herself and she wished it would help now since thoughts of the handsome Pinkerton refused to leave.

She sipped the fragrant hot chocolate and nibbled on a slice of pumpkin bread, enjoying the scattered cranberries in it. As she ate, she wondered why not only propriety went out the window but why she always lost her head when she encountered the Pinkerton.

"It's only when we're alone," she consoled herself. "I'll simply avoid placing myself in situations where I'm alone with him."

She didn't think that would be too difficult. Rye was slated to work as part of the touring company's work crew every day He would be reporting to the opera house and toiling long hours there. He would probably join in the evening meal at the Devinde mansion but others would be present. She couldn't think of a single situation where they might be alone together again, as they had been on the stairs the previous evening.

The thought depressed her.

She flung her napkin down on the tray, disgusted with herself. She had come to the West to discover herself. Find adventure. Learn about her growing country. Not pine after some handsome detective.

Even if he kissed divinely.

She dressed and decided that she needed to send a telegram to Daniel Mitchell today. She'd been remiss in not identifying her current whereabouts to him these past few days after being on the road for so long. She thought she might stay in Denver a month or even more, and she needed the attorney to wire funds to her. The cash he'd provided when she left the East coast had almost run out, which suited her. She'd been nervous carrying about a large amount of money in her reticule. After her transportation and food costs, a good chunk had gone as a deposit to Madame Drummond for her new wardrobe. Emma hadn't replenished her clothing in so long, and it surprised her how costly apparel and accessories had become.

Of course, it could be because Denver was so far from what most Americans would term civilization. Few dressmakers of Madame Drummond's talent were available this far west, despite the fact that the city's affluent population was growing rapidly. At least according to Walt Devinde, and she supposed the millionaire would know.

She still wondered at Bettina's parents and the strange arrangement they seemed to have regarding their marriage, leading separate lives in different cities for many years. She understood this was more common among the very wealthy, be it in New York or Paris or Rome. It would have been unthinkable to do so in the Bradford household in Connecticut. She knew her parents had been deeply in love, and her father mourned her mother every day after her death. That's why his choice to marry Louisa surprised her so.

First, she took the time to pen a long letter to her attorney, telling him about the various places she'd seen and the people she'd grown friendly with while on her travels since it would be impossible to relate all this information in a cable. Emma explained how she came to be staying at Walt Devinde's mansion and that she would be in Denver for several more weeks. She decided to mail it while she ran her various errands. As she came down the stairs, she discovered Renata and Ivar in the entryway and greeted them.

"We're off for fittings for my stage wardrobe," Renata said. "Rozalia is already there preparing for my arrival."

"We could drop you wherever you wish if you're going out," Larsen told her. "Walt has been kind enough to leave his carriage at Renata's disposal."

"Thank you for your offer. I need to send a telegram."

"Then we shall ask the coachman where the nearest office is located," Ivar said.

A maid appeared. "Your carriage is ready, Mr. Larsen." The servant saw them out the front door and asked Emma, "Shall I tell Miss Bettina when you'll return?"

"I'll probably be home before she arises. We have shopping plans and I know she won't want to miss that excursion."

"Bettina is a late rise?" asked Renata as they entered the carriage.

"Yes," Emma shared. "She is used to going to parties and other social occasions which can run far into the night. She prefers sleeping until she awakens. Sometimes, she's abed until noon," she confided.

The soprano sighed. "Ah, to lead a life of leisure. Maybe one day, eh, Ivar?"

He sniffed. "You would be bored silly, Renata. Besides, a talent as great as yours should be shared. I can't picture you sitting home as some *hausfrau*, with an army of children tugging on your embroidered gown."

Renata shivered as though someone had walked over her future grave. "That would be a living nightmare."

"You don't want to marry and have children?" Emma asked. "I thought all women searched for love."

"Ivar is right. I'm meant for the stage. *Matrimonio?* No. *E bambini?*" She shuddered. "No. *Ma l'amore?*" She laughed. "I will always have room for love. And *molti amanti.*"

Emma bit her tongue at the singer's words, feeling a blush rising up her neck. Renata didn't want marriage or children— but she had time for many lovers?

They arrived at Larimer Square and the telegraph office, and she said her goodbyes. She spied a bank and noted its name. Emma also noticed the post office adjacent to the telegraph office and decided to post her letter first. Once that task was completed, she entered the telegraph office, happy to see only one person in line. After a short wait, the clerk motioned her forward.

"I'd like to send a telegram to Plainfield, Connecticut. To Mr. Daniel Mitchell, attorney-at-law."

She filled out the short message and returned it to the clerk, who looked a bit cross-eyed to her. She hoped he would be able to send the correct message. He looked it over and read aloud:

Mr. Mitchell. In Denver at Walter Devinde's house for a

few weeks. Please wire sufficient funds to National Bank, Larimer Square. Letter to follow.

The operator frowned at her. "You didn't sign it, Miss."

"I don't need to. He will know it's from me."

It wasn't about saving money by omitting the few letters of her name. Emma still wanted to protect herself from John and Louisa at all cost. Her normally trusting nature might be a thing of the past.

He gave her an odd look but walked to his machine and sent the message. She closed her eyes as he did, listening to the dots and dashes. Emma's brother had taught her Morse code when she was a child and used to let her practice sending him secret messages that no one else understood. It surprised her that she still remembered the code so many years after David's death during the war.

Satisfied that the telegram had been sent correctly, she paid the operator and thanked him for his time. She stepped out onto the square and saw not only did it have a dry goods store but also a photographer's studio, a theater, and a bookstore. She would definitely stop by this bookstore when she had more time to browse. The Devinde library was simply a shell of a room, containing beautiful leather furniture and Aubusson rugs but very few books on the built-in shelves. She'd reread *Bleak House* before she and Bettina had discovered a wonderful bookstore in Denver upon their arrival. Emma had purchased a few more books from the place but she had already read them. It was time to start something new.

Thinking of books brought Rye to mind. Again. She remembered their very first conversation in the train station in New York, and how he'd expressed a love for Mr. Dickens. She shook her head, willing his image to exit her mind as she walked across the street to the bank.

As she entered, she admired the large lobby and airy ceilings and had to watch her step on the slippery marble floor. Once she stated her business to a clerk, she met with the bank manager himself, who helped her open an account. She explained she would have funds arriving shortly, and he welcomed her back to check on its arrival and add the total to the passbook he issued her.

Glancing at the watch pinned to her blouse, she decided to return to the Devinde mansion. Bettina would hopefully be awake by the time she arrived and they could plan the rest of their day.

As she caught a hack and gave the Devinde address, she looked longingly at the bookstore as she passed it.

~

"Johnny, you've got to do something. I think I'll go mad if I stay buried in the country like this," Louisa Bradford complained.

John Fairburn paced in front of the large picture windows that opened to a view of the gardens. *He* would be the one to go mad if Louisa didn't stop her constant harping.

"I don't know what you want me to do, darling. I questioned all the servants. You know how thorough a job I did." He gave her a hard look, silently reminding her of his actions with Molly.

"It wasn't your fault that maid knew something and wouldn't talk," she whined. "The girl was rather cheeky. Even disrespectful. And you did find out a little bit from her."

He snorted. "Enough to trace Emma to the city. Yes, I did locate her hotel. But nothing regarding her travel plans, other than she went to the train station. I questioned ticket agents there. I even went to the harbor and passed around bribes to see if she'd doubled back and taken a ship to Europe. No one remembered her. I'm at a loss, frankly. I don't know what we should do next. The chit has vanished without a trace."

"Along with all that money," Louisa said, bitterness oozing from her. "We've got to do something. We can't live on my clothing allowance in a small town in Connecticut the rest of our lives. People are talking, as it is."

"Let them," he said. "I'm your dear cousin, here to comfort you in your time of grief."

"Servants talk, Johnny. They know you don't sleep in your own bed, even if you do muss the sheets for them." She stood and went to the decanter, pouring herself a finger of whiskey. "Don't tell me it's too early. It's noon somewhere in the world."

"I think I'm desperate enough to try Mitchell again," he said. "I know that ornery lawyer knows something. Emma couldn't have disappeared without help— and especially without any funds. He must have arranged for her to receive money. Possibly even booked her trip for her, wherever she went."

Louisa drained the glass and poured another for herself. "Well, then go. Just do something. Anything. I can't stand the thought of all that money going to waste, especially on someone as foolish as Emma. The girl has no interest in her appearance. She actually enjoys spending time at the mill, talking to the workers and going over the books." Louisa's nose crinkled in disgust. "Besides, she quit going to parties ages ago. It's not as if she'll even use the money."

"I'm off. Hopefully, I'll discover something at Daniel Mitchell's office."

John left, glad to escape the tomb of a home. A bored Louisa, having to maintain her period of mourning, might be the worst thing he'd experienced in the past decade— though no match for his early years. His father, a charmer of the first degree, was rarely home and frequently out of work. Money had been tight, and his mother stretched food as much as she could to make it last. He shuddered, remembering the days of watery stew and moldy bread crusts and the hunger pangs as he lay awake at night.

At least he'd been blessed with not only his father's charm but the man's intelligence, which won John a scholarship to a fancy boarding school. He'd made the right connections there. Spent holidays with friends and their families whenever possible. He skated by on his good looks and white lies. He thought he'd found the easy life when he'd fallen in with Louisa, who married Dwight Bradford for his money.

Or at least Bradford thought they were married.

He was Louisa's true husband, a fact they'd kept quiet. God only knew what would have happened to the money willed to her if someone discovered that interesting tidbit.

John doubted Daniel Mitchell would give him the time of day but he wanted to visit the lawyer's office, nonetheless. It would allow him to investigate its layout, including the locks. He figured he might have to break in at some point to peruse the files and ascertain where Emma might have fled, if the information could be found. He also could meet whatever staff was in place. It wouldn't hurt to get friendly with any of them in hopes of learning something.

He believed he and Louisa had become careless and possibly Emma overheard something not meant for her ears. If that were the case, no amount of flattery and lies of love would cause her to fall at his feet, much less marry him.

Once he found Emma, he would simply kill her as

he had her maid. It would be easier to accomplish the task out of town. Emma didn't have the ties to a community as she did in Plainfield, a small town where everyone knew everyone's business. He doubted she would be missed by anyone, wherever she was hiding, even if she had made a few acquaintances.

One thing he'd become skilled in was forgery, so he knew with time and care he could reproduce a marriage and a death certificate for the courts, as well as Emma's last will and testament. First, though, he needed to find where she'd gone so he could take care of her. He didn't want to try and have the courts declare her dead and her inheritance transferred to Louisa, only to have a living Emma turn up and spoil things.

No, he needed to hunt her down. Eliminate her, then play the grieving widower after he returned to Connecticut. He and Louisa could then marry— again — and leave Plainfield immediately, selling the mill and house and whatever other properties Dwight Bradford had willed to his daughter. Let the communities along the Moosup River gossip. John and Louisa would be far from their moral condemnations.

Unless...

He wondered if he'd already tired of Louisa and her antics, and decided he had. If she were to suffer a tragic accident after Emma's death, he wouldn't have to share any of his inheritance from Emma with his real wife.

It was something to think about.

He arrived at Mitchell's law office, not surprised to find the building as stodgy as the man, and circled the place to get the lay of the land. John saw exactly what he was looking for. He knew Mitchell was the only attorney in the practice, so it didn't surprise him that the office was modest in size. A fair-haired man putting on his coat greeted John as he entered.

"May I be of service, sir?"

He thought how he wanted to play things since it looked as if the clerk were on his way out. "I don't have an appointment with Mr. Mitchell but I'd like to schedule one. Is he possibly available sometime today? Or even tomorrow?"

"Mr. Mitchell is in court this morning, but he will return this afternoon for office hours." The clerk opened a book and skimmed it. "You could see him at one-thirty if that's agreeable."

John began coughing but nodded. "That would be fine." He continued coughing and mimicked drinking something.

"Let me get you a glass of water right away, sir." The young man left and hurried down a hallway.

He continued the coughing fit and went around to the desk to see if anything useful might be lying about. He glanced over the items, disappointed at the neat stacks that sat there. None had anything to do with Emma. He returned to the other side of the desk just as the clerk brought him the water.

"Thank you," he got out and drank it greedily, deliberately spilling it down the front of his clothing. "Dash it all! This cold and bronchitis keep hanging on. May I use your lavatory, please?"

"Of course, sir. Down the hall and to the left."

He moved along the hall, coughing all the way, glimpsing a closed door and assuming it to be Mitchell's office. The lavatory was positioned directly across from it.

What he was looking for was at the end of the corridor. The rear exit from the building that he'd seen from outside. He entered the lavatory and quickly mopped the front of his shirt and coat the best he could before slipping out and stepping to the door. He quietly threw the lock, hoping the clerk would leave for his luncheon break or errand from the front door.

Returning up the hall, he gave a short cough to let the worker know he was coming. The clerk still had his coat on and stood patiently by his desk.

"Sorry for that. The coughing spells hit me at the oddest time. Usually if I drink something, I'm fine. I apologize if I made a mess."

"Not a problem, sir. May I jot your name down in Mr. Mitchell's appointment book for this afternoon?"

John paused as if he thought about it a moment. "You know, I believe I'm going to hit up that quack of a doctor first and see if he can give me something that will take care of this cough once and for all. My legal matter isn't pressing. My wife thought I needed to see about my will, is all." He chuckled. "Since I'm still in my mid-twenties, I think I can wait a few more days. Unless this cough kills me, that is."

The clerk laughed good-naturedly. "Then please stop by when you're in better health. I'll schedule you with Mr. Mitchell straightaway. He prepares quite a few wills. You'll be pleased at how thorough and efficient Mr. Mitchell is."

"Well, I'm off. Don't want to keep you. You look as if you were headed out yourself."

The young man grinned. "Actually, I was on my way to meet my fiancée for luncheon."

"Then I wish you a good day and a pleasant tomorrow."

Exiting the law office, John hustled across the street, heading around a corner to where he had the perfect vantage point. Less than a minute later, Mitchell's clerk appeared and locked the front door before strolling in the opposite direction.

He allowed two full minutes to pass in case the clerk had forgotten something and doubled back. When he felt sure the man was gone, John walked down the block, across the street, and then came up the rear. No one was in sight as he entered Mitchell's office. With the young man meeting his girl, John believed he had a good hour to search the place, but he didn't know when Daniel Mitchell might return to work. The lawyer could skip luncheon and head back to his office after his court appearance. Speed was of the essence.

Mitchell's office wasn't locked so that saved him time picking the lock. He went through each of four filing cabinet drawers, glancing at the labels along the edge of each file. He stopped at a large one marked "Bradford," pulling it out and skimming the contents. Nothing new struck him. It contained copies of Dwight Bradford's will and other transactions over the years, but no clues that indicated where Emma might be hiding. He searched through the rest of the files and in the lawyer's desk drawers, finishing with the two stacks atop the desk. One held files. The other appeared to be the morning's post, opened and placed in what looked like the order of importance.

Nothing. Absolutely nothing. He was angry at having wasted the trip. At least he hadn't given his name, which would arouse Mitchell's suspicions.

John returned to the clerk's desk and sat. *Was he missing something?* Or did the attorney keep anything to do with Emma at his home instead of his place of work?

If that were the case, he needed to find the man's address. He located an address book and opened it. As he flipped to the M's, a sudden rap on the door caused him to go still.

Had the visitor heard him?

He could open the door and pretend he worked here. If it were a long-time client, though, that scam would quickly play out. He remained frozen in place until he heard the mail slot open, an envelope thrust through. It fluttered to the ground.

It was a telegram.

His gut told him this came from Emma. Mitchell was a small-town attorney. He helped with land deeds and family wills. He doubted the lawyer received many telegrams. Once again, John counted off a full minute, waiting for whoever delivered the telegram to depart.

His heart in his throat, he reached for the envelope and slit it open. He assumed the normal practice would be for the clerk to open it as he had the mail received, especially if Mitchell were away from the office because it might prove to be something important.

Reading the contents, he smiled.

John took the telegram and returned to Mitchell's office. He laid it atop the stack of mail and left the room, closing the door behind him. He left the building the way he'd entered, happy that no one appeared in the alley.

Emma was in Denver, Colorado, the newest state in the Union. While he might not know the exact address, he certainly knew the Devinde name. It would be child's play to find where the millionaire resided.

He could taste the money.

CHAPTER SIXTEEN

Rye finished hammering at the same time Giovanni did, and the two men lifted the table, flipping it upright to stand. Another prop finished as the time drew closer for opening night.

"You wanna paint this, Rye?" the set designer asked. "Or you help Antonio paint the backdrop, *si?*"

He shrugged. "Either's fine with me. Or I can do both."

Giovanni nodded. "Finish backdrop. Two make it go faster. Then eat. We paint table and chairs after, you and me, okay?"

Rye grunted his approval and joined Antonio. The prop master showed him what needed to be done, and he dipped a brush into the can of blue paint and began filling in the massive portion of canvas dedicated to the sky.

He hummed under his breath as he worked. He enjoyed the people in Larsen's company. All were good-natured and made for fine companions. He had even begun picking up Italian phrases here and there. From listening to their stories, he longed to see Italy, especially the varying blues of the Mediterranean and the

Tuscan countryside, where a majority of the company's roots ran deep.

Yet boredom filled him at every turn. He was used to more excitement and challenge in his occupation as a Pinkerton agent. He didn't mind the manual labor involved in getting ready for the production but he'd much rather be chasing after lawbreakers, infiltrating gangs, building a case in order for an arrest to occur.

Renata Abetelli had no need of a protection detail. She wasn't a world leader, be it political or financial. The only reason Pinkerton detectives had been engaged was due to Ivar Larsen's jumpiness at bringing his diva to the American Wild West. Larsen had pressured Walt Devinde, which led to Devinde's seeking out his old friend Alan Pinkerton, and thus the present job.

Rye had half a mind to cable The Eye and let him know Larsen's fears were groundless. Maybe The Eye could assign him and Eddie a new job elsewhere for the duration of the run in Denver, then the detectives could return and accompany the soprano to her next engagement, be it Salt Lake or San Francisco. He figured that would be the only time she could possibly be in any type of danger. Train hold-ups did occur out West every now and then, and he wouldn't mind being aboard to offer protection under those circumstances.

Yet the thought of the Pinkerton chief giving Rye the okay to leave troubled him.

All because of Emma.

He put in long hours at the opera house so the only time he saw her was at dinner. Usually, he didn't make it back in time to enjoy those in the house gathering for an evening cocktail before they dined. He raced to make himself presentable and slide into his seat for the meal as it was.

Emma spoke to him occasionally. She was pleasant

and polite. But she never initiated any conversation between the two of them, despite the fact they faced each other at the table. While the others left dinner and went to Devinde's salon for entertainment, playing cards, listening to music, or reading, he and Eddie met and compared notes for the day. They often made a sweep around the Devinde property and discussed the activities of Renata, Ivar, and the company. Eddie also frequented several Denver establishments, making connections and hearing local gossip, trying to detect any threat that could affect their client's well-being, and he would inform Rye of any new developments.

He never found himself alone with Emma and was astute enough to realize it was on purpose. At least on her part. She probably didn't trust herself to be around him, especially since he couldn't seem to keep his hands off her.

It surprised him. He was a loner by nature, never having received nor given any affection. His assignments took him all over the country so he had no roots or ties to any community. Sometimes he worked undercover for weeks or months and deliberately chose not to get close to anyone. He had few friends, other than fellow detectives such as Eddie, and even then, Pinkertons rarely worked cases together. This protection detail guarding Renata proved to be an exception rather than the rule.

That's why it puzzled him why he was drawn to Emma. Physically, he understood it because she radiated beauty and energy. He'd never seen a more stunning woman than Emma, especially one so unaware of how beautiful she truly was. He was also drawn to her intelligence and charm, not to mention her musical laugh. He wasn't around women very often, much less ladies of her breeding. Emma epitomized everything the perfect woman should be. At least in his eyes.

But a future with Emma? That was next to impossible. She outclassed him in so many ways it made his head spin. Her gentility and education, her obvious access to money, and the fact that most Pinkertons never married only started a long list of why things could never work between them.

Yet she'd awakened a longing in him Rye didn't even know had existed. He wanted to get to know her. Explore every nook and cranny of her wonderful curves. Learn what her favorite foods were. How to make her laugh. What she thought about.

He laughed aloud at such outlandish musings and saw Antonio give him an odd look. Yes, Emma Bradford just might have driven him over the brink of sanity. But if he could tumble over into that abyss with her in his arms?

It would be well worth it.

Clearing his mind of any thoughts related to her, Rye concentrated on completing the canvas. When he finished, he cleaned the brush and decided instead of using his break to eat, he would explore the bookstore a couple of blocks over on Larimer Square. He had tired of the two books he'd brought with him and wanted to investigate something new.

Ten minutes later after a short walk in the beautiful late-May day, he inhaled the welcomed scent of musty books. He wiggled through the crowded, narrow aisles and soon lost himself as he browsed through Washington Irving's works.

Until he heard a giggle on the other side of the stack.

"I can't believe you dragged me in here, Emma. Who wants to be around old, moldy books? You have your nose in a book too much as it is when you aren't scribbling in that journal of yours."

"Let me browse for a few minutes, Bettina, then

we'll make our way over to the dry goods store and to our fitting. I haven't had a chance to visit this establishment and I'm in sore need of adding to my supply of books to read."

Rye stood rooted to the spot. He remembered first meeting Emma in the New York train station and how they'd bonded over their love of reading and favorite authors.

"Why read at all? There are a thousand things I'd rather do than read. Like talk about men."

"Men? Is that all you ever think about, Bettina?"

"Well, I have to do it for the two of us since you don't seem to be interested in them at all. I don't see why not. You're absolutely lovely, Emma. You should already be married at your age."

"I rather like my independence. The West is certainly an exciting place for women to be independent, with women voting and owning land. Don't you find that fascinating?"

A loud snort sounded. "I'm ready to become involved in Denver society. At least we'll be meeting all sorts of new people at the gala in a few days. I've told Papa he needs to entertain more. The only men I've met worth knowing since coming to Denver are Mr. McLeod and Mr. Callahan. Don't you think Mr. McLeod is dreamy?"

"While I'll admit Mr. McLeod is very nice-looking, he's almost twice your age, Bettina. I don't think your father would approve."

"Oh, Papa wouldn't care about age. He's at least a decade older than Mama. But Mr. McLeod is poor, else why would he be working for a living? I think Papa has higher aspirations for me. Still, Mr. McLeod is smart and very funny. Maybe he could go to work for Papa in one of his many businesses. That would make him more suitable, don't you agree?"

"I believe you should let Mr. McLeod do what he was hired to do. Let him concentrate on his job, while you focus on younger, more eligible men such as the ones you'll meet at the ball."

"Maybe I can convince Mr. McLeod to dance with me. At least once. That might make me seem more alluring to our guests, with an older, handsome man finding me attractive."

"I'm sure you'll be the belle of the ball whether Mr. McLeod dances with you or not."

"I know one thing. Mr. Callahan will certainly ask *you* to dance."

Rye waited at the long pause and wondered what Emma's answer would be.

"Why do you say that?" Her voice sounded guarded to him.

"Oh, Emma, that man is smitten with you. He can't keep his eyes off you at dinner each evening. He hangs on your every word yet you hardly give him the time of day."

"I do speak to Mr. Callahan. I don't ignore him."

"You know what I mean. I think you might actually like him. Are you pretending you don't and playing hard to get? Mama says men are attracted to the chase and enjoy pursuing a woman they think is beyond their grasp."

"Enough! How did we take up such an absurd topic? Give me ten minutes alone, Bettina. I promise I'll find the books I wish to purchase and then we can attend to our other errands."

"I'll be across the street at the dry goods store. Anything is better than inhaling the dust lingering in the air here. Do hurry, Emma."

Rye heard Bettina's footsteps tapping along the wooden floor as she moved away, then the jangling of the bell announcing her departure. He realized he was holding his breath, almost as if the women might have heard him on the other side of the stack of books as he eavesdropped on their conversation.

He needed to take advantage of seeing Emma. He didn't know what it would lead to, but he would regret it if he didn't.

Quietly, he stepped down the narrow passageway and weaved his way to the front door of the establishment. He opened it so the bell tinkled, as if he'd just come in. He then moved in Emma's direction and saw her perusing an opened book, a dreamy half-smile on her oval face.

"Hello, Emma."

~

EMMA LOOKED up to see Rye standing near her, bits of paint spattering his work clothes. She was used to seeing him in his suit and tie every night at dinner. This daytime Rye was very different, with shirtsleeves rolled to his elbows, revealing strong forearms. Without a coat and his shirt open at the throat, she realized just how broad his shoulders were as he stood taking up all the available room in the tight aisle. She swallowed hard.

"Good afternoon, Rye," she managed to get out, happy she didn't sound like a strangled cat.

"I'm here on my luncheon break, looking for something new to read. Do you have any recommendations for me?"

Those golden eyes, flecked with green, glimmered at her. She could get lost in those eyes.

"Umm... I... Have you read any of Mr. Cooper before?"

"The *Leatherstocking Tales*?"

"Yes. You might enjoy Natty Bumppo's adventures.

He's quite resourceful. I'm sure if he'd existed in a more civilized time such as now, he could even have been a Pinkerton."

"Is that a compliment, Emma?"

Heat crept into her cheeks. "Pinkerton detectives are widely known for being intelligent and capable."

"As is Mr. Bumppo."

"So, you have read Mr. Cooper before?"

His smile caused her heart to flutter wildly. "I'm partial to *The Last of the Mohicans*."

"Oh, that was my favorite, too."

"I was thinking about trying some Washington Irving. Have you read any of his works?"

Her pulse raced like a wildfire out of control as his eyes searched her face. She thought she might faint dead away at the piercing look he gave her.

"Yes," she uttered, trying to breathe— but he wasn't making that easy.

"I've read his short stories previously but I thought I might try one of his biographies. Perhaps the one on George Washington."

"I... I haven't read that. In fact, I haven't read many biographies at all."

She needed to escape. Now. Before she flung her arms around him and made a fool of herself in public.

"Then you must start. I find them fascinating." His eyes gleamed at her. "It's always so interesting seeing what events surrounding a person's life make him turn out a certain way."

"I suppose so. Family circumstances. Education. Even religion. I'm certain all of that factors into making a person turn out a certain way."

Emma fought her legs becoming jelly, praying they wouldn't give out and force her to plop to the floor. She locked her knees and gave a faint smile.

"I must excuse myself. Bettina is waiting for me across the street. We have a dress fitting to attend."

"I assume it's for the gala Walt is holding Friday evening?"

"Yes." Her voice came out a whisper.

In a low voice, he said, "I hope you'll save a dance for me, Emma."

The thought of being in Rye's arms nearly undid her. She stiffened her spine and nodded brusquely. "Yes. I'm sure that can be arranged." She licked her lips nervously. "I'll be off then."

"I'll see you at dinner tonight," he promised.

Emma fled the bookstore as fast as her feet could carry her without taking a tumble. She rushed across the street and into the dry goods store and spied Bettina.

As she joined her friend, Bettina gave her a puzzled look. "All that time browsing and you didn't even find a single book to buy, Emma?"

CHAPTER SEVENTEEN

$\mathcal{E}$mma dressed in a gown of mint green trimmed in delicate lace, the satin shimmering in the candlelight. She looked across the room at her ball gown set out for when she returned. Bettina insisted that she couldn't wear the same dress to both the opening night performance and the gala afterward at the Devinde mansion. While it seemed excessive to her small-town practicality, she knew high society demanded such rules of fashion be obeyed. Being a guest of Walt Devinde, she also knew how important this night was to her host, and would do nothing to reflect poorly on him or his daughter.

She heard the chime of the clock as she hurried down the staircase to the foyer. Mr. Devinde stood waiting, his elegant evening wear making him look quite distinguished. She greeted him as Bettina came floating down the stairs in a peach gown that made her complexion glow.

"Ready, Papa." She looked around. "Has Renata already left? I wanted to wish her good luck."

Her father laughed. "She and that dresser left hours ago, my dear. Ivar, as well. I'm sure you can go backstage and see Renata before the performance begins if you wish."

Somehow, Emma thought Bettina would be out of luck on that front. She couldn't imagine Renata wanting well-wishers hanging about before her Denver debut. The soprano was a true professional. Her mind would be focused on her upcoming performance.

In the carriage, Bettina turned to her. "You mentioned you could explain the storyline to me, Emma. Let me know the basics so I'll know what to watch for in tonight's performance."

She settled against the plush velvet and smiled. "*La traviata* is by Guiseppe Verdi, a famous Italian. It loosely means *the fallen woman*, although a closer translation would be *the woman gone astray*."

Her friend's look of dismay caused Walt Devinde to chuckle. "What Emma's trying to say is that Violetta, whom Renata plays, is a courtesan."

Bettina wrinkled her nose. "I have no idea what that is."

Devinde chuckled. "I, for one, am glad of it."

Emma hesitated a moment before she decided to plunge ahead. "This is a bit awkward to discuss in mixed company but a courtesan is a prostitute who has a wealthy clientele."

Bettina's eyes widened at the same time her jaw dropped. "Renata is portraying a… a… oh, I can't even say it," she proclaimed. "I can't imagine why she would do such a thing."

"Let's move past that and think about the story," Emma urged. "Violetta Valéry is famous throughout Paris, and she's recently recovered from an illness. A handsome young middle-class man named Alfredo Germont proclaims his love for her. She thinks he might be her one true love so she decides to give him a chance. She leaves her former life behind and moves with Alfredo to a small home in the country."

"That's much better." Then Bettina's eyes narrowed. "You didn't say anything about marriage."

She sighed. "No, I didn't. It does sound rather scandalous, though they do love each other completely. Sadly, Alfredo's father arrives and begs Violetta to break things off. His daughter's engagement may not occur due to Violetta's reputation. And though Violetta loves Alfredo with all her heart, she sacrifices for the good of his family, and ends things in a farewell letter."

"Oh! She isn't bad at all, is she?"

"No. Violetta has a good heart. She wants the best for Alfredo so she lies and tells him she loves another man, a baron. Then events take a turn when Alfredo denounces her in public and challenges the baron to a duel."

Bettina gasped. "He isn't killed, is he? Operas always seem to end tragically."

"No, he wounds the baron instead. Afterward, Alfredo's father confesses his role in ending his son's love affair and Alfredo races to Violetta's side. Unfortunately, she is dying with consumption by the time he reaches her. They proclaim their love for one another and then she dies in his arms."

Bettina sniffed. "I knew it wouldn't have a happy ending."

"But it is a great love story," Emma noted. "Even though it premiered only twenty-five or so years ago, playing Violetta is the dream of most sopranos. I've seen it performed in Europe and I believe Renata was born to play Violetta."

"She does have the fire and determination of the character," Walt said. "Also the beauty and vulnerability. That's why I wanted *La traviata* to be the first opera in my new house, with Renata as the perfect Violetta." He smiled at the women. "I hope you've both brought along your handkerchiefs. I doubt there'll be a dry eye in the house by the time the curtain falls tonight."

They arrived and alighted from the carriage. Emma saw Eddie McLeod standing at the top of the stairs leading up to the building, his eyes skimming the crowd that made their way into the new building.

He waved at them in greeting as they climbed to the top. "Good evening, Mr. Devinde. Ladies. It seems as if all of Denver society has turned out tonight for your grand opening."

Bettina smiled coyly at the Pinkerton. "Most of them plan to attend Papa's gala afterwards. You will be there, won't you, Mr. McLeod?"

Eddie returned her smile. "Of course. Miss Abetelli will make an appearance, so it seems I will, as well."

"I hope you'll have time to enjoy a dance or two," Bettina declared.

"No, I'll be working tonight, Miss Devinde. Your dance card will be filled nonetheless. If you'll excuse me." He tipped his hat.

Emma saw Bettina's face fall and whispered, "So many young men will be at tonight's ball that I'm sure you won't have time to fret about Mr. McLeod."

"I suppose." She looked to her father. "May we go wish Renata good luck?"

"Be my guest. I need to stop and speak to the box office manager about the governor's tickets. You two go ahead."

They left Devinde and made their way through the throngs gathered in the grand lobby. The chandeliers sparkled like diamonds and the marble floors gleamed from the many coats of polish applied. Bettina took Emma's gloved hand and weaved through the crowd until they arrived at a door that would lead them behind the stage and to the various dressing rooms.

Almost immediately as they entered the bustling backstage area, they bumped into Rye, who carried a vase of fresh flowers.

"Are those for Renata?" she asked.

"No. I just picked them up from the florist. They're for the first scene at the salon in Paris. Later, you'll see them slightly rearranged and in a completely different vase when Alfredo brings them to Violetta when they reunite in the last act."

"We thought we'd stop by and wish Renata well," Bettina said. "Emma's told me the entire story and I think Renata will do splendidly."

"You won't be granted access, Miss Devinde," Rye apologized. "Mr. Larsen explained to everyone that Miss Abetelli needs to concentrate on getting into character before the show opens. She isn't seeing any guests and has a stagehand posted at her door to keep visitors out."

"She's probably thinking about all that thunderous applause that will follow her stage death," Emma wryly noted, watching Rye try to hide a smile at her words.

"Emma, Renata is immensely talented. Don't be petty and sound jealous," her friend scolded. "I know others probably see her as arrogant, but she's simply confident."

"Supremely confident," added Rye. "And she should be. She has tremendous talent and has sounded wonderful in rehearsals. But excuse me, ladies. I've got a few more props to set up before show time. You might want to make your way to your box."

Emma kicked herself mentally for the comment she'd made about Renata as they left the area. She didn't mean to be petty but she'd noticed the extra attention the songstress had lavished upon Rye the past few nights at dinner. It didn't sit well with her. At all. She agreed that Renata possessed immense talent. But the woman could be temperamental, judgmental, and grate on anyone's nerves.

Walt Devinde's box, as the rest of his opera house, spared no expense. The wide, plush seats of burgundy were comfortable and they had a magnificent view of the stage. As they awaited the beginning of the performance, Devinde entered with a well-dressed couple.

"Governor. Mrs. Routt. May I present my daughter, Bettina, and her close friend, Miss Emma Bradford."

They greeted the couple, with Mrs. Routt proclaiming how lovely both women looked.

"Wait until you see them in their ball finery," Walt promised. "The men of Denver won't know what hit them."

"You'll have to share with me who your dressmaker is," Mrs. Routt said. "I'm always looking for a new one."

"And hats," proclaimed the governor. "Eliza's mad about hats."

"What woman isn't?" asked Emma, finding the governor charming. "Men might have needed a sword and shield to go into battle, but a lady in a superb hat can conquer the world."

Everyone laughed and Routt asked, his eyes twinkling, "You wouldn't happen to be a suffragette, Miss Bradford?"

"I view myself as an independent woman, Governor. I would be extremely interested in obtaining a vote so I'd have a better say in how our country is run."

Eliza Routt patted her arm. "My husband is interested in women's rights, dear. You know the West is quite liberal compared to our counterparts back East regarding women and the vote." She looked at her husband. "I'm hoping one day we ladies in Colorado will be granted the means to cast our ballots. When we are, I plan to be first in line."

"Give me time, darling. I've only been in office since last year."

The orchestra started the overture at that point and all turned their attention to the stage. By the time Renata's first aria had been sung, Emma looked over and saw Bettina was mesmerized by the soprano and Violetta's tragic story.

She remembered touring Europe with her father and seeing this opera for the very first time and thought back on when she took voice lessons and sang pieces from *La traviata* herself.

Maybe she was just a tad jealous of Renata Abetelli after all.

CHAPTER EIGHTEEN

*E*mma slipped out of the dress she'd worn to the opera and handed it to Ethel. She glanced at her reflection in the mirror and was happy no strands had come loose from her chignon. She noticed her flushed cheeks and chalked it up to the excitement from Renata's opening night performance. Or because she would be attending her first ball in years. Yet she knew she told herself a fib.

She was excited because Rye Callahan would be downstairs at the gala.

As Bettina's maid helped her into the elaborate ball gown, Emma tried to quell her nerves. She'd been jumpy ever since her chance encounter with Rye at the bookstore on Larimer Square. Tonight, though, she planned to take the bull by the horns, a phrase she'd picked up from Walt Devinde. She refused to shy away from the handsome detective. Although Eddie had mentioned to Bettina that the Pinkertons would be working at the ball, Emma knew Renata would wait until the gala was in full swing before she made her grand entrance. She hoped that would give her the opportunity to engage Rye in conversation— or perhaps even a dance before duty called. Her father had wanted her to enjoy life and step out from the shadows.

Maybe now was the time to throw caution to the wind.

"Oh, you look a sight, Miss Emma," Ethel remarked. "Denver men won't know what hit 'em when they see you in that dress."

"Thank you, Ethel. You've raised my spirits and my confidence. I've never worn something quite so extravagant."

"You're a sight for sore eyes. Do you need anything else, Miss?"

"No. I'm sure Bettina will be ready for you now."

The servant snorted. "Miss Bettina's probably still falling all over that singing woman, hanging on her every word."

She laughed. "Bettina is quite devoted to Miss Abetelli, but I think she'll be more than happy to put on a beautiful ball gown and help serve as the hostess of her father's gala. Thank you for your help, Ethel."

As the maid left, Emma decided to change her shoes. She located the pair she wanted and slipped into them, laughing to herself about Bettina's infatuation with Renata. The prima donna, along with Ivar and Eddie, had accompanied them home in the Devinde carriage, the young woman chattering away about the evening and Renata's performance, in particular. Bettina had trailed the opera singer up the stairs to her room, which is why Emma knew she had time to seek Ethel's help in changing gowns before Bettina needed her maid.

She took one last look in the mirror, happy at what she saw. The azure ball gown was worth every penny she'd spent on it. She left her room and moved down the carpeted hallway, spying Bettina standing in Renata's doorway. As she arrived, Emma saw the frustrated look on the soprano's face and knew the woman had come to the end of her rope.

Intervening before Renata hurt Bettina's feelings, Emma said, "Bettina, I just sent Ethel to your room. You must get ready for the gala. Your father will expect you downstairs soon. He'll need you by his side to greet his guests."

Her friend's eyes widened. "Oh, my! I lost track of the time. Forgive me, Renata, I must go dress." She hurried down the hall, calling over her shoulder, "I'll see you both soon!"

Renata gave a weary sigh and shook her head.

"She means well, Renata. You couldn't have a more dedicated and ardent supporter than Bettina Devinde."

Her eyebrows shot up. "The dear girl has worn me out, nonetheless. I shall have to have a little catnip before I venture downstairs to the party."

"I'm sure you'd rather have all the guests present before you make your appearance." Emma smiled. "I believe you mean a catnap. That's a brief period of sleep."

"*Si*. I cannot possibly be seen before midnight." The soprano studied her. "You look lovely this evening, Emma."

A compliment from Renata was rare. She decided to extend the olive branch the soprano offered.

"Thank you. I wanted to tell you how much I enjoyed tonight's performance. I've seen *La traviata* several times, but no soprano I saw in the role came close to your performance. Not only does your voice exhibit great range, but your acting skills are superb. I believed from the first moment that you *were* Violetta. *Magnifico, mio amico*."

Renata surprised Emma, embracing her. "Ah, my friend, I thank you for your kind words. High praise coming from Miss Emma Bradford." Renata smacked her noisily on each cheek and smiled.

Emma believed all was finally well between them. "I'll see you downstairs. After your catnap." She gave Renata a wink, which the singer playfully returned before closing her door.

She descended the stairs, hearing the strains of music beginning. She knew Walt had hired a string quartet for the evening and knew they must be warming up for the party. Her feet itched to dance in a way they never had back in her days of being introduced to Connecticut society. She hoped being out of practice wouldn't produce two left feet. Having studied voice and her years of playing the piano, she always had a sense of rhythm. She prayed it would return as the night progressed.

As she entered the ballroom, she stopped, marveling at the array of flowers that transformed the room, including the bluish-purple Friar's Cap, which she'd never seen until she arrived in Denver. Many of the arrangements consisted of wildflowers native to Colorado. Emma had pestered the butler about their names as they were delivered this afternoon, especially the orange flowers nicknamed Cowboy's Delight.

"You're a sight for sore eyes on this lovely June evening, Emma."

She turned and saw Walt Devinde standing behind her. On his arm was a beautiful woman in waves of golden chiffon. Though she guessed the woman must be in her forties, from a distance she could pass for much younger. Green eyes peered at her from a flawless face. Her hair, piled high on her head, was almost the same gold as her gown.

"Thank you. I'm delighted to be here. It's my first ball in simply ages."

He indicated his companion. "Emma, I'd like to introduce you to Miss Adele Walker. Adele, this is Emma Bradford, Bettina's closest friend."

The woman gave her a warm smile. "It's good to meet you, Miss Bradford. Walt tells me you've got a level head beneath all your beauty and he's delighted you're such a charming influence on Bettina."

"I'm blessed to have Bettina as my friend, Miss Walker. She's a lovely girl and very loyal."

Emma wondered why Bettina had never mentioned this woman before. She radiated poise and good manners, while at the same time making it obvious she was very possessive of Walt Devinde. She couldn't help but think how Renata Abetelli might react seeing Walt so cozy with another woman, much less one as beautiful as Adele Walker.

"What are your impressions of Denver? Walt tells me this is your first time in our part of the country."

They chatted a few minutes about the city and compared a few notes on millinery shops in town before Bettina joined them.

She greeted Adele in a friendly enough fashion so Emma supposed that whoever Adele was, Bettina seemed happy enough to have her present.

"There'll be no formal receiving line," her friend shared, as Walt and Adele excused themselves to greet the first arrivals. "Papa isn't overly fond of missing half the night's dancing while stuck receiving guests."

"I can't blame him. If he enjoys dancing, he should do it often," she proclaimed. "Actually, abandoning a receiving line fits in with the more relaxed rules of the West."

"There'll be no traditional dance cards, either. You're right. Papa doesn't stand much on ceremony. He's promised me there will be oodles of eligible men in attendance tonight. Single women can be scarce in this neck of the woods, even at the higher echelons of society. I hope you're prepared to dance often tonight."

Emma smiled. "I adore dancing. I haven't done so in a very long time."

A flurry of people arrived at that moment and the ballroom numbers swelled rapidly as the musicians struck up their first number. Emma thought that the idea of being fashionably late didn't apply in the West. A gala such as this wouldn't occur often, and she supposed people weren't about to miss a minute of the fun. She noticed Bettina being introduced around and smiled at the look of happiness radiating from her friend. Hopefully, Bettina would catch the interest of several suitors tonight.

"Enjoying yourself, Emma?"

She turned and found Eddie McLeod at her elbow. "I am. The music is divine and you should be relieved that Bettina's swamped with new admirers. I'm afraid she may have already forgotten her slight crush on you."

Eddie snapped his fingers. "Darn it all!" He laughed. "You wouldn't happen to know when the bird might make her appearance?"

"Actually, I spoke with Renata just before I came downstairs. Between tonight's first performance and Bettina's nonstop prattle, she told me she was going to lie down and rest a bit. She promised to join in the festivities around midnight."

He sighed. "I shouldn't feel relieved but I am." He brightened. "Would you like to take a spin around the dance floor? I'll be too busy staying on my toes once Miss Abetelli arrives. It seems a waste not to take advantage of the music."

She smiled. "I'd love to. I'm a bit rusty, so don't yelp too loudly if I step on your toes."

Eddie laughed and escorted her to the dance floor. Everything came back quickly to her and she enjoyed the dance immensely. When the music ended, she found another partner immediately and several more after that. Bettina had been correct in stating that being a single, unattached female put her in constant demand.

Then Emma saw Rye standing on the sidelines, watching her. She tried not to become self-conscious, knowing his eyes were on her. She threw herself into the dance, determined to have fun. If he really wanted to be with her, then let him ask for a dance. Maybe seeing her with other men might make him the slightest bit jealous.

Her newest partner introduced himself as Tad Carter.

"I've come to Colorado to seek my fortune," he explained. "I've recently graduated from Brown University in Providence. Miss Devinde told me that you were visiting from back East when I danced with her."

"Yes, I'm from a small town in Connecticut. My family owns a mill along the Moosup River. Denver is a long way from Providence, Mr. Carter. Why did you decide to come to Colorado?"

He shrugged. "My father has done some business with Mr. Devinde back in New York. I met him there last year while on a break from university and peppered him with questions regarding his ventures. He suggested that I make the journey here to speak to him in person about business opportunities once I completed my studies."

"Sounds as if you made an excellent impression on him. What have you discovered since your arrival?"

"Not a blessed thing." Carter smiled. "I literally got off the train an hour before *La traviata* began. Mr. Devinde had one of his men meet me at the depot. He passed along a ticket to the opera and told me to change into evening clothes right there at the station.

He then dropped me at the opera house and said he'd bring my trunk here."

"You'll be staying at the mansion?"

"Apparently so, but I've no clue as to where my room might be located. I barely had a chance to greet Mr. Devinde when I arrived, much less speak about business with him. He's been surrounded all night."

The dance came to a close. Emma said, "Let's remedy that. I see he's only with Miss Walker at present."

They wove through the crowd and approached Devinde and his companion. Walt greeted them heartily and pulled Tad Carter aside, wrapping an arm about him.

"It seems we've been abandoned," Emma told Adele Walker.

"I need to visit the retiring room as it is. Would you care to accompany me, Miss Bradford?"

"That would be an excellent idea."

The women made their way from the ballroom, passing directly in front of Rye. Emma nodded to him as they passed and he returned the nod. She sensed Adele falter slightly and then stumble beside her.

Suddenly, Rye was there, catching the older woman by the arm and righting her, holding on to steady her.

"Are you all right, ma'am?" he asked.

"Yes," she said, her breath coming rapidly, almost labored.

Emma noticed how the color seemed to have drained from her face. "Are you ill, Miss Walker? Would you care to lie down?"

Adele turned and looked at Emma, confusion on her face. "I seem to have gone lightheaded all of a sudden." A look of embarrassment crossed her face. "I haven't eaten much today. Vanity, you know. Wanting to squeeze into my lovely dress and look good in it."

Rye grinned at the older woman. "You accomplished your goal, ma'am. You're one of the loveliest women at the gala tonight."

The color began to return, as blotchy red spots crept up Miss Walker's neck and to her face. She placed a hand against her cheek.

"Perhaps I should go somewhere quiet for a few minutes."

Emma linked her arm through the older woman's. "Come with me, Miss Walker." She looked at Rye. "Would you stay on her other side, Mr. Callahan? Just in case."

He nodded and they escorted Miss Walker from the ballroom. Emma led them to Walt's library. As Rye settled Miss Walker on a sofa, Emma poured a generous portion of brandy into a Waterford tumbler and brought it over.

"Drink this. I'll see to bringing you something to eat. A little food might be just the thing to revive you."

"No, I can do that. Stay with Miss Walker." Rye left the room, closing the door behind him.

The ailing woman closed her eyes and sighed. She shook her head and then downed the brandy in a single gulp, grimacing after she swallowed.

She looked at Emma. "You said that was Mr. Callahan?"

"Yes. He's part of the opera company. I met him, along with other members of the troupe, on my trip west from New York."

She thought it best to keep to Rye's cover story. Though Miss Walker didn't seem like any kind of threat, she knew Rye would prefer no one outside their small circle know his real occupation, even if it were a good friend of Walt Devinde. What Miss Walker didn't know couldn't be accidentally divulged to the wrong person.

"His eyes. They're quite unusual," Adele remarked.

"I agree. I'd never seen eyes like them before making his acquaintance. They do draw in a person."

Her companion grew thoughtful. "I knew a man… long ago… with the same feature."

"That's interesting. You might want to share that information with Mr. Callahan. Fancy that you might know one of his relatives."

"No." Her protest came out as a whisper. "I'd… rather not. Frankly, it brings back unpleasant memories for me."

"I'm sorry to hear that. I won't mention it to him," she assured Adele.

"How well do you know this Mr. Callahan?" asked Adele.

Emma shrugged. "Not very well. He seems genuinely nice. Trustworthy. A hard worker. Why do you ask?"

Adele looked at her steadily. "Because he hasn't taken his eyes from you all night."

CHAPTER NINETEEN

$\mathcal{E}$mma sensed her face flame as Adele Walker stared at her.

"I believe you know him better than you're admitting to, Miss Bradford."

Before she could answer, Rye entered the library holding a plate. Hurrying behind him was Walt Devinde, concern etched on his face. He hurried to the leather sofa where Adele Walker sat and crouched beside her.

"What's wrong, dearest?"

She waved a hand in front of her. "Nothing, Walt. Please, don't worry on my account." She gave him a sheepish smile. "I wanted to look my best for you and your guests. I concerned myself with my hair and my dress and what jewels to wear. I'm afraid I neglected to eat anything all day and grew faint."

He frowned at her. "We can't have that." He motioned to Rye, who brought the dish of food over.

Rye handed the plate to Miss Walker. "I selected some of the meats and cheeses from the buffet. I thought something solid would be better than the sugary confections on display."

Miss Walker murmured her thanks as Walt picked up a cube of cheese and brought it to her lips. She nibbled on it, her eyes on his, no words necessary between them.

Emma found herself uncomfortable watching the couple. An intimacy existed between them and she thought it best to vacate the room to give them privacy.

"Mr. Callahan? Perhaps we can return to the party," she suggested.

"Of course." He looked at Walt. "Do you need anything else, sir?"

"No. Thank you for alerting me to the situation. If Bettina asks, I'll rejoin the gala shortly."

As they left the library and returned to the ballroom, Emma said, "Thank you for coming to Miss Walker's rescue. And for bringing back Mr. Devinde. Miss Walker is obviously someone important to him."

He shrugged. "My job is to observe. Watching the two of them together tonight, it was easy to ascertain that they are very...close."

She laughed. "You certainly danced delicately around that."

He chuckled. "Well, Walt *is* married. I didn't want to sound judgmental. I'm merely in his employ at present."

"Bettina tried to explain her parents' odd marriage to me. It's certainly not what I would want for myself, but she says it works for them. That they are very content leading separate lives."

He stopped. His gaze bored into her. "What would you expect in your husband, Emma?"

She bit her bottom lip in thought. "I'd want someone intelligent. Kind. Respectful. A man with a positive attitude and a sense of humor." She paused, deciding she might as well bare her soul. "And of course, I'd expect love. My husband would be the most important person in the world to me, and I would do any-thing for him because of the bonds of our love. I'd want fidelity. Monogamy. I hope he would cherish me as much as I did him."

She cleared her throat, his gaze still intense. "What's good for the gander should be good for the goose, as well. What about you, Rye? What would your ideal wife be like?"

He thought a moment. "You pretty much spoke of what I would wish for. Except you neglected to mention trust. I think honesty in a relationship is the most important thing in the world. To me, in order to love I would need to implicitly trust a woman and know she would always be truthful with me."

He looked at her steadily. "Marriage isn't meant for someone in my line of work. A Pinkerton is always on the move. Always traveling from city to city, across the United States, heading to the next assignment. That's not the way to build a life with someone, always absent. I love what I do. Because of that, I doubt I'll ever marry. It wouldn't be fair."

His words stunned her yet Emma realized they rang with truth. Rye relished his job as a Pinkerton detective. He seemed to have no close ties with anyone, moving from place to place as he did. In his way, he was letting her know that even though they'd shared a few stolen kisses, those wouldn't amount to anything permanent. He would finish his work on this case protecting Renata Abetelli and be on to the next assignment once his marching orders came through.

She should accept what he said without question and move on since it was obvious they would never share a future together. As a woman twenty-five years of age, however, she might never again experience the strong feelings she possessed for this man. She yearned to discover what her parents had shared. She knew the workings of physical love. This man had awakened something within her that needed to be fulfilled.

Emma intended to take that journey— if only once — with Rye Callahan. They would both know in advance that it couldn't lead anywhere but she decided in that moment that before either of them left Denver, she would become a woman in every sense of the word.

She gave him an enigmatic smile. "The music is tempting me. Would you care to dance?"

Tucking her arm through his, she began leading him back to the noise of the gala. She bit her lip to keep from laughing at the puzzled look that crossed his face. She knew she was being a bit forward but she didn't care.

In his mind, he had given her fair warning that nothing lasting would come from their friendship. She understood that— but she was ready for more from him.

As her father always said, she was the most determined, most stubborn person that walked the planet.

Emma intended to be with Rye Callahan, in every sense of the word.

She led him to the center of the dance floor.

EMMA BRADFORD CONFOUNDED him to no end. Rye was taken with her angelic beauty and intelligence, but she proved to be a mystery at every turn. A few minutes ago, he'd wanted to kiss her senseless, but as they spoke of marriage, the need to be a perfect gentleman arose within him. Emma needed a husband and a stable home. Children and pets. Not a brief encounter with the likes of him.

With sorrow, he made himself perfectly clear and let her know in no uncertain terms that he would never wed. He was married to his job at the agency. Addicted to the travel and excitement and constant change.

Rye thought that would be the end of it. He would see her over the next few weeks at dinner and possibly a few times in the house. Then he'd move on to wherever The Eye sent him next. He knew his words, though delivered gently, would probably hurt her— especially after the passionate kisses they'd shared— but she'd smiled at him with a sense of mystery.

Now, she wanted to dance with him. The last thing he wanted to do was hold Emma close in his arms and pretend nothing was wrong. She seemed totally unaffected by his declaration.

It frustrated him. It *infuriated* him. Did she think so little of what had passed between them as to brush it aside and then dance the night away? That didn't even take into account all the other men she had danced with at the gala. He had to admit jealousy had seethed through him all night, despite the fact that Emma didn't belong to him.

Hell. If she wasn't worried about anything permanent between them, then neither would he. Obviously, she hadn't placed as much emphasis on their kisses as he had. Maybe Emma was one of those women who never fully relinquished control of their heart so that it could never be broken. He might as well enjoy the night and not concern himself about the future.

Rye snorted under his breath as he took her in his arms and twirled her about. Then held her. A little too close.

But having her in his arms felt so right.

"You've danced quite a bit this evening," he remarked, his grip tightening on her hand. She winced and he immediately relaxed it, inhaling the scent of vanilla that swirled about her.

"Yes, I have. Bettina swears there's a shortage of women in Denver, and I believe she's correct." She smiled, her dimple creasing appealingly in her cheek. "I haven't danced in several years and I realize I've missed doing so. I suppose, tonight, I'm making up for lost time."

"You seemed to enjoy Mr. Carter's company."

She cocked her head. "Oh, you've met him?"

"Not officially. Walt Devinde let me know he would soon be a houseguest. I sent a telegram to our New York office and they vetted him for me."

Emma looked over his shoulder and smiled. "He's dancing with Bettina again. I do hope something comes of it. I feel they'd be a good match."

Before he could reply, the music stopped. Rye dropped his arms, albeit unwillingly. He wondered how to keep her in his company for a bit longer, at least until the bird made her appearance and his attention would need to be focused elsewhere.

"Would you care for some punch? Or perhaps something from the buffet?"

"I believe Mr. Devinde wants us," she said.

He glanced over and saw the millionaire had returned to the ballroom. Miss Walker was on his arm, looking much better. She had an air of familiarity about her but he couldn't place where he might have known her from. She hadn't spoken up about meeting him previously so he doubted they'd been introduced.

Rye guided Emma toward the couple and they were met by Bettina and Mr. Carter. At that moment, a hush fell over the room. He glanced up and saw Renata Abetelli floating down the stairs, as regal as any queen, dressed in a ball gown of rich amethyst. Applause spontaneously broke out. She paused and gave a slight smile, then bowed her head in acknowledgement before continuing her descent.

Ivar Larsen met his prima donna at the foot of the stairs and escorted her into the party. He steered them toward their host. Walt introduced Renata and Ivar to Adele Walker and Tad Carter. The songstress gave the young man a bright smile and then eyed Adele with open speculation.

"I couldn't have asked for a better opening night, Renata," Walt said. "You've stolen the hearts of Denver society in but a single performance."

Renata's brows rose. "Did I? Well, perhaps I might steal you away for a dance, Walt. You can tell me all about what everyone has said."

"Of course. Excuse me." He led her away.

An awkward silence hung as Miss Walker frowned and watched the couple walk away.

Ivar smoothed things over. "Miss Walker? I'm not an accomplished dancer but would you do me the honor?"

She nodded and allowed Larsen to escort her to the floor.

Rye turned to Emma. "I need to return to work."

"Of course. I understand."

"Work? At this time of night?" Tad Carter proclaimed. "What on earth do you do, Man, to want to leave a party," and looking to his companions, "much less two beautiful women?"

"You'll know soon enough, Mr. Carter. Now's not the time to go into the situation. Find me when the gala's over and I'll escort you to your room and explain. You're staying across the hallway from me."

Rye almost laughed aloud at the perplexed expression on Tad Carter's face as he walked away.

～

EMMA DANCED for another hour and then found herself growing weary. She'd need to soak her poor feet in hot water and salts tomorrow morning. She excused herself from her latest partner and noticed the room beginning to thin. She started to wave to Bettina, but her friend was deep in conversation, surrounded by a trio of young men who seemed to hang on her every word.

Exiting the ballroom, she decided though she was tired, it might prove difficult to fall asleep. The dancing had been exhilarating and she needed something to calm her racing mind. A boring book might do the trick. Nothing could put her to sleep faster than Pliny the Elder's *Natural History*, with the author espousing on topics such as the medicinal uses of cabbage. It had been the tome she frequently used to lull her father to sleep if he were restless or in pain.

Heading for the library, she knew exactly where the volume sat on a shelf, having passed over it several times in the past two weeks and giving it a wide berth. She reached the door and found it ajar. As she started to push it open, she heard voices and turned, ready to give the occupants privacy.

Until she heard Rye Callahan's name mentioned.

She stopped in her tracks and leaned toward the opening, reduced to eavesdropping as she had as a girl, but curiosity got the best of her.

"I don't know why you didn't tell me this before." Walt Devinde's voice. She was certain of that.

"There was no need to before. I'm telling you now. It's not as if you've shared everything with me," Adele Walker answered. "But I thought you should know about Rye."

"And no one suspects?"

Harsh laughter erupted. "No. How could they?"

"Then we'll keep this between us. Agreed?"

The conversation ceased. Emma was afraid she

would be discovered lingering at the door. She turned away and hurried up the nearby stairs to her room.

Sleep was a long time coming as she sat turning the fragment of conversation in her mind. Somehow, Adele Walker knew Rye or something about him.

And Rye didn't know anything about her.

ye busied himself mixing paint to repair a small table that had been accidentally toppled during the previous evening's performance. He'd already sanded the scraped surface and was about to give it a fresh coat of paint. Ivar Larsen had turned out to be a perfectionist and his eagle eye noticed it immediately. The manager informed Rye about the slight damage to the prop as soon as he'd arrived at the theater.

He noticed Larsen seemed in a surly mood and figured it was due to the bird's own state of mind. They were rehearsing the scene where Alfredo denounces Violetta, throwing his winnings at her feet. Larsen hadn't been happy with the way it had gone last night and had those involved in the scene at the opera house now, going over it until it satisfied him.

The more they rehearsed, the colder Renata became, withdrawing into herself. Larsen finally shouted at her, the first time Rye had heard the manager lose his temper. The soprano gave as good as she'd gotten and their argument escalated. The cast involved in the scene stepped aside, making themselves scarce as they peered from the wings. Rye couldn't blame them. He'd heard of artistic tempers before but the volume and length— not to mention the colorful language— of the argument made him wince.

Renata threw her hands in the air and stomped her foot. "Enough, Ivar! You have made my head ache." She glared at him, her eyes narrowing. An evil smile crossed her face. "So much that I simply cannot go on tonight."

"That isn't an option, my dear," Ivar told her through gritted teeth. "Your reviews have been nothing short of astounding. The house is sold out for the next week and beyond. I won't allow one of your tantrums to keep you from the stage. You owe it to Walt Devinde to appear. *He* has made it possible for you to have this new chance."

She looked at her director with malice. "I cannot go on. *I will not go on.*" Her voice dropped low, but thanks to the excellent acoustics of the opera house, Rye could hear every word she spit out. "If you wrapped a rope about me and dragged me onto the stage, I would say *nothing*. I would sing *nothing*. Not one line of a single aria."

Renata placed fisted hands on her waist. "Do not embarrass yourself, Ivar. Believe me, you would suffer embarrassment if I were to be brought on stage and chose to remain mute."

The venom of her words astonished Rye. He didn't think he'd ever heard a woman— no, anyone— speak with such direct spite. He watched as Renata stormed off the stage. He looked over at Eddie, who sat in the audience. His friend shrugged and stood.

"I'm betting the bird will want to go home now and rest that pretty little aching head of hers." The detective hurried down the aisle and went backstage.

Immediately, Larsen and the cast sprang into action, almost as if nothing out of the ordinary had occurred. Anna, a kind young woman who played Violetta's maid and served as Renata's understudy, immediately appeared and conferred with Larsen. Maria, the head of costumes and makeup, joined them for a brief conversation before hurrying off.

The director clapped his hands together. "We've done this before, ladies and gentlemen. Let's hope the headache does not last long this time."

A newly-hired stagehand named Hank appeared on Rye's left. He'd been one of two brothers that worked as gardeners on Devinde's estate and had been employed when Larsen needed a few extra hands on a part-time basis. Eddie discovered Hank and his brother George came from Kentucky and didn't have a dime between them after failing miserably at placer mining. They'd hired on to make enough money to return home to their parents' farm. It was all George ever talked about, though Rye sensed that Hank wasn't nearly as enthusiastic about the plan.

"You through painting that?" Hank indicated the table.

"Yes. Give it time to dry, though."

The fair-haired man shrugged. "I'll be sure it winds up where it's supposed to be. Giovanni said he needed your help with the lights right away." Hank took out a handkerchief and mopped his brow. "Ain't seen nothing like that before. They 'bout scared me to death with all their hollering and carrying on."

"I know what you mean," he agreed.

Rye spent the next few hours helping Giovanni run the lights. Anna differed in height from Renata by three inches and the electrician wanted to make adjustments as the company rehearsed.

"Does this happen very often?" he asked Giovanni.

"You mean *la nostra diva* refusing to go on?" The Italian shrugged. "Many times. It is like a mating ritual, *il mio amico*. She performs. The house sells out. The audiences are entranced. And then she is sick. And terribly missed. Usually arguing with *il mister*. Then he smooths things over. They forgive each other. She performs again. Beautifully."

"Until she does it again."

Giovanni nodded. "*Si*. You now understand opera and its divas, Rye."

Both men chuckled.

~

EMMA HAD NOT PLANNED on attending the opera that night until she passed Renata and Eddie returning early from rehearsal. Renata gave Emma a curt nod and breezed past her without a word. The Pinkerton stopped on the sidewalk and updated her on the falling out between the Italian and her manager and the very public tantrum witnessed by the cast and crew. He gathered it was part of a pattern and nothing to be concerned about.

Still, Emma wondered what the production would be like without its star and the magic she brought to the role of the sad heroine. She returned to the house and found Bettina and they made plans along with Tad Carter to see the show again with its new lead— if she went on.

The trio left the house and had Walt Devinde drop them off early at the opera house before he proceeded to Adele Walker's. They would meet up in his box for the performance and then have a late dinner together before returning home.

"I'm so glad you didn't mind coming with me," Bettina told Emma and Tad as they made their way backstage to the dressing rooms. "I've been at the theater so much and I've gotten to know Anna. She's a talented singer in her own right and I wanted to speak to her and wish her well before she goes on stage. This will be her first chance at a leading role, you know."

Bettina knocked at the door. Guila, the mezzo-soprano who played Flora in the opera, opened it. "Come in. Anna could use a friendly face."

Since she'd seen the opera three times in the past week, Emma immediately recognized the singer who played Annina, Violetta's maid. She hadn't known who Renata's understudy was, but it made sense. She smiled at the girl, who looked as if she was about to be led away to the gallows.

"Thank you for coming," she said in a whisper. "I'm just so frightened. What if they don't like me? All those paying customers came to see the great Renata Abetelli. Not me."

Bettina put an arm around Anna. "You will be splendid. I feel it in my bones. You have a lovely voice and this is a wonderful opportunity. Make the most of it, Anna."

Emma was proud at how encouraging her friend was toward the understudy. Although she idolized Renata, Bettina seemed to be maturing before everyone's eyes. The flighty young miss who'd arrived in Denver a short time ago was rapidly gaining an assurance about her. Maybe it was being out from under her mother's hand, or possibly it was due to the attention and responsibilities she'd gained in Denver helping manage the household. Regardless, Emma couldn't help but be impressed with Bettina's poise and encouragement toward the nervous young opera singer.

They made their way to the Devinde box and found Walt and Adele already seated. This was the first time she'd seen the woman since she'd accidentally over-heard her and Walt talking the night of the gala. Emma wondered what secret Adele had shared with her lover that no one suspected. Though Emma had heard Rye's name mentioned, she hadn't heard in what context. After pondering for hours, she thought it might be con-nected to a former case Rye had worked.

But what case? She was certain Rye hadn't recog-nized Adele but now she believed Adele somehow knew him. Or at least of him.

Emma was curious by nature and the fact that Rye was somehow involved in some secret he knew nothing about intrigued her even more. She determined at that moment to get to know Adele Walker better— and find out what the mystery revolved around.

The overture for *La traviata* began. She settled into the plush fabric, grateful for the view her box seat gave her of the production. Within minutes, she knew Anna was totally wrong for the role of Violetta Valéry, the famed courtesan sitting in her Paris salon. Violetta, while beautiful, had a world-weariness about her, due in part to her profession and also because she recov-ered from an illness.

Anna, while quite pretty in her own right, couldn't help but fare poorly when compared to the looks and self-assurance Renata Abetelli brought to the role. Anna's was more a farm-fresh beauty. She looked as if she'd just set foot in Paris for the first time, not like a woman who owned the city and had men falling spell-bound at her feet.

Emma could feel the restlessness spread across the crowd. Ivar Larsen had opted not to inform the audi-ence of Renata's illness, hoping until the last minute that the prima donna might arrive and take her place on stage. As a result, seeing an unexpected soprano playing Violetta, much less one who appeared naïve instead of sophisticated, caused the audience to murmur. As the whispers continued to gain in volume, she watched the poor understudy begin to fall apart.

By the second act, more than half the audience had vacated the theater. Emma expected a majority of them had asked for a refund of their ticket price. When the third act began, those left in the opera house openly cheered when the doctor told the new singer playing Annina that Violetta would soon die. They booed savagely when Alfredo's father expressed regret at separating the lovers.

Finally, Violetta died in Alfredo's arms. To silence. Emma knew poor Anna probably wished she had actually died.

As the cast rose and formed a line to receive acknowledgement for their performance, a light smattering of applause occurred. It quickly died out. No curtain call took place. Those remaining in the audience simply stood and shuffled out. Anna burst into tears and fled the stage.

Those in the Devinde box sat wordlessly, stunned at the events. Walt's eyes looked glassy and unfocused. Already, she could see him counting his losses. Anger rose in Emma as she thought how Renata played with not only people's feelings and expectations, but the very livelihood of the touring company and Walt Devinde's investment in them.

A throat cleared. All heads in the box turned and saw none other than Renata Abetelli standing there, the picture of health in a blood-red dress, her hair immaculately coiffed, diamonds sparkling at her neck and ears.

"I suppose Ivar has learned his lesson," she mused, then she beamed at Walt. "Do not worry. You will suffer a few losses tonight and poor Anna's confidence in her talent will have taken a blow or two. But the news will get out that the great Renata Abetelli will return tomorrow. Anticipation will build and all will be well again."

Renata brightened. "Are we going to supper as a group? I find myself famished."

CHAPTER TWENTY-ONE

*E*mma left the Devinde mansion and began walking in the warm sunshine, humming under her breath. She caught herself doing so and laughed. Ever since she'd seen *La traviata* repeatedly, she found the music swirling in her head. It reminded her of her voice lessons from years ago and how she'd dreamed of possibly going on stage one day. She'd now seen the production five times in the past couple of weeks, four with Renata in the starring role and the one ill-fated performance with poor Anna.

She continued to hum an aria as she made her way to Madame Drummond's shop. The last of the dresses she had ordered were ready for a final fitting before being delivered. Emma was eager to see the dressmaker, for Madame Drummond loved to gossip. If anyone in Denver might have information about Adele Walker, it would be the Frenchwoman.

She arrived and found herself the only customer present, grateful she would have Madame's entire attention. As she tried on the remainder of her new wardrobe, Emma nudged the woman into revealing what she knew about Adele Walker.

"Oh, that's lovely, Madame. I wouldn't have thought of using this shade of lavender."

"You look splendid in it, Mademoiselle Bradford. Of course, you look brilliant in any color, *n'est-pas?*"

"Thank you. Do you know who has a very unique sense of style? I met her recently. Adele Walker. Might you know Miss Walker? Or have you created any fashions for her?"

"Hmph. Turn around. Yes, *c'est parfait*. Let's slip it off."

As the shop owner lifted the dress from Emma, she said, "I know *Mademoiselle* Walker. All of Denver *knows* her. Or who she is."

"They do?"

"Yes. She arrived here several years ago. Eight? Maybe nine?"

"Where did she come from? I wasn't able to place her accent."

Madame shrugged. "I've heard California. San Francisco. Or *c'est possible* the East coast before that. There's a bit of mystery about her past. Still, that didn't keep Arthur Grover from taking up with her." She retrieved another morning dress and helped Emma into it.

"So…take up. I gather this Mr. Grover became involved with Miss Walker?"

"Hah! Involved. Yes, that is a polite way to say it." Madame waved her hands about dismissively. "Mr. Grover owned some of the largest mines in Colorado. Silver. Copper. He made a fortune after he arrived here." She lowered her voice in confidence. "Some men with money believe that gives them *carte blanche* to do as they wish, despite society's rules. I've seen it in Paris. In New York. And especially here in the West. If a man has money, then heads turn away when he…misbehaves."

"You're implying Mr. Grover was married, I suppose."

"*Oui. Non*, smooth it out. Like that. *Tres bien.* Yes, *Monsieur* Grover involved himself with Mademoiselle Walker. Drove poor *Madame* Grover out of town for close to three years. She retreated to Philadelphia, where they were originally from. She stayed there with her sister until Monsieur Grover passed away the Christmas before last. It was a good thing he died. I heard Madame Grover was fed up and ready to return to Denver to kill him."

"You don't say."

Madame's eyes widened. "Oh, it gets much worse, *mon cher*. Adele Walker showed up at the reading of Arthur Grover's will. She'd been invited by his attorney to do so. The poor wife was humiliated when her husband left the bulk of his fortune to his lover. It forced the poor wife to move in with her only son, Randolph, and his family."

"Randolph Grover? The bank manager at National Bank?"

Madame Drummond nodded sagely. "The one and the same. Ah, but don't you look lovely in that, Mademoiselle Bradford. I call it daffodil. It makes your skin positively glow."

Emma finished trying on the last outfit, steering the conversation in other directions. She thanked the dressmaker and then headed toward Larimer Square.

She already knew Randolph Grover. She'd met him when she opened her account at National Bank. The bank manager had been extremely kind to her, inviting her to return and check on the funds to be deposited in her account. She hadn't done so, trusting that Daniel Mitchell had wired them as requested. The attorney was nothing if not efficient.

This gave her a good excuse to stop by and pay a

visit to the executive and see if she could learn anything else beyond the balance in her checking account.

A clerk greeted her as she entered and she asked to speak with Mr. Grover. He led her directly to the manager's office, where Grover greeted her by name.

"Ah, Miss Bradford. What a delight to see you again. Have you brought your bank book? Your transaction occurred with no problems."

"That's good to know, Mr. Grover. I've been quite busy lately but I did want to stop by and see if things were in order."

"They are indeed. I'll have one of my clerks check to see what your exact balance is. Do you have your passbook with you?"

She handed it to him and he stepped to his opened door. He spoke briefly with his assistant and then returned to the seat behind his desk.

"How are you getting along in Denver?"

"Quite well," she told him. "I've been staying with my good friend, Bettina Devinde." She paused, putting the bait on the hook. "You may have heard of her father. She's the daughter of Walt Devinde."

A sour look crossed the bank manager's face. "I know of Mr. Devinde. I haven't met his daughter, however."

"She recently arrived from Chicago. Bettina is serving as her father's hostess although I gather a Miss Walker did so before Bettina came to town."

"I know for a fact that Miss Walker has been keeping company with Mr. Devinde for almost two years." He stared in the distance, his hands fisting and unfisting. "Despite having a large fortune, it hasn't stopped her from going after Walt Devinde and his. I hear he has a wife, too. That never seems to bother certain someones."

Grover came out of his reverie. "Please forgive me,

Miss Bradford. I'm not one prone to indiscretion but you've hit a sore spot with me. Miss Walker became involved with my late father. It practically destroyed my mother. My best advice to you would be to steer clear of her as best you can."

The bank manager became all business after his confession and Emma soon found herself on her way back to the Devinde mansion, pondering what she'd learned about Adele Walker. While she'd made some progress gaining information about the woman, she'd made absolutely none to the connection between Adele and Rye.

He worked long hours at the opera house and had missed dinner every night since the gala. Ivar Larsen had the crew working on new backdrops and props for a second production that would follow *La traviata*, so Rye's days were taken up with carpentry and painting. At night he helped with set changes and running the lights. She didn't know the last time she had even seen him, much less spoken to him.

As she entered the house, Rozalia Cattaneo came flying down the stairs.

"You must come. She need you. Come now!"

Emma groaned inwardly. Since Renata's pretend headache and missed performance, no one ever knew what mood the opera singer might be in. The household had learned to walk on eggshells. If the diva was in a great mood, things hummed along like a well-oiled machine. If she was in poor spirits, everyone gave her a wide berth. Emma had avoided taking luncheon in the dining room and asked for a tray in her room on two occasions, not wanting to be in the path of Renata's wrath.

She wondered what crisis awaited her as she followed Rozalia up the stairs. The maid ushered her into Renata's room. Heavy drapes were drawn, keeping out the day's sunlight. Though almost noon, the singer remained in her nightclothes, sitting in bed with half a dozen pillows propped behind her.

"Ah, Emma, *la mia dolcezza*. Where have you been? I've needed you."

"I'm here now, Renata. What's wrong? Are you ill?"

She pouted and then grimaced. "*E la mia bocca.*"

"Your mouth? Something's hurting your mouth?"

"*Si.* Look at it. Come close. Closer."

She stepped forward as Renata opened wide and held her tongue down as she pulled her bottom lip far to the side.

Even without strong light, Emma could see the swollen, red gums and guessed what the problem was.

"It looks as if you have an abscessed tooth, Renata."

The diva frowned. "What is this abscess, Emma? I do not understand the English."

She thought a moment. "*Infetto.* Infected. Your tooth — *il dente*— is infected. Are you in a lot of pain?"

Renata teared up. "*Si.* It gets worse by the minute."

"I'll be back."

When Emma returned, she brought warm salt water for Renata to rinse with. The diva frowned but followed instructions.

"Here. I'm going to put a clove on it now. This is an old home remedy. You'll need to leave it there for a few minutes. It will numb the area."

Renata did as she was told. Emma also held a warm compress against Renata's jaw, next to where the abscessed tooth was located. After a few minutes, she let Renata spit the clove out.

"Is better. But it still hurts. I cannot sing like this. It pains me when I open my mouth. What am I going to do?" Her voice rose in hysteria.

Eddie McLeod appeared in the doorway. Emma went to him and motioned for them to step into the hallway as she explained the situation. She didn't want Renata to overhear their conversation. She could only imagine the diva screaming about barbarians in the West and their backward methods.

"The only sure thing is to pull the tooth," he said. "It'll only continue to get worse if it doesn't come out."

"I remember back home that Farmer Kaye owned a turn-key. Anyone with a tooth that pained him would go see the farmer. He'd loosen their gum with the blade of his pocket knife and then set the hook of his turn-key under the tooth and pull with all his might until it came out." She chuckled. "He didn't even charge for his service."

"The bird isn't going to let anyone near her with a knife," Eddie proclaimed. "I doubt she'd see a barber either. I'm going to fetch a doctor. I'm not sure if Denver even has any dentists. The doctor will have to be the one to break it to her that she'll need to lose the tooth."

He left and she returned to sit with Renata. Emma climbed on the bed next to her and returned the compress to her jaw.

By the time Eddie returned, both Bettina and Walt were in the room. Eddie had asked Walt who his physician was, and Walt hightailed it to Renata's room to check on his investment and see if Renata toyed with another ploy that would cost him money.

Eddie entered with Dr. Paulson. Ivar Larsen trailed after them. Rozalia stood wringing her hands, muttering in Italian. Emma had Rozalia leave to fetch hot tea and the servant looked grateful for something to do.

The doctor tapped and probed inside Renata's mouth. He complimented Emma for using both the cloves and the hot compress.

"Do you have pain when you bite down? Or close tightly?"

Renata nodded sullenly. "And when I open wide. Like when I sing."

"Well, Miss Abetelli. We must extract your tooth. It's oozing pus along the gum line. You also have a few canker sores in there. They aren't helping the situation."

"Extract?" She looked to Emma. "What is this *extract*? It does not sound pleasant."

She braced herself for Renata's response. "Pull. Extract means to pull. Dr. Paulson wants to remove your tooth."

As expected, the diva began to hyperventilate. Then she began shouting. Moaning. Cursing in Italian. Rozalia entered the room and set the tea service down, running to her mistress and wrapping her arms around her. They jabbered in Italian so rapidly that Emma had no idea what was being said, only catching a word or two of their fervent conversation.

Dr. Paulson removed a bottle from his medical bag. Renata's wails quieted and she studied him carefully.

He held it up. "This, Miss Abetelli, is Dr. McBride's King of Pain. It has enough alcohol in it to put down a mule. I'm going to have you drink plenty of this. You won't even remember me extracting your tooth."

"No! I cannot. If you do this, I cannot sing!"

The physician shook his head. "The abscess will only grow larger and more painful. I guarantee you won't be able to chew or swallow— much less sing like the nightingale you are— unless you allow me to remove that tooth."

Renata began weeping. "But I must go on. I live to sing."

Ivar stepped up. "We are dark tonight, my dear, so you won't miss a performance this evening. You'll have this done and then rest." He looked at the doctor. "How soon can she sing after the procedure?"

Paulson shrugged. "I'd rest the area for three or four days. No irritations. That means no chewing. Just soft, invalid foods she can easily swallow. Little to no speaking, much less singing. The infection will subside. I have something topical that can be placed there once the tooth is gone. Cloves will help numb the area and the pain, as well."

"This can't be happening!" Walt Devinde proclaimed. "If Anna goes on again, it will be a disaster." He thought a moment. "We'll shut production down. Just for a few days. Until Renata can sing again."

"Emma sings like a songbird. I'm sure she could step in for Miss Abetelli."

She turned and saw Rye standing in the doorway.

CHAPTER TWENTY-TWO

*E*mma paced like a caged tiger in Renata's dressing room, panic filling every fiber of her body as the minutes ticked off.

"What am I supposed to *do*?" she asked herself.

She knew she loved to sing. She'd always enjoyed entertaining her father's guests back home. She thought how proud he would be of her now, seeing her dressed as Violetta, ready to take on Denver at Mr. Devinde's opera house.

Still, doubt filled her. Emma was no professional. The audience that awaited the rise of the curtain expected the divine Renata Abetelli to grace the stage. A world-renowned soprano. A woman of mystery, charm, and talent. Not a woman with no professional experience.

She gazed at her image in the mirror and tried to bolster her confidence.

"You don't value yourself enough, Emma. You have talent. You took years of voice lessons. You've seen *La traviata* many times, both here and abroad. You know every song Violetta sings. Every line that she speaks. And you rehearsed the role late into last night and for several hours today. You will fascinate this audience."

She paused. "And possibly the Pinkerton who believes in you."

She brought her shaking hands to her heart, trying to still them. Rye Callahan had gotten her into this impossible situation. He'd only heard her sing once to a little girl on a train. It was nothing compared to performing in an opera to a theater full of paying customers.

Emma bowed her head and fought the nerves. Rye believed in her.

She needed to believe in herself.

A hard rap on the door jolted her. She managed to get to the door on trembling legs and opened it.

Rye stood there, a bouquet of bright orange Cowboy's Delight in his hands. He handed the flowers to her as she ushered him in.

"I remember you said you liked these the night of the ball."

She nodded, touched by his gesture. "They're beautiful. Thank you." She set them down, knowing she should find water to put them in but too distracted by the whirlwind in her mind. It was almost time curtain time.

"What if I freeze?" she asked him. "What if I forget the words? How can I let Walt Devinde down after all his kindness toward me?"

Rye placed large, warm hands on her shoulders. "Look at me," he commanded, his voice low.

Her gaze met his. She shivered at both his touch and the powerful pull in those golden, green-flecked eyes.

"I know you're nervous. You think you can't do this."

She winced. "You saw how many mistakes I made during rehearsals. If only I had more time. This is happening too fast." She tried to pull away but his fingers remained firm, holding her in place.

"Those were mostly blocking errors, Emma. You knew the lines. And the notes to every aria." He smiled down at her. "Your voice is an amazing instrument. So you moved to a few wrong places on the stage. Even if you do so tonight, the audience won't realize that. They'll be wound inside the fantasy of the story you're weaving. The cast will accommodate you.

"I have utter faith in you and your talent. I would never have suggested you to Walt Devinde if I didn't. I believe in you, Emma. It's time for you to believe in yourself."

He echoed the very words she had thought just moments ago. Knowing Rye Callahan truly trusted her to go out and do her best allowed her to surrender her doubts. When she did, serenity poured through her, wrapping around her as if she were a small child blanketed by a loving mother. Confidence soared through her.

She could do this. And succeed.

When she looked at Rye again, a surge of desire poured through her, as slow and rich as warm honey. His pupils widened in understanding and his mouth came crashing down on hers.

His kiss stole her breath, stole her very soul, as if he sucked the life from her as greedily as a parched wanderer in the desert might draw water from a cut cactus. But even as he took from her, he gave. It was as if Rye poured every bit of his vitality and confidence and power into her.

When his lips finally left hers, Emma knew she could conquer the world. All because Rye had faith in her.

His hand cupped her cheek, his thumb slowing rubbing her lower lip. "I'd wish you good luck but I don't think you'll need it. It's as Seneca said— luck is a matter of preparation meeting opportunity."

She smiled. "So, you read philosophers as well as novelists?"

He squeezed her hand. "Everyone wants the best for you tonight, Emma. As that wise old bard Shakespeare said, *'All the world's a stage.'* Tonight, you own the world. I'll see you after."

He left without a backward glance. She brought her fingers to her mouth, the tips touching where his lips had rested next to hers only moments ago. She smiled at the thought.

A second knock sounded on the door. "Five minutes, Miss Billings." She had decided to use Billings as her stage name. Emma didn't want any reviews, advertising or gossip to possibly reach John Fairburn's eyes or ears.

She turned to the mirror to make certain her costume and hair were in place. Staring back, she no longer saw a woman afraid of failure. Instead, the reflection showed strength. Emma picked up Violetta's fan and made her way toward the wings.

JOHN FAIRBURN ENTERED the opera house, surprised by its richness and grandeur. It was apparent Walt Devinde hadn't spared any expense either outside or inside the building. The same with his mansion. He'd passed by it earlier today after having arrived on a late afternoon train yesterday. The architecture of the opera house reflected a Greek influence, much as the mansions of New York's Fifth Avenue did. With the kind of money Devinde had, its opulence didn't surprise him.

He wondered how Emma had made Devinde's acquaintance, much less how she'd become comfortable enough to reside in his home while she visited Denver.

Could she be the man's mistress?

Of course not. The thought was absurd. Prudish Emma Bradford, who'd kept her mouth tightly closed in the one chaste kiss they'd shared, wouldn't be spreading her legs for a married millionaire she had just met. Zebras didn't change their stripes. John would bet a pretty penny that Emma was the same naïve female she'd always been.

She was book smart, though. He'd give her credit for that. Emma also had an acute business sense from all those years shadowing Dwight Bradford around the mill and milking Stannis, the mill manager, for information. He chuckled at how easily he'd discovered her whereabouts, using the very telegram she'd sent to Mitchell at his law office.

Escaping Louisa's clutches had taken some finesse. He argued how they needed to keep things above board as far as their relationship went, at least until he could find Emma, marry her, and get her to create a will before he disposed of her. Louisa finally admitted it would be best if she remained behind in Connecticut and had no link to his trip to Colorado— and her step-daughter's subsequent marriage and death.

In truth, he planned to have Emma disappear without marrying him. Whether he could use all his immense Fairburn charm to have her accompanying him willingly was beside the point. He needed her gone from Denver, with no loose ends left. He didn't want Walt Devinde— or anyone in her new network of friends and acquaintances— to question why she left town, much less attempt to contact her down the line. He needed that door closed and no one coming to look for her at any point. His forgery skills would create all the necessary documents he needed to establish their marriage. And her death. His familiarity with both certificates wouldn't cause any problems.

He didn't know much about wills, however. Before he left to head west, he'd broken into a few law offices. Not Daniel Mitchell's. He wasn't taking any chances in that regard. John did enter three different places illegally, after hours, and perused copies of wills. He'd taken copious notes and believed he had enough of the language down for anything he created to sound authentic. If anyone questioned Emma's will, he himself could fill in the blanks. It was a young attorney, fresh out of law school, possibly the first will he'd written. The West was much different from the established East, so the language in the document might also reflect those differences. He had plenty of time to think about the false will and produce it before he returned and claimed his fortune.

Eventually, he would need to get rid of Louisa.

He saw now that her constant harping would never do. With plenty of money in hand, he refused to be tied down to one woman. Once the will was probated, he would sell the mill and Dwight Bradford's former home. Rid himself of any stocks and bonds or any property he might not be aware he possessed, via his dearly departed wife's death. Once everything had been liquidated, then he and Louisa could take an extended trip after breaking all ties in that little piss-ant town he'd grown to loathe.

John always fancied going to Europe, much as his schoolmates did with their wealthy families each summer, visiting Rome or Paris or London. While traveling, it would be easy for Louisa to have an accident if he wanted something official on the record. She might fall from atop the Colosseum while sightseeing or drown in the waves of the Mediterranean as they picnicked and swam along an isolated section of beach.

Or he could go another route and simply make sure her body never saw the light of day again, burying it deep in some Bavarian forest. He could then continue his trip abroad and return home alone, with no one the wiser.

But first, he had to find Emma Bradford and eliminate her.

He had stopped several places today, at shops he thought she might visit. He'd found a bookstore on Larimer Square that screamed her name. He never saw what she saw in those dusty tomes but he'd never been much of a reader. Soaking up life rather than reading about others and how they lived is what interested him. The bookstore's loquacious clerk had been more than helpful when he mentioned knowing her, confirming Miss Bradford was a regular customer, and even mentioning how she and her friend often attended the opera, where they sat in Walt Devinde's box.

John made his way here tonight, hoping to catch a glimpse of her. Wondering if she had changed since her mad flight from Connecticut. Dreaming of his hands around her swan-like neck, squeezing the very life from her, enjoying every moment of her fear and pain.

He consulted his pocket watch and saw the performance would soon begin. The Devinde box had several people seated in it but Emma wasn't one of the occupants. A distinguished man in black tie sat between two women along the front row. One was older but incredibly attractive with her milk-white skin and hair of spun gold, while the younger woman had beautiful, even features and a cloud of dark hair. He idly wondered if they were Devinde's wife and daughter. Maybe somehow Emma had become friends with one or both of them, which might explain her presence in the Devinde household.

The lights dimmed and the crowd's whispers fell. Before the orchestra began, a thin man in an immaculate, dark suit slipped from backstage to a few feet in front of the heavy maroon and gold curtains.

"I regret to inform you that Miss Abetelli has fallen ill and will not perform tonight, respecting her doctor's orders."

A low grumbling shimmered through the crowd. John had already heard from a local barkeep about the total failure that took place at the hands of an understudy that went on in place of an ailing Renata Abetelli. He glanced at the Devinde box to see how they were reacting to the news. Instead of shock or disappointment, the occupants' faces held smiles. It piqued his curiosity.

The man continued. "In Miss Abetelli's place is a new discovery, a soprano so talented that her voice will make you weep. I'm pleased to announce that Miss Emmeline Billings will perform tonight in the role of Violetta Valéry." He disappeared quickly.

The overture began with his departure, but the restless audience buzzed. He watched as a handful of patrons walked out, though the vast majority seemed willing to give the new prima donna a chance. The curtains rose to the scene of a Paris salon, full of people chatting quietly.

His jaw dropped in the next moment.

Emma walked out on the stage.

John tensed, his mouth dry, his pulse racing. Despite the elaborate dark wig and courtesan's blue silk gown, he knew the tilt of her head. The long, elegant neck. The high cheekbones and lush lips.

And yet apparently he had never known Emma Bradford at all. She opened her mouth and the words poured from her in song. Her voice was unlike any he'd ever heard, clear and angelic, drawing him in as intimately as any lover ever had.

When the performance ended, John rose to his feet

along with the rest of the crowd in a rare standing ovation. Outwardly, he applauded Emma's remarkable achievement. Inwardly, he seethed. Making Denver's adored new diva disappear after such a public introduction would be a difficult task.

But then again, he'd always been up for impossible challenges where money was concerned.

CHAPTER TWENTY-THREE

*E*mma awoke from another dream about Rye Callahan. Her fevered body longed for his touch.

The last time they'd spoken alone had been her opening night when his kiss gave her the courage to go on stage. Since then, she'd only caught glimpses of him at rehearsals and hadn't seen him at all at the Devinde mansion. While performing satisfied her to no end, she still knew the handsome Pinkerton could meet a need in her that had never been satisfied before.

She wondered if he could be as busy as he seemed or if he avoided her for some reason. She was determined to find the answer. The kisses they'd shared were fast becoming an obsession. She wanted more. She *needed* more— even if she didn't know exactly what her heart and body desired.

A knock as loud as an exploding cannon came from the other side of her door, startling her from her reverie. She quickly threw on a dressing gown and tightened the belt before opening her bedroom door. She found Rozalia standing there, her dour face as impenetrable as ever.

"You come. See her. Now."

Before she could respond, the servant turned and marched away along the carpeted hallway. Emma decided Renata could wait a few minutes. She splashed cold water on her face and proceeded to dress. She loosened her nighttime plait, brushing her hair before winding it into her usual chignon.

As she studied her image in the mirror, she steeled herself to do battle. She hadn't seen Renata since Monday, when she'd helped the diva with her painful tooth. The rest of that day had been reserved for the rehearsals she'd been thrown into, as well as more rehearsals and the performances over the last three nights. She dreaded meeting with the soprano but knew it was both inevitable and unavoidable.

She left her guest room and knocked on Renata's door. When no one called out to enter, Emma decided to open the door. The room was empty. Puzzled, she decided to make her way down to breakfast. When she entered the small dining room, she spied Renata in deep conversation with Walt Devinde and Ivar Larsen. She wondered what game the soprano was playing with her.

Nodding a greeting to everyone, she helped herself to the buffet the servants prepared each morning, lifting silver chafing dish lids and filling her plate with scrambled eggs, slices of ham, and biscuits smothered in sausage gravy. She found after a night of performing she was famished the next morning. Breakfast had become her main meal since she didn't like to eat much before she went on stage. She found it easier to sing—and fit into Violetta's costumes— if she ate sparingly. She did have a snack of fruit and cheese once she returned to the Devinde household after the evening performance, but breakfast now served as her largest meal.

The butler poured coffee and juice for her and had it waiting when she brought her heaping plate to the table. She thanked him and sat, wondering what Renata's next move would be. She didn't have long to wait.

"*Buongiorno*, Emma. We were just discussing my return to tonight's performance."

She winced, almost as if in pain. She realized all along she was simply a stand-in for Renata, and that the diva would return to her role as soon as she was able to sing without pain. Yet a sadness wrapped its arms about Emma, knowing she would never feel the freedom of the past few nights when she lost herself in the story of love and death.

The singer nodded sagely, as if she understood how deeply her words wounded Emma. "I thank you for helping Walt with his little problem. He said you've been good in the role."

"Good?"

She turned and saw Bettina standing in the doorway, an album in her hands. "She's better than good, Renata." Bettina seated herself at the table and opened the book. She scanned the clippings pasted inside and then began to read aloud.

"*Miss Emmeline Billings astounded Denver society last night with her remarkable voice. Both its range and clarity soared to the rafters of Walt Devinde's new opera house, bringing patrons to their feet in boisterous appreciation.*"

Bettina looked around the room. "I've been saving Emma's reviews and collecting them for her." Bettina's fingers skimmed the newsprint and located another passage to read to the assembled group.

"*Where Walt Devinde found Miss Emmeline Billings is a mystery; where she goes from here should be straight to the best opera houses in New York or abroad. Her range is that of a* lirico-spinto, *with great flexibility and power. Miss Billings projects with a rich timbre and dynamic control and easily can be heard above the orchestra. She is a delight to audiences.*"

"Enough!" proclaimed Renata, a frown creasing her brow. She looked from her host to her manager. "I understand that Emma is good in the singing, but *I* am the star of *La traviata*. I plan to return tonight. I have missed being Violetta and performing for the wonderful Denver audiences."

"But Emma has received rave reviews. Surely, she can somehow remain a part of the production," said Bettina.

The two men glanced at each other. Emma realized they'd come to some previous understanding. As Walt looked at her, she assumed whatever agreement had been made would not please Renata Abetelli in the least.

Ivar reached and took Renata's hand. "*Mio caro*, we have a wonderful plan. It will help rest your voice and still give Denver what they clamor for."

She looked suspiciously at her manager. "What is this? This plan?"

Walt joined in. "We want you to have center stage every evening, Renata. Your talent— your gift for music — is what I wanted to give to my newly-adopted city."

"I'm afraid this heavy performance schedule is wearing on your health," Ivar added. "We must protect our splendid songbird in every way. We want you to do all six evening performances. Emma will take on the matinees."

"They don't ever sell out," Walt said quickly. "It's almost a waste of your time to perform in them. Emma can easily handle the matinees without you having to worry about them. That way you can rest your voice and concentrate on what's important."

"*I* am what's important," Renata reiterated as she cocked her head and thought a moment. "Is true. The matinees aren't so important to me." She looked at Emma. "You may do these."

Emma realized two things quickly. One, they'd appealed to Renata's ego and vanity and actually gotten her to agree to giving up the matinee performances. More importantly, it allowed Emma to keep singing as Violetta for the foreseeable future, even if on a limited basis.

She tried to disguise her enthusiasm and contain the smile that threatened to beam brighter than the sun.

"I will do whatever you agree to, Renata. You are everyone's chief concern."

"Then we settle it," the diva said, waving a hand and smiling at those present. "I am happy that you make me so happy."

EMMA DESCENDED FROM THE CARRIAGE, Bettina chattering up a storm behind her.

"That was absolutely your best performance yet," her friend said. "I'm so glad Papa and Mr. Larsen thought it was a good idea for you to do the matinees."

They entered the house and saw Walt Devinde coming down the stairs. "May I have a word, Emma?"

"Of course."

"I'll see you at dinner," Bettina said. "Cook is doing her famous pot roast with baby carrots and English peas. And cherry pie to top it off."

Emma's stomach gurgled at the thought of it. Now that she performed in the afternoons, she came home and downed as much as any day laborer when dinner rolled around. She had given up the noon meal, though, so at least the seamstress hadn't had to adjust any of Violetta's costumes.

She followed Walt into his library.

"Have a seat, Emma. I'll get right to the point."

She perched on a camel velour divan, curious as to what the millionaire would say.

"I hope I haven't disappointed you during my run with the recent matinees."

He shook his head. "Far from it. We sold out both yesterday and today, which we hadn't done before with an afternoon performance. I think we would have on Friday, as well, but no one knew you'd be singing during it." He paused. "I have eyes and ears throughout Denver, Emma. It's the way I've always done business. The reports I'm receiving indicate people would rather see *you* as Violetta. Not Renata."

His words stunned her. "But Renata is a professional singer."

"It doesn't matter. I could let her go now and not see a difference in sales. I'm thinking about having the two of you alternate evening performances. I'd bill it as the *Battle of the Divas.*"

She bit her lip. "Have you discussed this with Mr. Larsen? Or Renata?"

"With Larsen, yes. He understands the situation I'm in. He's not only Renata's manager but it's his opera company. In the long run, making a profit is what counts."

She shuddered. "Not at the expense of what life would be like with a mad prima donna on the warpath."

"I know how temperamental Renata is— and what life will be like once we tell her about this new venture. Larsen thinks she'll move from here to the hotel. At the end of the day, though, she understands where her bread is buttered. Renata will have to go along with whatever we decide."

He pulled out a cigar and looked at her, brows raised, asking permission. She nodded and he lit it, inhaling deeply.

"I also haven't been paying you, Emma. I realized I've been remiss in that."

She waved the thought away. "Please. You've let me stay here all this time. You've given me a chance to have an opportunity I never dreamed of. That's payment enough."

"Then if you won't accept any compensation, perhaps you'd allow me to provide a donation in your name to a local charity. I'll give you time to think it over." He stood. "I'm off then. I have an early supper with Adele, and then we're taking in tonight's performance with Bettina and Tad Carter."

He studied her. "Not that you see her often but you might want to try and avoid contact with Renata during the next few days. Larsen and I will speak with her tomorrow about the new arrangements. Monday is dark anyway so that will give her time to cool her heels before she goes on Tuesday evening."

Emma watched him leave and thought just how explosive Renata's temper was. This time, it would all be directed at her. She stood and said to the empty room, "I'm not going to live my life in fear. I won't let her bully me."

She spent a pleasant evening, first dining with Bettina and Tad before they left for the opera house, and then writing a letter to Daniel Mitchell. She informed him of the sudden turn of events in her life and even invited him to Denver so he could see her perform. He had always been like a second father to her, and she hoped he would make the journey to Colorado.

Sleep refused to come. Emma thought it must be due to the excitement of returning to some of the evening performances. She decided to return to the library and find something to read within its limited collection. She spied exactly what she needed and picked up a copy of *Pride and Prejudice* from the shelf, smiling at her old friend. As much as she loved Dickens, no one wrote characters as vividly as Jane Austen did. Emma often wished she could be as witty and astute as Miss Elizabeth Bennet.

Opening the book, she snuggled into the chair that looked out the large window into the garden. Though night had fallen, the moon glowed brightly. Cradling the novel in her arms, she stared at the stars scattered across the sky. She'd studied those same constellations almost a continent away and found it hard to believe how far she'd traveled and how much her life had changed since her father's death.

Laughter startled her. Emma opened her eyes and, for a moment, didn't know where she was. Then she looked down and saw the book in her hands and remembered coming downstairs to the library.

"You know I love it when you do that."

More laughter again, this time low and seductive. She froze. She'd fallen asleep.

And now someone was in the library. Two someones.

Emma hesitated, not knowing if she should make her presence known. Then she realized it was too late. The noises that quickly occurred— a rustling of clothing, the low murmurs, then the heavy panting and gasps of pleasure— all let her know exactly what now occurred on the other side of her wingback chair. She curled into herself, wishing she could plug her ears. Her face heated with embarrassment, but she knew to remain still so she wouldn't be discovered.

Finally, the lovemaking stopped. She hoped whoever it was would vacate the room so she could escape to the safety of her own bed. She vowed never to speak of this to anyone.

"You should change your name from Devinde to Divine, my dear," Adele Walker said. "No man has quite your stamina. Or touch."

"And no woman has your wiles."

"Hmm. Do you believe I've tricked you? Deceived you in some manner?"

Walt growled low, sounding like a barely-tamed tiger. "You have ensnared me, my love. I'm drawn to you as a moth is to flame." He chuckled. "You have skills even a courtesan lacks."

Emma winced as she heard more kissing, wishing the ground would open and swallow her whole. She might never be able to look Walt Devinde in the face again without blushing.

"I want to marry you, Adele."

"What?"

"You heard me. I've never been without a woman and I'm not counting that dried-up prune back in Chicago. What I feel when I'm with you? I'm more alive than ever."

"You would divorce your wife— and marry me?"

"Yes. I don't care what Chicago society says. I'm in a city where I can live as I choose. I have enough money to insulate myself from anything unpleasant. Who cares what they say behind our backs?"

"You're serious, Walt."

"Damn straight. Marry me, Adele Walker. Let me make you Queen of Denver." He laughed. "Or Queen of the entire Wild West."

She sighed. "Then you better ask, Walt. This time you're asking Adeline Callahan for her hand in marriage. That's my real name."

CHAPTER TWENTY-FOUR

*J*ohn Fairburn drummed his fingers against his leg as he waited on the sidewalk for Fernanda, the opera company's assistant costumer and seamstress. He nodded to a few of the tour group's members as they left the rear entrance of the theater. He'd seen several of them over the past week as he'd wormed his way into Fernanda's good graces. An early lesson he had learned was that women always knew much more than men ever dreamed of— and John needed all the free information he could obtain.

Shadowing Emma and waiting for a chance to get her alone had proven impossible. She was escorted to and from the opera house in Walt Devinde's carriage. She always had someone with her, especially Devinde's chatty daughter, who seemed to stick to Emma like glue. He'd waited numerous times for her to leave the mansion to do some shopping or browse in one of her precious bookstores, but while she was singing, her time seemed to be filled.

Though Fernanda possessed a wealth of information, he hadn't been able to use any of it to his advantage. He did know the hours of rehearsals and performances, and she'd introduced him to many on the crew and in the cast. He'd received a private tour of the building, which did help him become familiar with the layout. That could turn out to be useful. At least he hoped it would.

She'd also pointed out Eddie McLeod, a Pinkerton detective that Devinde had hired to protect Renata Abetelli from any elements the soprano deemed unsuitable in the Wild West. John exercised caution and avoided McLeod. When he spirited Emma away, John didn't want the Pinkerton to connect him to the incident in any way.

"There you are, *carissima!*"

He turned and greeted Fernanda, kissing her on both cheeks in the European fashion. She spoke passable English, and he'd enjoyed exploring her curvaceous body after hours. Their brief affair had made up his mind— he would rid himself of Louisa at the first opportunity. With all the money he stood to gain from inheriting Emma's vast wealth, he didn't want to be limited to one woman. He hid his growing frustration with the situation and put on a smile for his companion.

"Is birthday of Giovanni. You remember him, *si?*"

"He does the lighting, I believe."

She nodded. "And he creates sets. Giovanni very good man. Very good at his job. We go with others and celebrate? You no mind, Stan?"

"Of course." He thought they might as well go. If he overheard some tidbit that would help him in his pursuit of Emma, it would be time well spent. He'd actually grown fond of Fernanda and didn't mind pleasing her in something small such as this little get-together.

They strolled arm-in-arm a few blocks until they reached a saloon. When they entered, he recognized various company members gathered at a group of tables in the rear. They made their way over and congratulated Giovanni before accepting mugs of beer from Antonio.

John looked across the room and saw another of the company's members enter the bar and glance around. He'd seen the man leaving the opera house a few times but he'd never been introduced to him. As the worker made his way toward them, his gait seemed familiar. He experienced an odd chill. It was almost as if he knew him.

The company member arrived to greetings from the group and turned in his direction. John spewed beer as their eyes met.

He has Da's eyes!

John immediately looked away and coughed as if choking. A hard pounding on his back almost did him in. He looked up into the man's eerie golden eyes, flecked with the same shade of green as Gerald Fairburn's. John had never seen eyes like that before.

Except in his worthless father's face.

"Are you all right?"

He nodded. "Swallowed and it went down the wrong way. Sorry if I got any beer on you. Hell of a first impression to make on someone." He held his hand out. "Stan Foster." He'd known better than to use his real name. Another way he'd never be traced to Emma's disappearance because John Fairburn had never been in Denver.

The man took it. "Rye Callahan."

Callahan stood as Da had, a few inches over six feet, as well as possessing Fairburn's powerful build. Even the man's jet-black hair mirrored Da's, though the old man's had started to gray a few years before his death. Standing this close, he knew without a doubt they shared the same blood. The worker was definitely one of Da's numerous bastards— but older than the rest.

"Here. Let me get you another beer." Callahan took

the mug from John's hand and reached for a pitcher on the table.

Gerald Fairburn had been long on charm and short on brains. He'd left a string of illegitimate children throughout Five Points. Probably beyond it, as well, since he'd crossed the country to California in the Gold Rush and then returned to New York City, neither richer nor wiser. He'd married John's mother in a literal shotgun wedding after he'd knocked her up— and then died when John was only nine.

Callahan turned back and handed him the ale. "What's your connection to Giovanni?"

He nodded in Fernanda's direction. "I've been seeing her. She invited me to tonight's little celebration. Can I get you a beer? Or something stronger?"

"No. I'm not much of a drinker. I just stopped by to make Giovanni happy. I'm one of his carpenters. He's a good boss and an honest man."

"Hmm." He studied Callahan and then raised his eyes to the ceiling and frowned as if deep in thought. Turning back slowly, he asked, "Have we met before tonight, Mr. Callahan? There's something familiar about you."

"No. I've got a good eye for faces. I would remember if we had."

"Are you certain?" He snapped his fingers and then pointed at Callahan. "New York City? I think I've seen you there."

The man's smile turned steely. Wariness filled those golden eyes. "I was born there but I grew up in Chicago. It's not possible that we've met. I'd remember."

Immediately, John knew the carpenter was hiding something. His body had stiffened at the mention of the city. But what? And why?

He shrugged. "I guess I'm mistaken." He started to

turn away and then looked back. "Except for your eyes. They're very unusual, Mr. Callahan."

"I get that a lot."

John narrowed his eyes at him as if in thought and then brightened. "I know. It's Mr. Fairburn. Gerald Fairburn. He was friends with my da long ago. His eyes were unusual. Very similar in color to yours. That's it. You remind me of Mr. Fairburn, God rest his soul."

He watched Callahan but didn't see a flicker of recognition at the mention of the Fairburn name. His gut told him Rye Callahan didn't know he was but one in a long line of Irish Fairburns born on the wrong side of the blanket. John couldn't believe he was speaking to a half-brother who hadn't a clue they were related. It gave him a perverse sort of pleasure.

"Nice to meet you, Mr. Callahan. I've ignored Fernanda long enough. Maybe I'll see you around."

He nodded and left his half-sibling to snuggle up to his new lover. As a man with secrets, he knew when someone else had one. He'd gamble a thousand in gold that Rye Callahan had a big one. He idly wondered just what it might be as he threw an arm around Fernanda and drew her close.

~

ADELINE CALLAHAN?

Emma didn't dare move from the library chair that hid her. Not when she knew that the woman just feet from her was related in some way to Rye.

She remembered back to the gala and how Adele Walker, as she called herself, had almost fainted after spying Rye in the crowd. No, Emma recalled Adele had noted Rye watching Emma. It was only when they had drawn close and passed Rye when Adele almost fainted. The woman had questioned Emma about Rye's unusual eyes, even going so far as to say she once knew a man who had the same feature but that it brought back painful memories for her. Emma had agreed not to bring it up to Rye, even after she'd overheard Adele and Walt mention him by name. She'd come in on the tail end of their conversation and had no idea why the two discussed the Pinkerton agent. Since she had nothing to tell Rye, she had remained quiet.

Then she'd totally forgotten about the incident because she became swept up in Renata's sudden illness and her own immersion in the opera's production.

She now wondered… who exactly *was* Adeline Callahan?

Emma held still, not even blinking. If discovered, she might never find out what connection this woman had with Rye. Holding her breath, she prayed for the lovers to continue their conversation.

"Ah, I'd already forgotten that you hold deep, dark secrets, my love."

"You know they're neither deep nor dark. Just the secrets a mature woman keeps of a foolish young girl who fell in love with the wrong man."

"When you told me earlier, Adele, I swore I would never betray you. I haven't. Rye Callahan is just another employee to me, one that's simply very good at his job."

"He can never know he's my child, Walt. Never. He was led to believe I was his aunt, one who left New York long ago, never to return. My brother is a kind man, and I know from seeing how Rye is that Seamus brought him up well. Seamus had an older son, Brian, but his wife couldn't have children after that. Rye was a gift to them, where he would've been a curse to me— unmarried, penniless, and immature."

"And foolishly traipsing after his father?"

Adele laughed but Emma heard no mirth in the sound. "Gerald could charm the snakes from Ireland better and faster than Saint Patrick ever imagined, all the while charming his way up the skirts of as many lasses, as well. I was a silly girl with no common sense. At least where Gerald was concerned. The only smart thing I did was leave Rye in Seamus's care while I rushed to California in hopes of finding Gerald. Why I bothered to do that after he abandoned me when I told him I was with child, I'll never truly fathom."

"You never located him?"

"No. By the time I arrived, only a handful of Forty-Niners had made their fortune. If Gerald had been one of them, I'd have heard. My gut tells me he eventually made his way back to New York. I was too humiliated to contemplate that. After a few letters, I told Seamus he wouldn't hear from me again. I needed to start fresh in a new life and not look back."

Adele's revelations startled Emma and she gripped her book tightly when it almost spilled from her arms.

"Well, I'm glad it all happened, even if it was long ago. You remained out West and that allowed us to meet. I'll ask you again. This time on bended knee and I'll get all the details right."

Emma heard movement and then, "Adeline Callahan, no one is more dear to my heart. I love you with great passion and ask you to marry me. I'll call you Adele or whatever you wish. Only know that I long for you by my side and in my bed."

Sobs began, and guilt ran through Emma for stealthily witnessing their private moment. Finally, they subsided.

"Yes, my love, I'll marry you. Even if your witch of a wife won't release you from the bonds of that marriage, I will love you and stay with you until my dying day."

Walt sighed. "I suppose I'll need to go to Chicago to ask for the divorce in person. I'm sure I'll have better luck that way than sending a telegram or a letter."

"Do you really think she'll give you one?"

"I'm not sure. I'll promise to take care of her financially, of course. I would never abandon my responsibility to her. If she wants to pretend to her friends that we're still married, I don't care. I have no need to return to Chicago once a divorce is granted, much less contradict her. If she refuses, it won't matter. I'll still put a ring on your finger and have the world call you Mrs. Devinde."

"What will Bettina think?"

"Frankly, it's not her life. She's not overly fond of her mother and she seems to get along quite nicely with you. Besides, I've noticed a growing attachment between her and Tad Carter. I'd bet my last dollar that they'll be engaged before we know it. She'll be so wrapped up in her own new life, she won't have time or inclination to meddle in ours."

Emma waited through another prolonged bout of noisy kissing before the couple finally vacated the library. She took a deep breath and let it out slowly before she stood and stretched. She'd been curled tightly in the chair for too long and her limbs ached and throbbed.

As did her heart. All she could think of was Rye. How he'd secretly been raised by his aunt and uncle, never knowing his real parents. How he had a good-for-nothing lothario of a father who had run off to seek his fortune in gold, leaving behind his newborn child and a mother more girl than woman. How Rye's own mother callously tossed away her own opportunity to raise him while she chased after a dream as ephemeral as smoke.

One thing Emma did know— she could never, ever reveal the truth to him. That remained Adele's responsibility alone. What Emma overheard had been in confidence. If Adele— no, Adeline— wished to share her secrets with the man she loved, it was her choice. No one else could force her hand to do the same, even if she kept her true relationship with her son a secret.

Yet she knew this new knowledge of Rye's beginnings would eat away at her. Worse, Rye himself had told her that he believed honesty— and the subsequent trust which grew from it— to be the most important quality between a man and a woman. If she broke that trust with him, especially over something so monumental, she would never regain it.

Her hands fisted in frustration. She wished she could hit something. Isn't that what a man did when he was angry and had no control? Throw a punch into a wall? She almost laughed aloud, thinking what might happen if she showed up with bruised knuckles or broken fingers when she arrived at tomorrow's performance. She supposed that's why temperamental women chased away their anger by throwing vases. Clean-up was minimal and not a mark remained behind. At least on the woman. She was certain a few walls might bear the fruits of impact.

She shook her head hard, trying to force her mind to go blank, and took a deep, cleansing breath. She would have to continue as if everything were the same. As if nothing had changed. She would act surprised when Walt left for Chicago and then returned to announce his engagement to Adele. She would be polite to Adele and as warm as always to Walt.

As for Rye?

That would be the most difficult of all. She had longed to take their relationship to a deeper level. That would be impossible with the secret she now held. Emma might sing well and even be able to speak Violetta's lines with reasonable emotion, but she was no actress. She couldn't look Rye in the face and tell him a lie.

For that's what it would be— a lie of omission.

War raged within her. She wanted Rye's kisses and friendship. Actually more. Much more. Yet she couldn't do him a disservice and be his friend when she kept secret his very origin and the fact he saw his mother several times a week. Rationally, she knew she should divorce herself from her strong feelings toward him. He'd already told her he had no interest in marriage. He was wedded to an exciting job that had him traveling all over the country, one that would never allow him to settle down and plant deep roots into a community and raise a family.

The choice was obvious. She would be polite yet distant. He might not even notice, as little as they saw one another since she'd become involved in *La traviata*. He would finish his protection detail in Denver and move on. She would complete her engagement at the opera house and do the same. Hopefully, they would head in opposite directions and never run into each other again. She realized it was the only solution to an incredibly difficult situation.

Satisfied that she'd drawn the only conclusion possible, she replaced *Pride and Prejudice* on the shelf she'd taken it from. It was long past her bedtime. Though she doubted sleep would come easily, she wanted to retreat to the comfort and quiet of her bedroom. Maybe she would find some solace writing in the pages of her journal. It seemed the one constant that comforted her.

She opened the library doors and stepped into the foyer.

Straight into Rye's chest.

CHAPTER TWENTY-FIVE

ye reached out and grabbed Emma. The minute he touched her, desire flamed in him. He pulled her close, wrapping his arms about her, savoring the feel of her in his arms after so long a time. She smelled subtly of roses and he inhaled deeply, wanting her with a primal ache that would never be satisfied.

She turned her face up to his, a question written across it. In answer, his mouth came down on hers. Hard. Demanding. Greedy. He had never wanted a woman more than he did Emma in this moment. He plundered and took and possessed her mouth with his, never letting up, satisfaction oozing from his pores at her throaty whimpers and moans.

His hands began caressing her through the silk of her robe, dropping to slide along the curve of her hips and down to cup her tantalizing bottom. He squeezed and kneaded it and then in a fog, realized she mirrored his actions. Her nails raked along his own buttocks and then tightened, squeezing and releasing. His manhood began to swell. He had to put a stop to this— before he couldn't.

Rye tried to push her away, even as his mouth still

held hers captive, but her grip on him tightened. She pulled him even closer, running her hands up his back and around to his chest. She stroked him until his senses were afire, every nerve tingling with anticipation.

He broke the kiss, his breathing harsh. "We...should stop." But his willpower fled and he kissed her again, longer, deeply, more intense than before.

"No," she murmured into his mouth. "Not this time."

Their tongues danced as flames of a fire burning bright, leaping, twisting, stroking, mating as one.

He tried again. "Emma. I... I..."

She bit his lower lip, holding it prisoner. A surge rushed through him, pulsating. "No. Don't stop," she murmured. "I want this, Rye. I *need* this." Her gaze pinned him. "I need you."

She released him and grabbed his hand, pulling him into the library, closing the door. She turned the lock and leaned her back against the door, her glorious strawberry blond hair spilling about her, a look of triumph in her eyes. As if she'd already won.

And she had.

All protests died before he could speak them. She stood before him, her lips already swollen from their love play, and smiled. Just a ghost of a smile. But one that let him realize it was Emma who was in control.

She took his hand and linked her fingers with his, drawing him across the room to an oversized camelback sofa. A single fluorescent lamp glowed near a chair in the far corner, leaving most of the room in silhouette.

She released his hand and reached for the tie on her robe.

"Wait."

She stopped, her gaze searching his. "It's what I want, Rye. What I've wanted for a long time." He saw the pulse in her throat dancing nervously. "I know you don't want anything lasting. I don't either. All I know is that I've wanted you for what seems like forever. I'm twenty-five. Already on the shelf as far as women go." She smiled. "But tonight, it's my chance to *live*. To come *alive*. To celebrate that I'm in control of my life and my destiny.

"I may never have a chance to come together with a man. I want this, Rye. I want this. With you. Please. Say you want me, too."

"Oh God, Emma."

He closed the gap between them, sweeping her in his arms. He sat on the sofa with her in his lap, his hand tenderly cupping her cheek, his thumb stroking the alabaster skin. She reached her palm to his cheek and rested it there, drinking him in.

"I don't believe in love, Emma. I don't know if it even exists. But I believe in here. And now. I believe in you. In us. For these stolen moments only we can share."

She pressed a finger to his lips, silencing him. "No more talk, Rye. Just show me what's in your heart."

She untied the knot of her robe, parting it to reveal a matching silk nightgown in soft peach. The curve of her breasts called his name softly. He pushed the robe from her shoulders. It fell to her elbows, trapping her arms. He slipped his fingers along the straps of her nightgown and slowly slid them down her arms, pulling the flimsy silk to her waist. Her eyes never left his. She remained as still as a doe in the forest, waiting to see the hunter's next move.

She had hunted him as much as he had her. Now, she was his. If only for a little while.

His hands went to her bare shoulders and then dropped to the perfect globes of her breasts. His palms touched them and they filled his hands, pulsating with a life all their own. He began kneading one, flicking his thumb over her nipple, which pebbled in need. He drew the other breast into his mouth, his tongue teasing and laving. Her gasps of pleasure radiated through him and she encircled his head with her hands, drawing him closer to her.

Rye worshipped each breast, giving both equal time, pleasuring her with his tongue and hands. As good as they tasted, he longed for her mouth again and kissed his way up the slender column of her neck and back to her honeyed mouth.

He kissed her until he was sure both their lips would fall off as she pushed his coat from his shoulders and unbuttoned the simple wool vest and workman's cotton shirt he wore. He shrugged out of them and tossed them aside, now bare to his waist, and caught the satisfied look of approval in her eyes.

She reached out a hand to explore and her light touch caused his muscles to jump. Laughing in delight, she continued the game, her fingers stretching farther until she'd touched every inch of his chest. Then she pressed hot lips to his collarbone, her kiss almost scalding him. His breathing grew shallow and rapid, matching hers.

Rye pushed her down onto the sofa, hovering above her. He pulled her sleepwear from her waist, gliding it down slowly over the curve of her hips, his pulse quickening as the fleeing material exposed more of her creamy flesh. When it reached her calves, he became impatient and yanked suddenly, tossing it over his shoulder. Mirth bubbled up in her.

He locked a hand around her slender ankle as he sat drinking her in.

"Do you know how beautiful you are?" His fingers dragged slowly up her calf, by itself stunning, but the whole of her caused his heart to sing.

"I was thinking just the same thing about you," she purred.

"You don't seem self-conscious at all," he noted.

Her dimple only increased her beauty as a smile lit her face. "I'm not," she said. "I would have thought this would have turned me shy— but I feel safe with you, Rye. And utterly content."

"Hmm. I think I can do better than content."

He unfolded himself until he lay fully stretched out next to her. He stroked her belly lightly and allowed his fingers to move down to her soft, golden-red curls. She frowned, more in curiosity as she cocked her head slightly.

"Still feeling safe?"

She nodded.

"I don't want you to feel safe," he growled. "I want you to feel desire." His voice dropped, low. "I want you to writhe and moan and lose your breath. I want you to long and ache and want more than you've ever dreamed of wanting."

Her eyes widened. Then she smiled at him, a womanly smile that told him she was discovering the power of her femininity.

"Let's see if you're a man of his word."

"I guarantee I am."

His fingers played a tune upon her, finding her sweet spot, strumming and stroking her until he kept his promise. She gulped air as she twisted and bucked and moaned under his touch. When he feared she would cry out, he covered her mouth with his. Both his fingers and tongue plunged ruthlessly in a rapid rhythm.

He sensed her passion as it burst forth, her cries of ecstasy absorbed, the quivers shaking her body in a newfound joy. He encouraged her to ride the wave and she did, mindlessly giving herself over to him.

Then she lay spent, trembling, her chest rising and falling quickly. Her eyelids batted rapidly several times and then closed before languidly opening. She stared at him, those azure eyes flickering with content.

And desire.

Rye couldn't take it any further. Though he physically ached and needed to find release himself, Emma didn't truly know what she asked of him. If they joined together, it might be impossible to walk away from her.

He kissed her deeply before he sat up and lifted her clothes from the floor. He pulled the wadded material apart and shook out the nightgown. He bunched it up and pulled it over her head and then stood. His hands grasped hers and brought her to her feet, the gown skimming the length of her.

Handing her the robe, he caught the scent of roses everywhere. He'd never be able to see a rosebush again without thinking of Emma in this moment, her hair tousled, her lips rosy and swollen. She took the robe and he stepped away and threw on his shirt, his back to her. He was glad his pants had remained on. The bulge in them strained the material. He took his time buttoning the shirt and then his vest before he picked up his coat and held it front of him, hiding the evidence of his arousal.

"You haven't asked." She tied the robe's belt and stared at him.

"Asked what?"

"If I was satisfied." A mischievous look danced across her features. "I shall simply say that you are a man of your word." She took a few steps toward him, closing the gap between them. "But...how do I satisfy you?"

He raked a hand through his hair. "Knowing I fulfilled you makes me happy, Emma."

She laid a hand on his forearm. Even though his

coat was draped over it, an electric bolt ran through him at her touch.

"I want to pleasure you as you did me, Rye."

He leaned down and kissed her brow, closing his eyes to savor the last moment of intimate contact between them. Then he stepped back. "I hope you do find love someday, Emma. I pray that you find a man that can make you happy and give you babies and be everything you wish for."

He paused for a moment. "But I told you— I'm not that man. I've never really known love. I wasn't happy growing up. The war showed me just how cruel men can be. I've found something I enjoy— something that makes me feel whole— and that's being a Pinkerton. It's my life, Emma."

He smiled, knowing it held an air of sadness. "I'll never forget you. Or this night."

Rye turned and left the library. Every step away from Emma made him realize he was a liar.

He had known love. He'd know it for the rest of his days.

Because Emma would forever be the love of his life.

"Why can't we go home, Hank? I miss Kentucky. I miss Mama. And her cobbler. And her stew. We ain't had anything close to Mama's stew since we came to Colorado. Why did we come so far? We got nothing to show for it. And that opera lady's so mean. She yells all the time. It hurts my ears."

Hank Penland put the finishing touches on his appearance as his brother grumbled and then ushered him out the door. He'd listened to George's complaints all his life. Older than George by a mere eleven months, the brothers were night and day different, from their appearance and personality to their level of intelligence. He bemoaned the fact that George got all the height and good looks, but at least Hank got the lion's share of brains. He'd wanted to leave his simple-minded brother behind in Kentucky when he came west to seek his fortune, but Mama insisted they not split up.

No one ever crossed Mama.

Placer mining had been a bust. They'd bought their supplies— pans, rock boxes, various tools, even a tent— but the only thing that seem to last or be of any value were the Levi Strauss denim work pants that everyone recommended. They'd bummed around, seeking odd jobs here and there to pick up cash after the mining effort fizzled, while he contemplated a way to make some real money. He'd promised George they'd return to Kentucky one day soon, but Hank had no doubt it would be George alone on the eastbound train. Not him. Farming sucked the very life from his soul and he knew he could find a better way to make a living—honest or otherwise.

"Why are we going to see Mr. Devinde? Are we in trouble? Did I do something wrong, Hank?"

The brothers had run into Devinde by chance soon after they reached Denver. He hired them on as handymen and gardeners on his newly-completed estate, allowing them use of a small cottage on the far edge of his land, rent-free. George, in particular, possessed a green thumb and had done wonders with the landscaping in the few short months they'd been in Denver. Working outdoors came naturally to George. Thinking did not. That was Hank's specialty.

When Ivar Larsen needed extra hands for a few carpentry projects at Devinde's opera house, the millionaire volunteered the Penland brothers' services. He had been pleased with their work on the estate and vouched for them to the Pinkerton agent assigned to protect Renata Abetelli. Devinde promised to keep them on after the opera company left, in order to do maintenance around both his residence and the opera house, as well as continue with their landscaping efforts. They'd also help other companies that came in, be they opera or theater, to transition to using the facility.

In Hank's eyes, it wasn't enough. Sure, most men would jump at the chance for steady work in a growing city but he had bigger dreams. He wanted to be like a Walt Devinde someday. He needed to figure out a way to raise a stake and move to the next level. One beyond physical labor. Something that used his mind. He had a proposition for Devinde so they were on their way to see the millionaire now. Hank would even throw George in to do any extra work Devinde might have around his mansion.

"I've got to see Mr. Devinde on some special business."

"Will it make us money? To go home? I really wanna go home, Hank."

"I know you do."

They continued to make their way to the main house, passing through the gardens. As they got closer, he spied the magnificent mansion. Envy ate away at him as he took in its opulence. The rear view included the same tall Greek columns as did the front, creating a spacious porch that looked out over the immense lawn and gardens. That's what he wanted. To live in a fine palace like a king. To boss around a hundred employees. Maybe more. To dress in fine clothes and carry a walking stick and have everyone whisper and point as he walked down the streets of Denver. Hank was just as good as Walt Devinde or any other man. He wanted his fair share.

He was determined to get it.

As they reached the entrance to the gardens, a door swung open. Renata Abetelli came flying across the porch and down the stairs. Tears streamed down the soprano's face as she held her skirts high, running blindly toward them.

Alone.

Opportunity knocked.

And Hank Penland was smart enough to answer when it did. His chance at a bigger scheme had arrived without warning. He needed to play his cards right. If he did, he knew he could make a handsome profit. For no work at all.

He called out to her, which caused her to stop in her tracks, startled. He tipped his hat. "Miss Abetelli. What's wrong? You look sorely distressed."

Her brow furrowed. "Do I know you?"

Before George could speak and ruin everything, he said smoothly, "I'm Hank Penland, one of the men Mr. Devinde hired to look after his opera house." He tossed a thumb, gesturing to George. "My brother George and I have been assisting the crew the last few weeks, as well as managing affairs on the Devinde estate."

She sniffed, her mouth setting hard. He figured it was another of her famous tantrums and decided to play on her obvious anger and coat her in sympathy at the same time.

"Are they taking advantage of you and your generosity again? Is it that dreadful Mr. Larsen that's giving you problems?"

"*Si*," she spat out. "It's a *conspirazione* against me. Ivar and Walt. They pretend I'm some delicate flower that needs rest. But I know better. I am *the* soprano. Not Emma. No one *ma me*."

He tried not to laugh. Renata only acted as a delicate flower when she wanted to get her way about something. Hank thought Emmeline Billings actually had a better voice than the Italian diva. She brought innocence balanced with a world-weary wisdom to the role of Violetta Valéry.

But he needed to soothe the savage beast in front of him.

"What have they done now? Do they not recognize your immense talents over that silly Billings woman? She can't hold a candle to you, Miss Abetelli."

Renata's chin went up haughtily. "They want to alternate our performances. *Che sciocchezza!* I didn't care about her taking on the matinees. No one of importance attends those. But to cut my schedule in half? They might as well cut out my heart. I *live* to perform."

"That's rubbish," he agreed. "For Mr. Devinde to bring you all this way and then not have you sing? Why, I'd say that's downright criminal." He paused. "You need to show him who's in charge."

"I will not stay under his roof another second. I will go to the hotel, as I should have when I arrived." A diabolical smile swept over her face. "I will run up the bill and have him pay for it. In fact, I will purchase a new wardrobe at his expense. Renata Abetelli will not be treated in this shameful way."

He looked over her shoulder, surprised to see that no one had come outside after her. Time was of the essence. He had to convince her. Fast. "What about your luggage?"

She shrugged. "I told Rozalia to pack my things. She will bring everything to the hotel."

"And Mr. Larsen?"

"That coward? He's nothing to me. He did nothing to defend me. For all I know, he concocted this outrageous scheme with Walt Devinde. I'll show them all. I'll refuse to go on. Let's see just how long it takes for them to lose their precious money. They'll come crawling. Begging. I'll see them suffer for such an injustice. No one trifles with Renata Abetelli."

He shook his head and decided to ice the cake. "It's outrageous how they've treated you. You're so kind. So beautiful and humble, yet so talented. They have taken advantage of your sweet disposition, Miss Abetelli. That's monstrous behavior."

He offered her his arm. "May I escort you to the hotel?" He turned to see George's jaw drop in amazement. One look silenced anything his brother might have said to ruin this moment.

She batted her eyelashes at him. "You are too kind."

She slipped her arm through the crook of his elbow, giving him a blinding smile.

He returned it and then shook his head. "I doubt you'll want to use Devinde's carriage to ride into town."

She spat in disgust. "I'd rather die than prey on his hospitality."

Hank had no intention of taking the diva to town.

"Since Mr. Devinde lives several miles from town, it would be too much to ask you to walk so far. The wind would chap your beautiful complexion and it wouldn't do to have your feet swell with all that walking."

The corners of her mouth turned down in disgust.

Before she could change her mind about using Devinde's carriage, he added, "We live nearby. Just beyond the gardens at the edge of the property. I'd be happy to entertain you there while I send George out to summon a cab. I can offer you a cool drink and allow you to rest and calm your poor nerves. George can also go ahead and notify the hotel that you'll be joining them later today. You'll be luxuriating in their best suite in no time. Is that agreeable?"

"*Si*. You read my mind."

He beamed at her. "It's my honor to serve you, Miss Abetelli."

EMMA STILL FOUND herself walking in a daze since Renata's disappearance three days earlier. The soprano had balked at alternating performances with Emma and stalked from the house after screaming obscenities at Walt and Ivar and ordering Eddie to see to the carriage so he could escort her into town. Of course, she'd taken time to calmly instruct Rozalia to collect her trunks and have them sent to the hotel before she stormed out.

But Renata never arrived there. Walt was convinced it was another ploy of the diva's, missing her scheduled performances in the rotation and deliberately not sending word of her whereabouts. Ivar totally disagreed, stating that he knew Renata better than anyone. She would have lounged in the lap of luxury and wanted Devinde to sweat the losses that stacked up at the opera house, gloating publicly. The fact that she never arrived at the hotel and hadn't been seen since she left the mansion assured him foul play was at hand.

The trouble was, audiences didn't seem to notice that Renata was no longer appearing in *La traviata*. Emmeline Billings stepped in without hesitation and she earned a sell-out crowd both of the previous two nights. Devinde said he didn't care if Renata crawled back on hands and knees and begged to be placed back into the production. The Pinkertons could choose to waste their time looking for her if they wished but he'd washed his hands of her and her antics.

Emma came across Rye and Eddie discussing the case. Whether Devinde believed foul play had occurred or not, the detectives possessed responsibility for Renata and were actively searching for her. Rye even resigned from the company, much to Giovanni and Antonio's disappointment, in order to devote all his time to locating the soprano.

Emma came downstairs as Rye entered the mansion, looking like the walking dead. Dark circles were painted under his hollow eyes. His disheveled clothing and mussed hair led her to believe he'd been out all night in a futile search and now returned for a few hours of much-needed sleep.

Their gazes met and she saw that guilt ate at him.

"I never took it seriously," he said, his voice barely above a whisper. "I didn't see any threat to her well-being. I was remiss in my duties."

She wanted to comfort him but he was all about business at this point. She couldn't blame him.

"I know you and Eddie will find her," she said with conviction.

He shook his head. "We've interviewed everyone in town, from respectable citizens to the disreputable. It's as if she vanished from the face of the earth." He closed his eyes, his brow furrowed as if in deep pain.

"You'll find her. She'll be safe. And you'll punish whoever took her."

Rye opened his eyes and looked at her. "I wish I could believe you." He raked a hand through his hair. "I think it's time I cabled The Eye and updated him on the situation."

"Who's that?" Emma asked.

"My employer. He founded the Pinkerton Detective Agency. He still enjoys being out in the field more than sitting behind a desk. Once he receives the news, he'll hightail it to Denver. He'll probably fire me on the spot." His head fell in resignation.

She grabbed his arm and shook him. "Don't you give up, Rye Callahan. You're better than that. I have faith in you. Just like you've believed in me. I know you'll solve this case and bring Renata back safely."

Those golden eyes glittered with new determination at her words, which pleased her. She saw him draw from a well of reserved steel.

"Thank you. You're right. I'm a trained professional. I will find her." He yawned. "Once I get a little shut-eye." He looked at her. "Wait. Are you going somewhere? Alone?"

She nodded. "My attorney, Daniel Mitchell, is arriving in Denver today. He's been a good friend and like a second father to me over the years. I received a cable from him several days ago, just before this crisis began. I invited him to come see me perform. We also have business to discuss. About my future."

"I'm pleased for you that he's able to visit but I can't let you go meet him alone. Not with what's happened with Renata. I'll come with you."

She observed how bone-weary he looked and thought she couldn't ask him to accompany her. Besides, no one had threatened her. She was simply Emma Bradford. No one important or famous. Without the elaborate costumes and bold stage makeup and wigs, she didn't resemble Emmeline Billings in the least bit.

Guilt already oozed through her at not sharing what she knew of his connection to Adele Walker, though she still believed it was Adele's story to tell. What was another little white lie? Especially if it would help Rye get the needed rest he deserved.

"Bettina and Tad Carter are in the carriage. Rest assured, I will have company."

What she omitted was that the lovebirds would be dropped off for a special picnic luncheon that Tad had planned at the gazebo in the town square. From the hints he'd dropped, Emma was certain the young man would be proposing to her friend. She wouldn't impose upon their plans.

"All right. As long as you're with them, I'm satisfied."

Emma left the house as Rye ascended the stairs. As she ventured outside, she noticed a plain envelope with only a name scrawled upon it. She reached to where it sat, propped against a column, and saw it was addressed to Walt. Her gut told her it had something to do with Renata.

She snatched it up and rushed back inside.

"Rye!"

He turned, having made it to the top of the stairs. She held the envelope up.

"You need to see this."

He hurried back down and took it from her, turning it over and studying it carefully. "Where did you find this?"

"It was on the porch, leaning against one of the columns, facing the house. Any messenger would have knocked and delivered this straight into the butler's hands. This strikes me as being odd, someone unknown leaving it in the open to be discovered. Do you think it could be a ransom note?"

"Ransom note?"

They turned and saw Walt, accompanied by Adele Walker, coming out from his study. He crossed the foyer and stuck out a hand. Rye handed the envelope to him. The millionaire ripped it open and removed a single sheet. With Adele reading over his shoulder, he scanned the message quickly and then handed it to Rye, who did the same.

"It's another of her tricks," Walt proclaimed. "I'll be damned if she thinks she can milk any money out of me, especially for faking her kidnapping."

Emma shuddered at his vehement words. She sided with Ivar Larsen, who believed something had happened to Renata.

"It's not a prank, Mr. Devinde. Miss Abetelli is intelligent but I don't think she would take a deception to this length. I believe it's a serious matter and you should consider paying the ransom." Rye paused. "Or at least send me with what looks like a ransom payment. It'll draw the kidnappers out and Eddie and I will be able to capture them and hand them over to the authorities."

"No." Devinde's voice held a firm resolve. "I won't even pretend to raise a penny for her. She's made her own bed. Let her lie in her lies. I've washed my hands of the matter. You should, too. In fact, Mr. Callahan, I think you and Mr. McLeod can call it a day. Your work for me in Denver is over, as far as I'm concerned."

He turned and consulted his pocket watch. "It's time for my noon meal. You're welcome to join us." Devinde turned to walk away as if he hadn't a care in the world.

"Walt!" Adele Walker, usually so quiet and passive, barked out his name. "You come back here. Right now."

Devinde's jaw dropped as he stared at her.

His mistress narrowed her eyes as she literally shook a finger at him. "You *will* pay whatever ransom is demanded. Is that understood?"

He shook his head. "No, my dear. I'm not wasting a dime on—"

"It's not about wasting your precious money. You've got more of it than King Midas ever did. It's your reputation that's at stake." She softened her tone. "What if it got out that Miss Abetelli was in peril, held by vicious kidnappers, and you chose not to lift a finger and come to her aid by paying a ransom that would free her?"

Devinde cleared his throat. "When have I cared about what others thought? You know I'm planning to divorce my wife for you. I don't care a hoot what others will think about that move."

"This is different." Adele gave him a tender look. "You've had conflicts with Renata. Both professionally and personally. Now, she's disappeared. That won't look good to the authorities."

She raised a hand when he tried to interrupt. "I know her disappearance hasn't been made public. But when a note arrives demanding a specific amount of money for her release and you refuse to pay it, Ivar Larsen will hightail to the police. Believe me, they will take a hard look at you, Walt. It's no secret the problems you've had with Renata."

Adele took his hands in hers. "Do this. For me, love. Let Rye and Eddie stay on the case."

Emma watched the millionaire melt at the tender words. "All right. For you, Adele. No one else." He raised her hands to his lips and brushed them against her knuckles before he looked to Rye. "Stay on it. Let me know when another note arrives and the details. I pledge I'll pay whatever they ask."

The couple left the hallway. Emma couldn't believe what she'd witnessed. "How can he be so callous?" she asked.

Rye shrugged. "He's a businessman. Profit is his bottom line. He doesn't like confrontation or complications and Renata creates both. He has you as her replacement. The box office isn't suffering."

"Then I'll refuse to go on."

He gave her a wry smile. "And be like Renata? I doubt it. Think of all the people in Ivar's company. They need the job. Ivar's done everything in his power to keep the troupe going, even with Renata missing. Don't let them down, Emma. Hopefully, we'll hear from the kidnappers soon with where they want the ransom to be delivered and then this nightmare will be over."

She sighed. "You're right. Are you going to inform Ivar about this development?"

"I'll head over to the opera house to let him know the kidnappers have made their first move. Eddie is with Larsen now so I'll share this note with both of them. Larsen doesn't have that kind of cash but he needs to know that Devinde has agreed to front the money."

"Where are you supposed to take it? When?"

"It doesn't say. The note explains that Renata is being held, that she's safe, and it makes a demand for a large sum of cash. I have experience in these matters. The kidnappers will let us worry for a few days. But now that they've made contact, I'm sure another note will follow soon. Eddie and I can take turns watching for whoever delivers it and even follow them."

"Then come with us now. The carriage is waiting out front. We can drop you off first so you can formulate a plan with Ivar."

He slipped the letter into the inside pocket of his suit coat. "I know it's asking a lot but don't say anything to Bettina or Tad. The fewer who know about this, the better."

"I understand."

He escorted her to the carriage. Emma had an odd feeling of being watched. She looked around and saw no one, just Jamey, the driver, waiting to assist her. She shook it off and told him that their first destination would be the opera house to allow Rye to see Mr. Larsen. She took the hand Jamey offered and stepped into the carriage. Rye climbed in behind her. Bettina and Tad separated quickly, both their faces flush with embarrassment.

She chose to ignore it and greeted them. "I'm sorry I was late. I ran into Rye in the foyer and spoke to him for a few minutes. We need to drop him at the opera house if you don't mind."

"Any news about Renata?" Bettina asked.

"No," the detective lied smoothly. "Eddie and I have run ourselves ragged around Denver and haven't found any clues at all."

"I think the witch just went into hiding," Tad remarked. "She's a spiteful creature and would relish the fact she's driving everyone mad with worry."

"Tad!" admonished Bettina. "Something frightful could have happened to her. Please, don't talk like that."

"I'm sorry, Bettina. I do hope it's simply some game she plays and that nothing awful has happened to her."

They chatted about other things as they drove into town. Emma kept the conversation rolling, jumping from topic to topic, hoping to get Rye out of the carriage before the other couple mentioned their plans. Her strategy worked and they left the Pinkerton at the opera house. Jamey drove on for a couple of blocks before the carriage halted again. Tad helped Bettina from the coach and then reached back for the picnic basket sitting on the floor. She hoped Rye had been too absorbed in his thoughts about the kidnapper's demands to notice it.

After Bettina exited the carriage, Tad said, "Wish me luck, Emma. I'm going to ask Bettina to marry me." He winked at her and swung the basket around before closing the door.

She was pleased that the two had found one another. They were well-suited in both their interests and their dispositions, and both were so attractive. They would have beautiful children. Emma hoped Bettina would ask for her help in planning the wedding. She said a fervent prayer, wishing that Renata would soon return and be able to celebrate the happy news.

The carriage arrived at the train station and Jamey helped her down. She glanced at the watch pinned to her dress and saw she still had time to spare.

"Mr. Mitchell's train won't arrive for another half-hour," she said. "I think I'll stroll back to the bookstore and purchase a present for him."

"I can take you, Miss. No trouble at all."

"No, don't bother. It's a lovely summer day and I'll enjoy the exercise. The train arrives just before two o'clock, so come out to the platform then to help with the luggage. I'll meet you there."

Emma walked the short distance to the bookstore, happy to be visiting a cherished place. She'd had no time for shopping, much less reading, since she stepped into her role as Violetta. She hoped that would change, especially with Daniel Mitchell's arrival. She wanted to be able to spend time with the attorney and catch him up on all that had gone on since she'd fled home. She was also eager to learn if anything had been discovered in regard to Molly's death.

As she entered the bookstore, tingles vibrated through her. She looked over her shoulder at the crowded sidewalk but saw no one familiar, much less anyone looking directly at her. She shrugged off the odd feeling of being watched. She had to be jumpy due to her knowledge that the kidnappers were out there. But they had no interest in her. She moved deeper into the stacks of books and lost herself in the comforting, musty smell. It took a while but she found the perfect gift, a volume on railroads. Mr. Mitchell had a fondness for trains and he would enjoy this book tremendously.

Emma paid for her purchase and had the clerk wrap it in tissue and place it in a small box. Leaving the bookstore, she headed for the train depot. She glanced down at her watch and saw she'd taken longer browsing for the present than she'd anticipated. She hurried back to the Devinde carriage, where she thought she could leave her package inside. Jamey was nowhere in sight. He must have already gone into the depot.

As she reached for the handle on the carriage's door, someone roughly grabbed her arm and wrenched her around, causing the parcel to slip from her hands.

"Hello, Emma."

CHAPTER TWENTY-SEVEN

*H*ank Penland stared at all the workers scattered across the brightly lit stage, busy as beavers building a dam in preparation for winter. Ivar Larsen had them working on sets for a new opera that he said they would be performing after they left Denver. The manager played his cards close to the vest and hadn't mentioned a word to the company about Renata's disappearance. Many of them had worked for the Swede for several years, so Hank supposed they were accustomed to the prima donna's frequent absences from the stage. As long as they were being paid, most of them didn't care who sang every night as Violetta Valéry.

He couldn't help but feel the power coursing through his veins. He'd delivered the ransom note to the Devinde mansion and planned a second one to follow with precise instructions on handing over the money in exchange for Renata Abetelli.

It couldn't be soon enough.

The soprano had driven George and him mad with her shrill voice and weeping. She had turned out to be the most spiteful, vindictive woman who ever walked the earth— and that included Mama Penland. He'd resorted to keeping her gagged most of the time in order to stop her constant jabbering and cursing. Even then, she grunted and mumbled nonstop behind the gag, never giving them a moment of peace these past few days. Thank goodness their cottage was isolated enough from the main house to prevent her from being heard.

She'd worked hard at the rope that bound her, almost loosening it enough to escape early this morning. Hank was certain she would have stabbed both brothers in their sleep with one of their gardening tools before fleeing if she'd gotten the chance. That's why he insisted that his brother stay home with her today. They'd left the diva on her own the previous days but couldn't afford to take any chances at this point.

Enough time had passed. He was ready for the scheme to run its course. He'd given Devinde and Larsen plenty of time to worry about their star's disappearance. It was time to cash in and leave Denver in the dust.

He spied George entering the theater and quickly made his way over to him.

"What are you doing here?" he hissed as he pulled his brother into the shadows at the back of the darkened theater.

"I can't take it anymore, Hank. You know I'm a big guy. I can take a blow. Give as good as I get. But I can't hit her. She's a woman. If I have to be around her another minute, I might pick up whatever's handy— an iron skillet, a kerosene lamp— and keep smashing her in the mouth until she's quiet."

George trembled as he spoke. "She started having trouble breathing. I had to take the gag off. It's been awful, Hank. We need to give her back. Today. Right now."

"Are you crazy? We can't do that. We're about to

earn the biggest payday of our lives." Hank played his ace. "Don't you want to go back to Kentucky?"

His brother nodded, tears welling in his eyes. "Do we have to do it this way? It's wrong, Hank. Mama wouldn't like this at all."

"Look around. Go ahead. Look." He gave time for George's gaze to sweep across the interior of the opera house. "Do you see how happy everyone is? It's because she's not here, with all her biting sarcasm, chopping good people into tiny bits. We're doing people a favor, George."

He put an arm around his simple-minded brother. "Look. When we get our money, she can come back and torment these people again. We'll be long gone by then." He gave George a squeeze. "Go home. You can put the gag back on her. She's had enough time without it. If she fusses, tell her I said so."

George shuddered. "But her eyes, Hank. They're spooky. It's like they're talking to me. Even when she can't."

He tended to agree with George on that. The diva's eyes spoke volumes and it was obvious that retaliation on her kidnappers weighed heavily on her mind.

"Try not to look at her. Hurry home. I don't like that she's alone." He reached into his pocket and pulled out a coin. "Stop by the bakery. Get a treat for her and you, too. If one thing shuts her up, it's sugar."

George left reluctantly, dragging his feet like an unenthusiastic boy headed to another first day of school. Hank watched him exit the rear doors, passing Rye Callahan. He wondered why Callahan had quit without notice. The man worked hard. Kept his head down. Yet Hank always thought the carpenter knew everything going on around him. That's the kind of partner he wished he had in this venture.

Callahan hustled over to Larsen. The acoustics in the place were so good that Hank heard him say, "We need to talk. Alone."

They came up the center aisle and Hank plastered himself against the darkened corner wall. The men stopped at the last row and slipped in, taking a seat. He edged closer, curious as to what a former employee might say to Larsen that needed privacy.

"A ransom note arrived. It confirmed Renata's been taken. In exchange for her, they want money. A lot of it."

Larsen gasped. "Is she all right?"

"The letter guaranteed so. It also demanded a lot of cash from Devinde."

"How much?"

"We don't know yet. This was just an opening move, letting us know she's been taken and is safe for now. Another note will follow, naming the exact amount."

"What did Walt say about this?"

"His immediate reaction? He refused to pay it. He feels Emma's his ace in the hole. He's actually made more money off her performances than Renata's."

Hank moved back along the wall into the shadows again and slipped out the door into the foyer. He couldn't stand to hear anything more of their conversation.

He'd taken the wrong one.

He wouldn't see a nickel from Devinde. He knew Larsen didn't have it. Damn. He would have to give that Italian witch back right away. At least that would please George.

Instead, he needed to take Emmeline Billings. Fast. He had no idea where she lived but she was the true moneymaker. He would find her. His plan would still work. God helped those who helped themselves. That's what Mama always preached. Well, Hank was a doer. He'd make it happen.

Then doubt filled him. Could he really return the uppity soprano? She'd seen both their faces and knew where they lived. She could identify them to the authorities. Hank had some shady dealings in the past—but he'd never killed before.

Could he?

He left the lobby and headed up the stairs to the business office. Maybe he'd find information about Emmeline Billings' address there. If not, he would need to set a trap for her arrival at the opera house.

He smiled. If Devinde had no soprano to go on and was forced to return ticketholders' money, that would definitely loosen his grip on his wallet.

Maybe he should double the ransom.

~

"REST ASSURED. I've spoken with my attorney, Ivar. He's authorized to give the Pinkertons whatever sum the kidnappers request. My mind's made up, however. Once Renata has been returned, I insist you keep up the alternating performances. The box office hasn't suffered a whit while she's been gone."

Walt Devinde stood and tamped out his cigar. "If you'll excuse me, gentlemen. I'm leaving for Chicago in the morning. I have an important matter regarding my wife that I need to see to immediately."

He held out a hand to Rye. "Take care, Mr. Callahan, Mr. McLeod. I don't want anything happening to either of you. I'm sure you'll bring this kidnapper to justice." Devinde exited the study.

Rye took the next few minutes to fill Eddie in on what had happened that morning, with the discovery of the note detailing Renata's well-being and how Adele

Walker convinced her lover to pay whatever ransom demand was made by the kidnappers.

"Now, we need to decide our next move," he concluded.

"Oh, Papa—" Bettina Devinde stepped in with Tad Carter following like a lovesick puppy dog. She looked around the room expectantly and then frowned. "I'm sorry for interrupting, gentlemen. I'm looking for Papa. He's usually in his study at this time of day. Do you know where he is?" She gave Carter a blazing smile. "We have the most amazing news for him."

It hit Rye that Emma wasn't with them. "Where's Emma? I thought she was with you two."

The couple shrugged in unison. Carter said, "We're not sure. We've been on a picnic. Emma was supposed to meet her friend coming from the east coast. His train was due in just after two. I assumed she'd be here by now. Maybe they've stopped by the opera house first. I know she's eager to show him the place."

He remembered Emma telling him about the attorney's visit and relaxed. At least she'd be with Jamey. The driver was a good man and Rye had gotten to know him fairly well during his stay in Denver. They had even discussed the particulars about Jamey becoming an employee of the Pinkerton Detective Agency. He thought Jamey would be a good fit for the organization and had encouraged the coachman to submit his application, telling Jamey he'd put in a good word with The Eye if he applied to the agency.

A commotion in the foyer drew everyone's attention as a loud voice stated, "It's not right. I must speak to someone immediately."

Those remarks were followed by a man poking his head into the study. Finding a group gathered there, he entered. Even without knowing his description, Rye had a good idea who the man was.

"Are you Mr. Mitchell?" he asked.

"Yes, as a matter of fact, I am he. Where the devil is Emma? She never met my train. The girl's never been late a day in her life. It's not like her to forget."

Rye felt as if he'd been punched in the gut.

CHAPTER TWENTY-EIGHT

ohn Fairburn smiled at Emma, his grip tightening on her. He enjoyed seeing the conflicting emotions that flitted across her face.

"Surprised to see I finally caught up with you, Emma?"

She yanked her arm but he held it firmly.

"Get in the carriage."

"No." Defiance lit a fire in her eyes.

He tightened his fingers until she winced. A little whimper escaped those full, rosy lips. He liked that she saw the real John Fairburn. Not the kind, polished gentleman he'd played in order to win her affections. A frisson of excitement rushed through him at the look of fright in her eyes.

Just like Molly.

He smiled at the memory. Soon, he would add more of the same to his recollections. Except this time, Emma would dominate them. His fantasies would become reality. He couldn't wait to begin. But first things first.

"Did I forget proper manners, my love? *Please* get in the carriage. Now."

He opened the door and forced her in, giving her a swift shove before he climbed up after her. She landed on her hands and knees but scrambled to the cushioned seat opposite where he chose to sit. She glared at him as she gingerly rubbed her arm. She might not live long enough to see the bruises that formed there.

"How did you find me?" she demanded. "Only Daniel Mitchell knew where I was."

"You cabled him, my dear. I happened to come across the telegram you sent. I couldn't pass up the opportunity to visit Colorado. To see you. The grand Devinde mansion. And hear you sing." He beamed at her. "You're quite the performer, Emma. Or should I say *Emmeline Billings?*"

He leaned back and studied her. "I must say that I was a bit shocked to see you on stage, but your voice is beautiful. You're almost as talented as the lovely Renata Abetelli."

Her eyes narrowed at that comment. "I'm sure that's *another* opportunity you couldn't pass up. Why did you kidnap Renata?" She shook her head in anger. "You think you're so clever, sending a ransom note to Walt Devinde. Is there nothing you'll stoop to?"

Her words surprised him but he kept his poker face. Apparently, he wasn't the only enterprising man in town. He rather admired the man who'd thought to make some easy money by sweeping up the Italian singer. He didn't have Renata— but Emma thought he did. More importantly, could he use this to his advantage?

His thoughts raced. Emma had proven so hard to get close to, he hadn't really firmed up his plans. When this opportunity to snatch her arose, he'd taken it. Unfortunately, he didn't have a place to stash her. The room he rented at a local hotel wouldn't do.

In a flash, he knew exactly where to hold her. Fernanda had revealed every nook and cranny of Walt Devinde's fancy opera house to him. They'd put several of the more hidden-away spots to good use. He had an idea where he could keep Emma for a short while as he made plans to spirit her out of town. He couldn't afford to have her death investigated by the authorities in Denver. Instead, he wanted her corpse far from here. It was easier to get rid of a body in the rough country miles away. He could bury her, throw her in a river, or even leave her remains for wild animals to scatter and devour.

What he needed was her cooperation. They were in an area with lots of traffic. He couldn't have her causing a scene or making them memorable in any way. He must play his cards just right. Besides, there would be more money in it for him beyond her considerable fortune if he took Emma hostage and demanded a ransom for her release. With Renata Abetelli also missing, Walt Devinde would be without a star for his opera house. He'd already heard gossip of the disaster the understudy had made of the production during her lone appearance. The millionaire would pay up so his box office wouldn't suffer.

This unexpected windfall would be icing on the cake. He would collect the ransom and access her fortune and then disappear— after taking care of Louisa. No more John Fairburn. He could become anyone he desired. Live anywhere he chose. He wished he could pat himself on the back for such a well-played move.

"You're clever to figure out that I took the diva." He shrugged modestly and gave her a sad look. "I needed money to win back your affection, Emma. I'm not sure why you fled Connecticut. You left poor Louisa in a panic and me heartbroken."

She snorted. "You don't have a heart, John. What you do have is a liaison with Louisa. I overheard the two of you plotting. I valued my life and Papa's hard-earned money too much to turn either over to you."

"Hmm." He drummed his fingers against his thigh. "You're not the innocent you seemed to be. Maybe this western adventure has matured you."

The stubborn set of her mouth told him he needed to act fast in order to convince her to come quietly with him.

"Sorry my idea didn't work." He eyed her speculatively. "Although I still think we would have been good together."

"Never!"

"Then I'll move on to my impromptu back-up plan, my dear. I guess I'll leave you and return to that sweet piece of tempting flesh. Ah, Italian women. They are a passionate lot."

Her eyes widened. "You haven't hurt Renata, have you? Is she safe?" Emma hesitated. Her cheeks pinkened. "Is her...integrity intact?"

He laughed. "I doubt her integrity was intact before she came into my possession. She is uninjured. Though she's quite the spitfire."

She crossed her arms. "Good. You deserve any harassment she's given you."

"But she won't stay like that."

Panic filled Emma's face. "What do you mean? Oh, please, John. Don't hurt her," she pleaded. "Walt will pay for her safe return. I heard him guarantee it not two hours ago."

He wondered how long the true kidnapper planned on holding the diva hostage. It didn't matter. If the millionaire would pay for one woman's return, he'd pay for another. What was money to someone who had more than he could count? Besides, Emma might be more valuable. Not only could she appear on stage and draw a crowd, she was a close family friend.

"John? John? You wouldn't hurt Renata, would you? Like…you did Molly."

Her words took him aback. "You know about that?"

She nodded. "I suspected as much after Mr. Mitchell met me in New York and told me about Molly's murder." She edged away from him, pushing until she backed into the corner of the carriage's bench seat.

"Then you know exactly what I could do to Renata Abetelli." He paused and gave her a ghost of a smile. "And that I would enjoy doing it."

She trembled. Tears brimmed in her eyes. "Please, John. Don't. I beg you."

Emma must have made friends with the opera singer, possibly while they both stayed at Devinde's house, or during the rehearsals and run of the production. It made it easier to play on her tender heart.

"Then I have a proposition. I'll release Renata— but I'll trade her— for you. I'll bet Walt Devinde would compensate me more for your return than hers. You're friends with his daughter. Everyone knows what a spoiled brat she is because he gives her everything she desires. She'll be certain her father pays."

Her jaw dropped. Tears spilled down her cheeks as she shivered in fear. Or revulsion. But John needed to reassure her. String her along in order to convince her to come with him willingly. He didn't want any public display that would arouse suspicion.

"Don't worry. You can pay Devinde back. Daddy Bradford left you enough money to do so. Devinde won't have to be out a dime."

He straightened his tie. Brushed imaginary dust from his pants. He wanted to give her time to process what he'd said and buy into it. If Emma thought he'd release an unharmed Renata back to Walt Devinde, then wouldn't he do the same with her?

"So. Is it settled? Come with me of your own accord. I'll be sure Miss Abetelli is returned to the Devinde mansion with every hair on her head still in place. Then when Devinde pays *your* ransom, I'll be off. Out of your life. You'll never have to see me again."

He leaned toward her as if sharing a confidence. "I'll be honest, Emma. I've grown tired of Louisa. I have no reason to return to her. And I like the West. I can start a new life here. Make a fresh start."

He watched the wheels turning in her head as she tried to find fault with his logic, biting her bottom lip as she thought. He didn't doubt that he'd successfully hooked her. She'd come with him. He'd done a masterful job persuading her.

"I'll agree to your demand, but you must first release Renata."

"I'm glad you've come to your senses, my dear. We need to be off now. I'll want you to write your own ransom note. I want it in your hand so there's no doubt in Devinde's mind of the gravity of the situation. You can even guarantee to reimburse him in the note itself to assure he'll follow through with the payment."

John paused, reeling her in with a final, brilliant idea. "I'll even have Miss Abetelli be the one to deliver it to him. In person. I hope that will satisfy you."

She swallowed hard. She looked so vulnerable in that moment. God, he wanted to touch her! Seal their unholy deal by claiming her virginity, but now was neither the time nor the place. That would come after he'd isolated her and this new scheme was in motion. He'd use her up, more than he had that delicious morsel Molly.

And enjoy every moment.

Until then, he would play the gentleman kidnapper and treat Emma Bradford with kid gloves.

CHAPTER TWENTY-NINE

George didn't know what to do. He loved Hank. He did everything his brother told him. Hank was smart. Hank knew stuff. All kinds of stuff. But he felt so bad.

The mean opera lady looked at him again. This time, she had tears in her eyes. She hadn't cried before now. Oh, she pretended to. Hank called those crocodile tears. He said she didn't mean them. That she was trying to make them feel sorry for her.

George looked at her. This time, even he knew she was really crying. She sobbed behind the gag he'd put on her again. It made his eyes sting. He blinked to make it go away but it wouldn't. He started crying, too, which made the lady cry even harder. He wiped his eyes with his sleeve. Hank said your heart didn't hurt. It wasn't like you could bump it and bruise it or break it. But his hurt. Real bad.

He couldn't take it anymore.

He reached over and untied the handkerchief and then pulled out the other one he'd forced between her teeth.

She gave him a weak smile. *"Grazie, Giorgio."*

She talked some more in Italian but he didn't understand what she said. She kept crying. His heart hurt more. And his head. Mama wouldn't be proud of him at all. It didn't matter what Hank said about going home. This was wrong.

"Don't cry," he told her. "I'm gonna take you home."

Her eyes widened. Quickly, her head bobbed up and down as her tears flowed more freely.

"*Si, si, Giorgio!*"

He pulled out the pocketknife Mama had given him before they'd left Kentucky. She'd told him to always be careful when he used it. He went behind the opera lady and sliced through the rope bound about her wrists. She brought her arms around and shook her hands. He moved to her front side and dropped to his knees. He cut through the restraints about her ankles. As he pulled the ropes away, he smiled up at her.

She kicked him in the teeth.

George fell onto his back, stunned. She kicked him hard in the ribs. He rolled and gasped for air. Then she stomped on his hand. His pocketknife dropped to the floor.

She picked it up and waved it around like a crazy lady, shouting words he didn't understand, as she sliced the blade through the air. He did the first thing that came to mind.

He ran.

~

RYE ASKED for the carriage driver to come to the study. He wanted to question Jamey about Emma's activities and pick his brain to see if he might have noticed anything unusual at the train station.

First Renata. Now Emma. What was happening?

Jamey arrived and described how they'd arrived earlier at the depot.

"Miss Bradford decided to walk to the bookstore to purchase a gift for Mr. Mitchell. I offered to drive her but she said it was only a few blocks and that she'd enjoy the walk. She instructed me as to what time to be on the platform to gather Mr. Mitchell's luggage. When she didn't return to the carriage, I figured she'd gone straightaway to meet the train directly."

"But that wasn't the case."

"No, Mr. Callahan. The passengers disembarked and nary a sight of Miss Bradford. I figured out who Mr. Mitchell was since no one met him and he looked about as if he expected someone to do so. I introduced myself to him and we waited for Miss Bradford to appear. Since she never showed, I thought it best to get back to the house immediately and let you know."

He placed a hand on Jamey's shoulder. "You did the right thing."

"Where the dickens *is* Emma?" Mitchell demanded.

Loud shrieks startled the group in the study. Rye hurried to the door and flung it open.

Renata Abetelli stood in the foyer, hollering to the high heavens and waving a pocketknife about. Disheveled, dirty, with dark circles under her eyes, the Italian singer's screams pierced the air. Before he could react, Bettina Devinde threw herself at the woman. Renata dropped the knife and latched on to the girl, holding on to her as if her life depended upon it.

Ivar Larsen rushed to embrace both women and all three of them began crying. Larsen began jabbering in Italian to Renata.

Rye looked at Tad Carter. "Send for a doctor. Ring for some tea. No, she'll need something stronger than that. And get word to that maid of hers at the hotel. In fact, go in person and bring her back here yourself." Carter shot off on his errands without a backward glance.

Eddie poured out a brandy and brought it over. Renata jerked it from his hands and downed it in a single swallow.

"What the devil's going on?"

Walt and Adele stood in the doorway. At the sight of them, Renata broke into fresh tears. Bettina and Ivar guided Renata to a plush sofa, while Adele grabbed a throw from a chair and wrapped it around the diva's shoulders.

His eyes met Eddie's and he held up a hand. He wanted to give Renata a minute to calm herself before trying to question her. Gradually, she quieted, her tears spent. All eyes in the room turned to him.

He pulled a handkerchief from his pocket and handed it to Renata. She accepted it and dried her eyes.

"Miss Abetelli, we need to know everything you can tell us about the man or men who took you. We want to bring them to justice."

Rye decided not to tell her that Emma has also turned up missing. If she didn't know about that incident, he didn't want anything to set off her hysterics again. Right now, Renata was calm and lucid so he needed to gain as much information from her as he could.

He glanced at Daniel Mitchell, who looked as if he were about to let that cat out of the bag. His stare warned the attorney against doing that very thing.

Renata's fingers clasped the crocheted blanket about her. Her back straightened with resolve. Rye could see the steel in her eyes as she remembered her ordeal.

"There were two of them. They work sometimes at the opera house and sometimes at this house. They stink of earth and plants and paint and wood."

"The Penland brothers?" Walt asked, surprise evident in his voice. "Surely not. They've been so reliable."

Her eyes burned as she turned on the businessman.

"They live on *your* property. They keep me prisoner in a dirty hovel, bound and gagged and helpless. Renata Abetelli is *not* helpless."

"You got away from them?" Rye interjected.

"*Si.* The one who thinks he's so smart, Hank. He wasn't there. The idiot, *Giorgio*, was. I had fought and growled like an animal, trying for days to escape." She smiled eerily, sending a chill up Rye's back. "Then I play the victim. I cry prettily. The stupid one says he will let me go. He cuts me loose and I beat on him with all my might."

She stood and began pacing, gesturing with the throw wrapped about her. "I, Renata Abetelli, escaped from their clutches. He ran away like a cowardly little boy." She stopped in her tracks and faced him. "I want them caught. *Punito. Morte* is too good for them."

"Do you know why they took you?" Rye asked.

"I hear them talk. They want money for me. The other one. He write a note. He bragged to me how I will make him rich."

The time had come. He had to know. "Did they also take Emma?"

Renata's jaw dropped. "Emma? Emma is gone, too?" She shook her head vigorously. "No, they did not have Emma." She sniffed in disgust. "They aren't smart enough to take two women."

He turned to Eddie. "I know Hank and George. George is very simple-minded. If he fled, he's gone to the opera house to find his brother."

"Maybe we'll find Emma there, too," Eddie added hopefully.

"Then I'm coming with you," said Daniel Mitchell. "If these brothers don't have her, there may be some clue there as to her whereabouts."

"Count me in," Jamey added. "Miss Bradford's been nothing but kind to me since the day she arrived. I feel responsible since she disappeared on my watch."

Renata flung the throw from her shoulders as if it were a theatrical prop. "I must go with you. I will confront these brothers and have them grovel on their knees. I want to see their faces when Renata Abetelli hands them over to justice."

Ivar put an arm around her. "I'm not letting you out of my sight, my darling girl."

"Hell's bells," Walt Devinde declared. "I guess we all are going."

CHAPTER THIRTY

mma's heart thumped against her ribs, hard and rapid, as John led her up the steps of Walt Devinde's opera house.

This was where he kept Renata?

They entered the lobby. Her heart sank when she saw it was empty. She'd held out hope that even though the crew wasn't scheduled to arrive for another hour or more, maybe someone might be here early and catch sight of her. Immediately, John rushed her across the length of the room and to the far right corner. He pushed through a doorway that she hadn't even realized was there. She saw a set of stairs a few feet in front of them.

"Grab on to the rail to steady yourself," he commanded as he lit a kerosene lantern sitting on a table inside the doorway. "Keep walking down the stairs until we reach bottom."

She clutched the handrail as the door clicked behind them. John kept hold of her upper arm as they moved along the staircase. When she had toured the building weeks ago, they hadn't gone into the basement area so she didn't know what to expect.

They reached the bottom. Emma quickly became

confused by the many quick turns he made but John definitely knew his destination. As it was, the basement's size mirrored the floor above them. With the expansive lobby, roomy theater, large stage and backstage areas above them, who only knew how many square feet the basement held. She knew a handful of the larger props, as well as some costumes and sets were stored on this level, but she supposed they would be located in areas close by the stairs for convenience.

He grabbed a few items, including a length of rope, as he dragged her along the passageway before he finally paused at a door and opened it. He ushered her inside and closed the door behind them. Emma noticed a chair next to a small table and what appeared to be a large tarp lying in the corner. Other than that, the room lay bare.

"Where's Renata?" she demanded, proud that her voice sounded strong. She didn't want John to know how terrified she was, with her knees knocking and her heart pounding. Even beneath her gloves, her damp palms gave away how frightened she was. John had always acted in such an urbane, gentlemanly fashion—but the man now before her had proven to be a monster.

His eyes lit up. "She's close by." He grinned. "You don't think I'd put the two of you together? She's already been a handful as it is. I don't need the pair of you conspiring against me."

He reached and yanked her reticule from where the strings sat tucked in the crook of her arm. He stepped to the table and set down the lantern before opening the drawstring and dumping the contents of her reticule onto the desk. He picked up her small, leatherbound journal and then dug through the items until he found a pencil, sweeping off the rest of her belongings onto the floor.

"Ah, predictable Emma. Always prepared with your journal and trusty little pencil. You constantly jotted down random thoughts in this." He laughed as he flipped through the pages. "Louisa slipped it from your reticule once. We had ourselves a fine time reading your amusing little scribblings. I must thank you for providing the supplies needed to write your own ransom note."

He smirked at her. She wanted to claw out his eyes. His gaze returned to the pages and he stopped abruptly. She wondered what had caught his eye.

"Hmmm." His eyes widened as he read, then he looked up and burst into laughter. "So, you're keeping secrets, Emma. I see you're quite conflicted with what you know about this Rye Callahan."

"That's none of your business," she snapped. She moved toward him and snatched the journal from his hands, holding it close.

He cocked his head. "When I meet this Mr. Callahan, I'll solve your dilemma. I'll let him know who his mama is— since neither you nor she has shared that knowledge with him. I'm sure he'd be delighted to find out that piece of information."

Anguish filled her. "Please, John. Don't. I beg you."

"I'll think about it." He crooked his finger at her. "Now, come here. Sit. You'll write exactly what I say and no more. Then we'll let Renata Abetelli make her delivery to Walt Devinde."

He opened the journal again and ripped a blank page from it, setting the paper and pencil on the table.

Reluctantly, Emma went to the chair and sat before her knees buckled and sent her tumbling to the floor. She removed her gloves and smoothed her hands along her skirts before she picked up the pencil. She stared down at the page because she couldn't trust herself to look at him. She might burst into tears at any moment and didn't want to give him the satisfaction of seeing her weak and cowering.

He dictated slowly, making sure she captured every word he uttered as he leaned over her shoulder. As she wrote, her fear subsided. In its place, anger began to rage inside her. She finished with her signature and sat back in the chair.

John picked up the page and read through it again, his lips moving silently. He nodded to himself and folded it in half, placing it back on the table.

"Address it to Devinde."

"I'm sorry. I don't carry envelopes with me. Maybe you can remove your ugly countenance from my presence and purchase one at a nearby stationer."

She saw the blur but didn't recognize the meaning behind it. The slap knocked her from the chair. The right side of her face enflamed and began throbbing. Her eyes watered. She blinked back any tears that threatened to fall and sprang to her feet. She wanted to return the slap to remove the smugness resting across his features but realized she had pushed him far enough.

"I won't tolerate insolence from you, Emma. I understand if you're frightened. It's not every day that a well-bred young woman finds herself in your position."

He paused and cracked his knuckles one at a time. She knew he meant to scare her into submission.

That wasn't going to happen.

Though she wanted to bring her palm to her now-tender cheek and hold it there, she kept her arms by her sides. She returned to the chair and scrawled Walt Devinde's name across the page. She thrust the ransom note at John and seethed when he chuckled as he took it. He slipped it into an inside pocket of his suit coat.

"I want to see Renata now. Before you release her to make this delivery."

He shook his head. "You aren't the one in charge. I'll take it to her as soon as you're secured."

"You're a fool if you think you'll get away with this, John."

"I've been called worse."

"You won't see a penny from Walt. I promise you that."

He studied her a moment. "Why wouldn't Devinde pay for your return? You even offer to reimburse him in the note itself. Surely, he knows you are an heiress and possess a fortune yourself."

Emma crossed her arms and glared at him. "He won't need to pay. The Pinkertons will take care of you. You'll go to prison, John. Or even hang. For kidnapping Renata and me. And for Molly."

He laughed. "You think that Pinkerton Devinde hired will stop me? I've seen him about, escorting the little songbird to and from the opera house. He hasn't found her before now. Why would he find you?"

"I know they'll stop you. And they'll rescue me."

He tilted his head. "They?"

"Yes," she spit out. "They. Eddie McLeod *and* Rye Callahan."

He started. "Callahan? You mean the poor soul who hasn't a clue who his real parents are? I thought he was just a carpenter. I've actually met your Mr. Callahan, Emma. Along with others on the crew."

"Then you know just how capable he is."

"Interesting. Devinde hired two of them and kept one a secret." He looked lost in thought. Then he turned back to her. "So, you mean Mr. McLeod and my brother will somehow magically save you."

My brother?

"What do you mean? You're not making any sense, John. You're not related to Rye. You're nothing alike. He's fine and upstanding and intelligent and polite. On the other hand, *you* are a deceitful cad. A kidnapper and murderer."

His eyes narrowed. "Rye Callahan *is* my brother, Emma. Or I should say half-brother. He doesn't know it, of course. You seem to think quite highly of him. Perhaps… you're friendly with him?"

Shock ran through her as she tried to process what John had revealed. Rye and John— related? Impossible!

He chuckled. "I see you're surprised by this interesting twist. Ah, my darling Emma. Are you in love with Rye Callahan?"

John reached out and brushed a curl from her cheek. She cringed and sprang from the chair, taking a step back.

"I see how it is. You've always telegraphed every emotion across your face, my dear. It's clear as day. You want this half-brother of mine. But not me."

He grabbed the chair and swung it around. He seated himself backward on it, resting his forearms along the top.

"Let me tell you an ugly story, Emma dearest. Gerald Fairburn was long on charm and looks, but he had the morals of an alley cat. He shot his seed up the skirts of countless women throughout Five Points. I have half-brothers by a slew of women."

He raked a hand through his fair hair. "Your Mr. Callahan has Da's muscular build. His Black Irish hair. What confirmed his identity to me were those odd eyes of his. The gold with the flecks of green. I've never seen eyes like Da had, not in any of his by-blows in the Points.

"But Rye Callahan's eyes are a match for his da's. *My* da. Gerald Fairburn."

~

JOHN ENJOYED BEING able to tell Emma about her wonderful Mr. Callahan's roots. As always, her emotions flitted across her face as fast as lightning. Shock. Surprise. Disgust. He loved the power of being the bearer of such news.

"To think you want him. Not me. Tsk-tsk, Emma. What would your dear papa say about you falling in love with someone so inappropriate? The bastard son of a dissolute lecher. A man who doesn't even know his own heritage. At least Gerald Fairburn married my mother. Her da forced him to. At least I can say I'm legitimate."

He took a perverse pleasure in seeing how his news shattered her. He also knew now was the time to secure her when she was so traumatized. He grabbed the rope he'd snagged from a pile of goods as they'd entered. From his frisky basement encounters with Fernanda, he'd remembered what was there— paint cans, some boards, a few tools.

And the rope. Oh, everything was coming together so easily. He knew it was meant to be.

Before she could react, he wrapped the rope around her wrists several times. Then he brought it down to her ankles and circled them a half-dozen times before bringing the line back up. He lifted the wriggling Emma into the lone chair and wound the remaining length around her torso and the chair, finally knotting it in the rear.

He smiled down at his work, knowing she wouldn't be going anywhere.

"John, this hurts," she pleaded. "You've secured me too well. It's too tight. I can't feel my hands. And I can hardly breathe."

"That's exactly what I wanted to do, my sweet. I don't want you working your way out from your bonds."

Again, he could read her face like a sentence from a book. He knew the minute he was gone, she'd begin to scream her head off. He returned to the objects from her reticule that he'd tossed on the floor and chose the items he needed.

Pulling a handkerchief from his pocket, he waded it up and thrust it into her mouth. Her eyes widened. She immediately pushed her tongue against it, causing it to slip out. He pushed it back again and used her own handkerchief to tie the first one in place. Then he removed a long skein of yarn that was wound on a small reel. He wrapped the yarn around her head several times and tied it off. Now the gag was firmly in place.

He stepped back, admiring his handiwork. Then he lifted the tarp in the corner and tossed it aside. He tilted the chair Emma was attached to and rested its back against the ground before he placed the tarp over her. He heard her protests, little more than weak grunts behind the gag. The tarp muffled the sound she made. Anyone opening the door— and he seriously doubted that would occur— would more than likely miss her.

"Behave, my love. I'll return shortly."

He retrieved the lantern from the table and left the room, closing the door behind him. He wished he had a key so that he could lock her in, but very few of the crew came down here. Those that did only stayed a few minutes, stopping at the first room or two where goods were stored. No one made their way through the maze of the basement, certainly not this deep.

She would not be found.

He broke into a smile. It might be months, even years, before workers brought sets or props back to this portion of the building. He wouldn't have to smuggle Emma out of Denver. He had no need to bury her body in the hills. She could remain exactly where she was for a very long time.

John made his way along the myriad of passageways until he arrived back at the staircase leading up to the main floor. He would claim the ransom. Create the wedding and death certificate forgeries. Head back to Plainfield. Assert his legal right to Emma's estate, being her only heir.

Life was good.

Extinguishing the lantern, he entered the theater's lobby. No one from the crew lingered there. Just to be sure, he exited the building quickly, humming to himself as he glided down the stairs. As he reached the sidewalk, he spied a young boy tossing a ball up in the air. He would be perfect.

"Young man!" he called out.

The boy rushed over to him. "Yes, sir?"

He pulled a bill from his pocket and handed it and the ransom note Emma authored to the child. "Would you run that into the opera house for me? It goes to Mr. Larsen."

The boy looked down at the letter and frowned. "But it says *'Walt Devinde'* on it."

"Yes, I know. Mr. Devinde is out of town and so Mr. Larsen is handling his business affairs for him. Be a good lad and put this in Mr. Larsen's hands. He should arrive shortly so you may have to wait a bit for him. Can you do that for me?"

The boy glanced at the money and then smiled up at him. "Right away, sir!" and bounded up the stairs.

He hurried away. He knew if a ransom note had been delivered to the Devinde estate by Renata Abetelli's true kidnapper, then those damned Pinkertons would be watching the place like hawks. He couldn't afford to get caught at this point. Getting the note to Larsen was the next best thing. The fact that it wasn't sealed meant Larsen would read it and act upon it immediately. John wanted to be far away when the pot began to boil over.

Just before he reached the corner, he heard his alias called out.

"Stan? What are you doing here?"

He stopped and smiled broadly. "Fernanda! You're just the person I've been looking for."

Hank Penland tiptoed away from the closed door. He'd heard enough. More than enough.

Stan Foster was *not* Stan Foster. Fernanda's new swain was someone named John. He was definitely someone from Emmeline Billings' past.

And *he* claimed to be the one who'd kidnapped Renata Abetelli. Or at least that's what he told the Billings woman and she obviously believed him capable of it. Hank didn't know if that was a ploy this John fellow used to get Billings to come with him. If so, it had worked.

He turned the corner and began to move more quickly now that he was well out of earshot range. He had to think how to turn this new twist to his advantage. He had Renata Abetelli at the cottage and Emmeline Billings was here. That meant Devinde had no prima donna for the performance tonight. Hank glanced at his pocket watch. It was a little less than four hours before the curtain went up.

He'd save Billings for later because he knew he could get more for her. The question was, could he get Devinde to pay for Abetelli's return in so short a time?

He chuckled, thinking even if he did, the Italian would never go on tonight. She'd be distraught from her recent experience. He didn't care as long as he could milk the money from Devinde. Though he'd overheard Rye Callahan tell Ivar Larsen that the millionaire wouldn't pay up, circumstances had changed. Devinde needed a soprano for tonight— and Hank was willing to produce one.

He reached the foot of the staircase that led up to the main floor. He decided to carry the kerosene lantern with him. If he extinguished it, the smell would linger. That might tip off good old John that someone had followed him and his treasure down to the basement. He chortled. He'd come to learn every inch of this building after Devinde sent him and George to work here part-time for Larsen. Today, that knowledge came in handy.

His problem was how to get quick word to Devinde and then come back and claim the Billings woman. That had him rattled. Hank wanted ransom money for Renata Abetelli, but now Emmeline Billings had practically fallen in his lap. His new friend John had done the hard work. Hank Penland just needed to take advantage of it. He would also need a place to hide in between. Abetelli knew who he was. He wouldn't be able to go back to the cottage once she was released.

Climbing the stairs, Hank came out into the lobby area. He spied his brother pacing, blood staining the front of his light gray work shirt. His stomach dropped.

What had the idiot done now?

He marched over and grabbed George's sleeve. "Why aren't you with our guest?" he hissed.

George threw his hands against his face. "Hank! Oh, Hank!" his voice quivered.

He heard the panicked tone and fought to calm himself. His gut told him George had done something terrible. He needed to know fast so he could fix whatever mess his brother had created.

"Where is she?" he asked.

George shook his head back and forth. He dropped his hands. His face screwed up like a small child who was about to burst into tears. A ragged gap revealed his missing front teeth.

"She's gone."

"Gone? Where? Where did she go?" His grip tightened. "Tell me."

"She got loose. She hit me and kicked me. My teeth came out, Hank. How'm I gonna eat?" He brought a hand back to his mouth and covered it. "It hurts."

"She escaped." A dull roar began in Hank's ears.

George nodded. He rubbed his ribs with his free hand. "She kicked me here, too. She screamed at me. And then she ran. I didn't know what to do, Hank. I came here. You're so smart. You'll know what to do."

All his plans. Ruined. Thanks to this imbecile. He couldn't stand the sight of his brother.

"Go wait back at the cottage. I got some things I need to do. Then we'll go home."

"To Mama?"

"Yes. Hurry."

"Okay, Hank." George ran to the doors and left the building.

He hoped that damned Pinkerton was waiting back at the Devinde estate. Let him arrest George and hand him over to the authorities. That might gain him some time.

Hank went to the grand staircase that led to the fancy boxes and raced up the stairs. He moved out of sight and crouched on the ground after he reached the top. He waited for John now. Once the man left the theater, he would return to the basement and move Emmeline Billings. He knew this place better than the architect who designed it. He'd find a spot to hide her for a few hours. Then he'd figure out how to get the ransom money for her. Since he'd lost the other ransom, he'd definitely raise his asking price. His only regret was that he wouldn't get to see the look on John's face when he came back and found his little prize gone.

He waited less than two minutes before the man slipped out the basement door and hurried to the exit. Hank ran down the hallway to a window that overlooked the front of the building and watched him as he went down the stairs. Hank started to turn to leave but saw John stop a boy and hand him something. He decided to see what would happen next.

After a short exchange, the boy ran up the outside stairs, a piece of paper in his hand. Hank moved to where he had a vantage point and saw the child enter the lobby and cross to the entrance leading into the auditorium.

"It's the ransom note," Hank said aloud.

He hurried down to the main level and made his way to the basement entrance. He had a brilliant idea where he could stash the Billings woman.

RYE FORCED down the bile again as the carriage bumped along the road, heading into downtown Denver. He looked at the occupants— Eddie, Daniel Mitchell, Larsen, Devinde, Adele Walker, and a surprisingly quiet Renata Abetelli— and wanted to lash out at them all.

He couldn't. He was a professional. Pinkerton agents were trained to think quickly and act accordingly.

And keep their thoughts and feelings to themselves.

Eddie caught his eye. He saw the sympathy in his

friend's eyes. Rye turned away and gazed out the window. He wanted Emma there, next to him. He would sacrifice anything, anyone, to have her by his side.

He knew the Penland brothers weren't responsible for her disappearance. Poor George was a sweet, overgrown boy in a man's body. Hank, the older of the two, was whip-smart, but he doubted Hank could execute a plan that involved kidnapping both women at the same time. The small cottage on Devinde's estate had been a perfect place to hold Renata, one that they'd never thought to search since the Penlands were trusted employees. If Hank had taken Emma, she would also have been hidden at the cottage. Renata's confirmation that she was the only prisoner there let Rye know someone far more cunning than Hank Penland had abducted Emma.

But who? And why?

He believed Daniel Mitchell knew the answer. He'd wanted to discuss it with the visiting attorney on the way to the opera house, but practically everyone at Devinde's house, short of the cook, had gone on this venture. He would get the older man alone once they arrived and then question him.

In the meantime, the wheels couldn't turn fast enough.

Emma's disappearance created a gaping hole in his heart. He'd told her he was married to his job. That he didn't have time for what she wanted. But he'd lied to her. And himself.

The truth was that he loved Emma Bradford. He'd do whatever it took to find her. Then he'd spend the rest of his life making it up to her. It didn't matter where they lived. What he chose to do for a living. The important thing was he had found the love of his life. He couldn't lose her, not now, not when he'd never told her how he felt about her.

The vehicle began to slow. He saw they approached the opera house. Across from him, Mitchell looked out the window— and gasped aloud.

"What?" Rye demanded.

The carriage came to a halt. All eyes focused on Emma's friend.

"I was afraid of this." Mitchell pointed. "See that man standing at the corner of the block? In the gray coat, talking to the woman in blue."

He spotted the pair the attorney motioned to and recognized Maria's pretty assistant, Fernanda. She conversed with the man she was stepping out with. Foster. Stan Foster. "What about him?"

The lawyer cut his eyes from the window and looked into Rye's. "That man is John Fairburn. He tried to court Emma back in Connecticut, before her father passed." Mitchell paused. "And he wanted to marry her. Then kill her. John Fairburn is the reason Emma fled and came to the West."

CHAPTER THIRTY-TWO

ury filled Rye as he processed Mitchell's words. He wanted to wring the life out of the man who'd threatened Emma's well-being. *Kill her?* Oh, he would do that— and more— to this Fairburn fellow.

But he had to keep his head.

He looked to Mitchell. "I'll follow Fairburn. Do *not* leave this carriage. I don't want him to see you and flee."

He glanced at Eddie. "The crew arrives soon to set up for tonight's performance. Find Hank and George."

"If Fairburn just left the opera house, Emma might be inside, Rye. If she is, we'll find her."

He nodded and exited the carriage. The couple still stood on the corner, though it looked as if Fairburn were about to leave. He would tail Fairburn, hoping the man would lead him to the missing Emma. He headed in their direction.

As he drew near, they parted. Fernanda took a few steps away and then called out a greeting when she recognized him.

"Hello, Rye. Are you returning to your job? We've missed you."

Fairburn looked quickly over his shoulder. Their gazes locked. He didn't bother to hide his rage. Fairburn took off running.

Rye sped past Fernanda, his eyes fastened on the gray coat barely ahead of him. He gained on Fairburn and launched himself when he was within range. He tackled the man to the pavement, slamming Fairburn's face into the ground. Whipping out his handcuffs, Rye secured Fairburn's wrists behind him.

He dragged the man to his feet and forced him back down the block toward the opera house, past a stunned Fernanda. When they reached the Devinde carriage, Daniel Mitchell stepped out, his face mottled in anger.

"Damn you, John Fairburn! What have you done with Emma?"

Fairburn glared at the old man and then smiled eerily, like Lewis Carroll's Cheshire Cat. "Oh. Is the lovely Emma in Denver?"

Rye spun him around and punched him square in the nose. Blood spurted as Fairburn cried out, as much in surprise as pain.

"Let's get him inside," he told Mitchell. "I'll question him there. Believe me. He'll talk."

Mitchell frowned at the delay but nodded his agreement, stepping to take one of Fairburn's outturned elbows as Rye latched on to the other. They marched their prisoner up the steps and inside the opera house.

As they entered the lobby, they passed a young boy leaving. He took one look at the handcuffed Fairburn and sped out the door. Rye spied the group who'd come in the Devinde carriage standing in a circle. Ivar Larsen held a sheet of paper in his hands. The Swede saw Rye coming and waved the page about.

"This note was just delivered, Rye. Emma wrote it. She's been taken hostage."

"I know." He gestured to Fairburn. "This is the man

that kidnapped her. I believe he's hidden her somewhere inside the theater."

He looked to Devinde. "If you'll allow, I'll take Fairburn to your office and interrogate him. Eddie, find whatever crew is on the premises. Check in the theater and backstage. There's no need to keep them in the dark. Have them fan out and find Emma."

"And that horrible Hank," Renata chimed in. "That scoundrel must pay for what he did to me." She tapped her chest. "I will lead the search for *questo bastardo*."

"I'll also send a crew member for the police," Eddie said. "Let's go, Miss Abetelli."

Rye and Mitchell ascended the stairs and took John Fairburn to Walt Devinde's office. The millionaire and his mistress followed closely behind them.

HANK OPENED the door that Fairburn had gone into with Emmeline Billings. He raised the lantern he carried and scanned the space. Practically empty, it contained a single table and a tarp tossed in the corner.

"Hello?" he called softly.

Immediately, the tarp moved slightly and he heard a whimper. He smiled and closed the door behind him.

He set the light on the table and squatted beside the tarp. Pulling it back, it revealed the Billings woman, gagged and tightly fastened to a chair. Her eyes widened as she saw him then relief flooded them. They filled with unshed tears.

He patted her head gently, stroking her hair a few times in a calming motion.

"It's all right," he comforted. "You're going to be fine. Just fine." Hank smiled down at her. "I'm sorry that fellow trussed you up like this. But don't worry.

You won't have to stay this way forever. Just until Walt Devinde pays me to return you."

She blinked rapidly at his words and then began protesting behind the gag, angry grunts coming in spurts. Her eyes flashed at him with such animosity, he believed she could give Renata Abetelli lessons in hatred. She whipped her head back and forth and he removed his hand, chuckling.

"I gather from what I overheard that you knew Mr. Foster. Oh, yes. Stan Foster's the name he's been going by while he's squired that pretty little Fernanda around the last couple of weeks. Betcha didn't even know he was in town."

His knees ached from perching so he sat beside her. "I gather that this feller John used to be your beau." He shook his head. "He's a fickle one, for sure, but he's also a bald-faced liar." He thumped his chest hard. "*I'm* the one what took that crazy Italian. Him trying to take credit for my work is plain wrong."

She looked confused for a moment.

"Take time to put the pieces together. He wanted you to think he'd stolen the Abetelli woman when it was George and me who took her all along. Well, me for the most part. George is a fool. He does what I tell him. I've always been the smart one in the family."

She glared daggers at him.

"That's right. He tricked you into coming here. He had no diva to release. No, my idiot brother's already gone and done that. I decided as long as you were already tied up, so to speak, that I would make it my business and profit from it before he can."

He eased to his feet. "That means I've gotta move you. Can't have old John coming back here and finding you haven't moved an inch. Don't worry, though. I've got a little nook to put you in, nice and tidy."

Hank bent and grabbed a portion of the tarp with

each hand and slid her across the length of the room. He eased the door open and paused. Something was going on. He heard noise. Footsteps. Men hollering out. He cursed under his breath. He knew in his bones that Gentleman John had already been compromised. Didn't the dolt have enough sense to run a quick con?

He shut the door and leaned down to the woman. "I've a hunch your beau's shenanigans have already been found out. Maybe by that Pinkerton fellow."

Hank returned her to where he'd found her, sliding her to the far corner. He tossed the tarp over her again. It pleased him how muffled her protests sounded.

"I better go join in on the hunt for you. Or rather, lead the search party as far away as I can." He laughed at his cleverness.

He wadded the tarp up more and slid the table in front of it. If anyone opened the door and gave a cursory glance, they might miss her altogether. He hoped that was the case. And if someone discovered her, then he'd have to cut his losses and leave Denver as fast as possible.

He grabbed the kerosene lantern from the table and slipped out the door. He wound his way down the corridors toward the voices so he could join in the action. He started to call out when he heard a loud shriek and stopped in his tracks.

He'd come face-to-face with Renata Abetelli.

The jig was up.

CHAPTER THIRTY-THREE

Rye wanted more than anything to be involved in the search for Emma but he knew if she were here, he trusted that Eddie would find her. He looked to the sullen John Fairburn and knew he would have to persuade Emma's kidnapper to talk. It wasn't something that required an audience.

He turned to Devinde. "I appreciate being able to use your office, Walt, but this might be the time for you and Miss Walker to step out."

"No." Adele met his eyes. Something glittered in them that frightened him. He'd been to hell and back through the war— but he'd never seen a look like this before.

"Darling, if—"

"No, Walt. I refuse to leave." She looked at Rye. "We'll sit on the sofa over there. I promise not to say a word."

Devinde look at him and shrugged. He led Adele away and seated her.

Before Rye could continue, Daniel Mitchell went to stand in front of Fairburn.

"I knew you were no gentleman from the time you showed up in Plainfield, claiming to be Louisa's cousin.

I tried to warn Dwight but Louisa already had her claws in him." The attorney tapped his cane on the floor for emphasis.

"You didn't know anything, old man. You're as blind and naive as Emma. Or should I say as Emma was. She surprised me when she fled." He smiled. "Just as I was ready to get cozy with her and her inheritance."

Mitchell glared down at Fairburn like an archangel. "I know the lengths you went to. To try and find her. I know you're the one who violated poor Molly and beat her to death, trying to find out where Emma was."

Rye's stomach turned sour. "Who was Molly?"

The attorney said, "She was Emma's maid. *And* her friend. Emma trusted Molly and was going to have the two of them leave Connecticut and get as far as possible from that one's clutches. Molly stayed behind to cover for Emma and pretend she was in her room, grieving over her father's death. Molly was to take a train into New York and meet up with Emma."

Mitchell turned to face Fairburn. "But she never showed up. This man— this monster— assaulted her and then murdered her. All to find out where Emma went." He took out his handkerchief and moped his brow.

Rye studied the man in the chair. If he'd done that to a servant girl, who knew what he would've done to Emma? His rage erupted. He balled his fists, ready to pummel Fairburn into revealing where Emma was, when Eddie came through the door with Hank Penland in tow.

Hank's eyes scanned the room and widened when he spied Fairburn. His knees folded and Eddie jerked him back to his feet. He looked at Rye, and Rye saw the last bit of hope fade from Hank's eyes.

Before he could ask, Hank began babbling.

"I'll tell you. I'll tell you everything. Everything you

want to know. That man is pure evil. I saw him. I saw him bring Miss Billings into the opera house. I could tell she didn't want to be with him. He was latched on to her like a leech on a leg."

Hank took a step toward Rye. "I followed them. Down to the basement. They went inside a room. I was scared of him, Rye. He's a big guy. But I listened at the door. I heard him say awful things to Miss Billings. I ran upstairs to get help but he was fast on my heels. I hid while he left and I saw him stop a boy and give him a note. I knew it had to be a ransom note. And then I—"

Rye grabbed Hank's shirt and yanked him close. "Where is she? I don't care about your longwinded story. *Where is Emma?*"

Hank cringed. "Don't beat me. I'll take you to her. I'll take you. You. No one else."

Rye turned to Eddie. An unspoken message passed between them. He knew his fellow Pinkerton would follow at a discreet distance.

He released his grip. "Then let's go to the basement." He grabbed Hank's arm and marched him from the office.

Renata and Ivar stood outside. The soprano stepped up, slapping Hank. She began jabbering in Italian, berating him. Larsen came and pulled her away.

"My love, calm down. You have a performance to prepare for."

Her jaw dropped. "Are you joking, Ivar? Surely, you don't think I can go on after what I've suffered through."

Her manager smiled. "I believe you can do anything, my darling. Conquer any fear. Any stage. You are the bravest woman I know. Think of the emotions you can draw upon from this experience. Yes, there was terror and helplessness— but you survived— and you will thrive," he promised.

Rye watched the soprano puff up as she thought about Larsen's words.

With conviction she said, "Of course I shall sing tonight. I have been gone too long from my beloved audience." She looked at her manager. "Come, Ivar. I will ready myself. I plan to give the performance of my life."

As they walked away, she looked back over her shoulder. "I trust that you will take care of this *bastardo*, Rye."

"Don't worry, Miss Abetelli. He'll be taken care of."

He watched them leave and stayed in place a minute before escorting Hank Penland to the basement.

"It's in good faith that I'm revealing where Miss Billings is, Rye. Possibly you might overlook it if I slip away while you free her?"

He glared at Hank but didn't give him a yes or no. With Eddie as his back-up, he knew Hank would be in police custody soon. Besides, he'd seen Renata's wrath on more than one occasion. He would not be the man to let her kidnapper escape. He did make a mental note to see if she might let poor George off the hook. He doubted George had even understood what the kidnapping was all about. Rye didn't think it fair to punish the man for being simple and following the lead of his domineering brother.

Hank pointed out the kerosene lanterns and Rye lit one. The two men descended the long staircase. Once they reached the basement, the carpenter led him down several twists and turns. He was about to ask Hank what game he thought he was playing when Hank stopped in front of a door.

"This is the one. This is where he took her. I'm sure, Rye."

He released his hold on Hank and opened the door. He held the lantern high as his eyes scanned the room. A prop table. A bulky tarp.

No Emma.

Hank took off running. Before he could follow and beat Hank to a pulp for leading him down a primrose path to nowhere, he heard a faint noise. His gut told him that somehow Emma *was* here. He rushed into the room, thoughts of chasing Hank gone in an instant.

He threw the flimsy table aside. It shattered against the wall. He dropped to his knees and rested the lantern on the ground. He pulled at the tarp, folding it back.

And there she was.

Anger fueled him— but he had to turn it off. He didn't want to frighten her. She'd already been through a traumatic experience. He didn't want to magnify it.

He righted the chair she was lashed to and reached around her head to untie the gag, his eyes never leaving hers. He pulled out the handkerchief wadded into a ball and thrust into her mouth.

"Rye," she said hoarsely. "I knew you'd come." Total faith in him shone in her eyes. Her belief in him almost shattered him into pieces.

He tried to reply but his voice broke. When words failed, action spoke volumes. He cradled her face with his hands and kissed her. Again. And again. Heated, passionate, searing kisses that spoke of the love he had for her. *This* is what he wanted. For the rest of his life.

"Rye?" she murmured against his mouth. He ended one last, deep kiss and lifted his lips from hers, his palms still framing her face, and emerged from the fog of passion.

"Do you think you could loosen these ropes? It's a little hard to breathe with these around me while we're doing all this kissing."

He caught the teasing light in her voice but felt awful just the same. He pulled his knife from his boot and sliced through the ropes that restrained her. She sucked in a quick breath when he loosened her hands. Tears formed in her eyes.

"It stings. Oh, it hurts," she moaned.

He gently rubbed her wrists, then her ankles. She trembled as he did so. Their eyes met, and he yanked her to her feet, smashing her against him. He lost count of their hot, heated kisses. His hand roamed her body, stroking, touching. She groaned.

He pulled away. "Am I hurting you?"

"No. I'm just so out of breath."

He gave her a crooked smile. "Good," and began kissing her all over again until he, too, was breathless.

He finally broke their embrace. "Emma Bradford, I want to make love with you all night." He watched her turn pink at his bold words. "That will have to wait. A lot of people upstairs are concerned about your whereabouts. Daniel Mitchell is worried sick."

Rye paused. "I'm sure you'll want to confront the man in custody— John Fairburn."

She whispered a mild curse, disgust wrinkling her nose. He laughed and kissed her hard. God, he would never get tired of kissing this woman.

"Let's go."

He wrapped his arm about her waist and led her back to Walt Devinde's office.

CHAPTER THIRTY-FOUR

*E*mma put a hand on Rye's arm as they reached Devinde's office. "Wait a moment." She took a deep breath, composing herself. She wanted to be in full charge of her emotions when she walked through that door. She nodded and Rye opened the door.

Daniel Mitchell broke out into a huge smile. She ran to him and fell into his arms. The attorney hugged her tightly. She smiled. He had always been so reserved and formal. She liked this new side of him.

Then Walt Devinde and Adele Walker were there, welcoming her, asking her if she was all right. Even Eddie McLeod gave her a quick wink as he stood watch over a handcuffed Hank Penland. She glared at the carpenter and he withered into a small lump.

"I'm fine," she assured everyone. "However, there is someone I need to speak with."

They stepped back and she moved to stand in front of John Fairburn. He was sitting in a chair, his arms restrained behind him.

Emma held nothing back.

"You thought to play me for a fool— but you were the fool, John Fairburn. You believed you could marry me and do away with me so you could steal my fortune and share it with Louisa."

She placed her hands on the chair's armrests and leaned close. "I outwitted you and I will outlast you. You will be brought to justice for my kidnapping, but more importantly, you will pay for Molly's death. I hope you rot in hell until the end of time."

She stepped back, giving him a cold look. She abhorred violence, but almost wished she could see him dangle from the hangman's noose.

John looked up at her and laughed. "I gambled and lost." He shrugged. "Nothing ventured, nothing gained. I hope you'll be happy with your papa's money...and my brother."

She froze. The room grew silent.

"What's he talking about, Emma?"

She turned to Rye, speechless.

"She's looking awfully guilty, Rye Callahan," John taunted. "Go ahead, Emma. Don't you want him to know the truth? That he's the spitting image of my da, with his frightening golden eyes and height and build."

John glanced to Rye. "You and I, we've got bastard half-brothers scattered throughout the Five Points, boyo. Gerald Fairburn was quite the ladies' man, with his swagger and magical Black Irish charm. He bewitched half the lasses in the Points and the other half were enamored of him."

Emma watched Rye's face as John's venomous words spilled out. Shock— then a dawning realization — crossed his features.

From the corner, a voice said, "Shut your mouth, John Fairburn! *You* are more like Gerald Fairburn than Rye could ever be."

Adele Walker rose from the sofa and walked straight to the prisoner. She stopped before him, her eyes narrowing as she studied him. She looked back at Rye and then focused on John again.

"*You* are the one with his silky charm and smooth words. You also have his despicable character. I should know— because I was one of those featherheaded fools who let him dazzle me with his good looks. I lacked the maturity and judgment at sixteen to be more discriminating. Gerald Fairburn sold me a worthless bill of goods."

Adele turned to Rye. "I gave birth to Gerald Fairburn's son, while he ran off to strike it rich in the Gold Rush. Senseless ninny that I was, I left that sweet babe and traipsed after my lover to California. I never found him— but I realized that my son needed something I could never give him. A stable home. So, I wrote to my brother and begged him and his wife to watch over my boy as their own."

Emma saw the tears glistening in Adele's eyes. Her voice softened. "That boy was you, Zachariah. I'm your mother, Adeline Callahan. Seamus was my brother."

ADELE WALKER WAS HIS MOTHER? John Fairburn was his half-brother?

Rye stood frozen to the spot.

"I know I don't deserve your forgiveness, Rye. I don't deserve any kind of relationship with you. But I hope you'll see it in your heart to give me a chance to get to know you."

He saw the desperate hope in her eyes. "You knew who I was when we first met. That night at the ball."

She nodded. "You're very like him. Physically. You have Black Irish written all over you. And your eyes. I'd never seen them in anyone other than Gerald Fairburn." Her mouth trembled. "When I heard your name, I had no doubt. I knew you were my son."

Hurt filled him. "You chose not to tell me. Why? It seems so...cruel."

John Fairburn burst out laughing. "Cruel? Ask your piece of sweet meat over there. *Her* not telling you. That's what I'd call cruel."

Rye turned in confusion and looked at Emma. Tears streamed down her cheeks.

"No, John. No. Please."

Fairburn snorted. "If this is the end of the ride for me, I'll dare to put the last nail in your coffin, Emma. I've lost everything." He gave her a malevolent smile. "And now, so have you."

Rye stared at Emma. Their gazes met. He knew from the look on her face that she had known.

She had known...and hadn't told him.

"Rye." His whispered name from her lips felt like a blasphemy. Honesty meant everything to him. Since that day when he returned home from the war and learned that his parents had lied to him his entire life, it changed him. Emma had broken that trust that he believed to be the bond between them.

"You lied to me."

"No! No, I didn't. I wouldn't lie to you, Rye. You know that. I... I... just couldn't tell you. Yes, I found out. I accidentally overheard Adele telling Walt that she was your mother. It was a private conversation between the two of them, behind closed doors, but it wasn't my story to tell."

"It was a lie of omission, Emma." Anger raced through his veins. "A lie, nonetheless." He threw a hand up to silence her before she could twist the truth anymore.

"This son of a bitch is my half-brother. This woman

abandoned me. I can live with that." He narrowed his eyes. "What I can't live with is the fact that the woman I love betrayed me."

Without a backward glance, he stormed from the room.

"Rye! Rye!" Emma called out in anguish. Her sobs sounded like a wounded animal in the moment before its death.

He kept on walking. He strode down the hall, looking neither left nor right. He didn't dare stop. For if he did, he would shatter into a thousand pieces. He reached the staircase and raced down it, not knowing where he was headed.

"Stop!"

He turned. Adele Walker— *his mother*— stood at the top, looking down at him. Although he longed to turn his back on her, something made him stay.

She lifted her skirts and hurried to the bottom until she stood on the last step, making them eye-level to one other.

"You don't owe me a blessed thing. I do owe you an apology. I was so young and mesmerized by Gerald Fairburn. It was as if he held a spell over me. He left and I gave birth to you, Rye. You were the most beautiful baby in the world. But I was headstrong and foolish and took off after Gerald, thinking I could change his mind. That we could be a family.

Tears brimmed in her eyes. "I realized that you already had a family. I entrusted you with my beloved brother. I knew he would treat you as a child of his own flesh. That you would have an older brother to get into mischief with. That you would be wanted and loved. Seamus had a steady job. Even if Gerald had come back and we'd settled down as a family, it never would have lasted. He was a shiftless scoundrel and didn't deserve a bonny lad like you."

"But—"

"No. The best decision I made thirty years ago was to stay out of your life. You see me now. I wasn't mother material then and that never changed." She put her hands on his shoulders and squeezed. "But that decision was the absolute hardest one of my life, Rye. Because I loved you. I loved those ten little fingers and ten sweet toes. Your smooth skin. That plump baby fat that I wanted to kiss every minute of every day."

She blinked back her tears. "I loved my sweet boy— enough to let him go."

A lump formed in his throat. His eyes stung. Rye wanted to say something but he hadn't a clue where to begin.

"I'm giving you some advice. Not motherly advice. That would be wrong." She placed her palm tenderly against his cheek. "Don't cut off your nose to spite your face. You said you love Emma. Don't be miserable for the rest of your life by walking away from the woman you love."

His jaw tightened as much as his resolve. "She lied to me. I can't forgive that. I won't."

"You can. If you choose to. Emma overheard me talking with Walt. He asked me to marry him. I didn't want any secrets between us so I told him about you. I've never shared that with another soul. I've carried that heartbreak around for three decades. Your Emma was being respectful to me when she didn't betray the confidence that I'd shared in private with the man I've come to love.

"I know it had to be hard on her but she was right to want *me* to be the one to tell you. It was my place. I was wrong not to have done so. Please, don't take your anger and frustration with me out on her. You have a chance at love, Rye. To build a life with a good woman. Don't let your stubborn pride keep you from her.

Choose love, Rye. *Choose love.* You'll never regret that choice."

Adele dropped her hand and turned. She went back up the grand staircase.

He stood, his thoughts swirling, as if he'd been swimming far from shore and suddenly yanked underwater by a hidden undertow that swept him out to sea.

"You the Pinkerton?"

He turned and saw two Denver policemen had entered the lobby and stopped just feet from him. He had to banish the turmoil raging within him. He was a Pinkerton— and had a job to complete. Quickly, he collected his thoughts, shutting the door to his emotions in order to focus on the business at hand.

"Yes. I'm Rye Callahan. My fellow agent, Eddie McLeod, has two men in custody upstairs. Hank Penland, who kidnapped Renata Abetelli, and John Fairburn, who abducted Emma Bradford." He paused. "Fairburn's also wanted for questioning for a murder back in Connecticut."

The broader of the two said, "We've got a Black Maria out front to transport them to headquarters. We'll need you and Mr. McLeod at the station to give your statements. And the two ladies, of course, if they're up to speaking with us."

"Miss Bradford is upstairs and can accompany you now. Miss Abetelli has insisted that she sing at tonight's performance, but I can bring her to the station tomorrow morning if that's convenient."

The taller policeman whistled low. "Performing after being kidnapped? That's incredible."

"Several witnesses are also upstairs and can contribute to building your cases against Penland and Fairburn. They're all in Walt Devinde's office. I'm sure Mr. Devinde will offer his carriage to see that everyone is brought to police headquarters in a timely fashion. I'll meet you there."

Rye turned away from the men and hurried through the doors.

CHAPTER THIRTY-FIVE

*E*mma pushed away the breakfast tray, her food cold and untouched. She hadn't been brave enough to attend the morning meal downstairs, fearing she would run into Rye and crumple like a sodden heap into the carpet.

As she finished dressing, fresh tears spilled down her cheeks. She didn't know she had any tears left in her after last night, which had been interminable. The police arrived and arrested John and Hank Penland, taking them into custody. The group gathered in Devinde's office had followed the paddy wagon to police headquarters, where she caught a last glimpse of John Fairburn and overheard him blaming Louisa for everything that had occurred, implicating her in his crimes. The arrogant look had finally worn off his face, replaced by one of utter despair.

Much like what she now wore on hers.

Daniel Mitchell never left her side in the hours that followed, serving both as trusted friend and counsel as she was interviewed by a group of Denver police detectives. The attorney also filled in the blanks regarding Molly's death in Connecticut and the officer in command promised they would be in touch with the Plainfield authorities. Either way, John Fairburn would be permanently gone from her life.

As would Rye.

She caught sight of him as they left the interview room. Walt and Adele had already completed their statements and waited for her. As Adele enfolded Emma in her arms, Emma looked across the room and saw Rye standing beside a door. Cold fury shone in his eyes as he took her in before he turned away as Eddie McLeod joined him. They walked down a hallway and disappeared from her sight. Her heart wrenched as if an iron vise had latched on to it, turning it cruelly. She dissolved into tears, which continued throughout the carriage ride home.

Adele sat with her as she tried to fall asleep. Emma appreciated the effort to comfort her but finally begged to be left alone. She wallowed in misery until she fell into a restless sleep.

Now she needed to make some changes in her life.

A knocked sounded on her door. Before she could answer, Bettina entered. Emma could tell by the look on her friend's face that someone had filled her in on the events of last night.

A new wave of tears began as Bettina rushed to her. She fell into Bettina's arms and cried for all she had lost. More than anything, she could hear Rye's final words that continually echoed in her mind.

"I can't live with the fact that the woman I love betrayed me."

Rye loved her. *Had* loved her. And she'd foolishly squandered his love. His face, hard as granite as he'd ground out those last words, shouted that there would be no second chances— no tomorrows— for them. Emma knew how he valued honesty. She'd hurt him deeply by keeping the truth about his origins from him.

She pulled away from Bettina, who brought a hand

to her face in order to brush away a wayward curl. The flash of a diamond engagement ring caught Emma's eye. It was like being stabbed directly in her heart. She wanted to wallow in her unhappiness but chose not to. She couldn't dampen Bettina's spirits.

"I'm leaving Denver," she announced.

"What? You can't go, Emma. I won't let you. I need you. Papa's leaving today for Chicago. There's so much to do, so much planning for the wedding. I need your help. I can't do it without you."

She brushed the tears from her cheeks and strengthened her resolve. "I have to go, Bettina. I am as unhappy as a soul will ever be. I don't want my misery to rain upon your happiness."

Taking her friend's hand, she added, "I am happy for you, dearest. Tad is a wonderful man and so in love with you."

"But...you're like the sister I never had, Emma. I don't want to be married unless you stand up with me."

She sighed. "Then I promise I'll return for the ceremony."

Bettina squealed and hugged her.

"I must leave for now, though. Can you understand that? My heart has shattered. I need time for it to heal. I can't do that in Denver, not with Rye living in this household, having to see him here or at the opera house. I have to get away.

"But I promise to be back for your wedding." She squeezed Bettina's hands. "I wouldn't miss it for the world."

They chatted for a few minutes about Tad's proposal and possible wedding venues and dates and then Emma excused herself.

"I must see your father."

She stepped into the hallway and walked with trepidation. She told herself even if she did run into Rye, it wouldn't make any difference. He'd washed his hands of her. Nothing she could say would ever bring him back to her. She ventured down the staircase and went quickly to Walt Devinde's study and knocked.

"Come."

She entered, closing the door behind her. Facing him, she said, "I cannot thank you enough. For so many things. For taking me in and making me feel a part of your family. For giving me the opportunity to go on stage and perform. But if I don't get away, I'll lose the grasp I have on my sanity. I'm sure you understand why."

He came from behind his desk and placed his hands on her shoulders.

"You are like a daughter to me, Emma. You always shall be. And you will always have a place waiting here for you in Denver." He placed a chaste kiss on her forehead. "I'm leaving for Chicago this afternoon. If you have need of an escort, I'd be happy if you accompanied me there."

"I may do that. I need to send a note to Mr. Mitchell to let him know of my plans to leave immediately. We may go as far as Chicago with you. After that, I'm not sure where I'll go."

~

RYE WENT UP THE STAIRS, wondering where Renata might be. He'd informed her when she arrived home after last night's performance that he would take her to the police station at ten this morning in order for her to give her statement regarding her kidnapping. The diva readily agreed, happy to do whatever it took to see Hank Penland behind bars.

Renata hadn't made an appearance at breakfast. That didn't surprise him since she often took a tray in her room. As usual, she ran late. He decided to go to her room to remind her of their appointment.

He raised a hand to knock on her door but it opened before he could. Rozalia Cattaneo, her arms full of rumpled bedding, gave him a quizzical look.

"I'm looking for Miss Abetelli."

"She go. No here." The dresser brushed past him and went down the hall toward the servants' staircase. He assumed she had laundry to do.

Rye wondered where the diva could be and returned downstairs. He glanced out the French doors he passed and saw George Penland on his knees, working in the garden. He turned and held a plant up and seemed to be explaining something.

To Renata.

Rye started to rush out and then stopped in his tracks. The soprano wore a look he'd never seen on her face. He caught a softness about her mouth, a wistfulness as Renata cocked her head, nodding as George earnestly spoke to her.

He opened the door and slipped outside. George looked to Renata and said something else before he stood and went to a wheelbarrow. He pushed it in the opposite direction. The Italian watched him as he rounded a corner and slipped from view.

And smiled.

She stood and saw Rye watching her. He hurried to her.

"I'm so sorry, Miss Abetelli. In all of the excitement last night, it seems we all forgot about George Penland." He shook his head. "I suppose he's just gone about his business. I'll have Eddie round him up and bring him downtown. You won't have to see or speak to him again. Are you ready for—"

"I had a sister. Much like George. So simple. So kind. So trusting."

Renata sighed. "She was my shadow. I used to run all over her. Made her dance to my tune. She waited on me, hand and foot. Did everything for me. Her name was Domenica. It means *belongs to the Lord*. I'm afraid I was the one who lorded over her. And then I lost her."

The opera singer grew pensive. "I regret it. So much of what I said and did. I can never take it back." She brought her hands to her temples, letting her fingers rub them as she closed her eyes. "I cannot do this. To this man. This simple soul who only wants to go home to *sua madre*. I must be the better person. I must forgive him. He didn't know he made such a mistake. Do not let Mr. McLeod take him to the police. He shouldn't be punished. I forgive him."

She opened her eyes and stared at him intently. "Your heart has hardened, Rye Callahan. You are at a crossroads. Don't make a mistake that will ruin the rest of your life— and that of others you love."

He followed Renata in from the garden, astonished at the change in her, never dreaming she had an ounce of forgiveness in her volatile nature. As he closed the door behind them, he saw Emma step out from Devinde's study, heartbreak frozen on her angelic features. She stopped and looked at him with such longing that his gut twisted as if rammed with a sledgehammer.

Then she turned and raced up the stairs without a backward glance.

CHAPTER THIRTY-SIX

Rye sat in the Devinde carriage with Renata as they returned from police headquarters. The diva had basked in the numerous compliments tossed her way by the admiring males who'd fawned over her throughout the interview. She'd also raged against the treatment she had endured at Hank Penland's hands during the days she went missing.

Renata never mentioned a word about George's role in the fiasco.

He glanced over at Eddie. The detective shrugged nonchalantly as they arrived back at the Devinde mansion. Rye was sure they would discuss Renata's change of heart outside her presence. The diva's about-face regarding George pleased him. He'd dreaded seeing George taken into custody and was certain the gardener wouldn't understand the reason why. Renata's reversal came as an unexpected but pleasant surprise.

The coachman stopped the vehicle directly at the front entrance and opened the door. Eddie jumped down and both men offered a hand to aid Renata's exit from the carriage. She seemed back to her usual selfish ways, not thanking either one as she made her way inside the mansion.

As Rye exited the carriage, Jamey asked, "Do you have a minute, sir? Both of you, actually?"

He nodded. "What's on your mind, Jamey?"

The driver said, "Well, I've given a lot of thought as to what you said, Mr. Callahan. I would like to apply to be a Pinkerton."

"I'm glad you've made up your mind, Jamey. I think you'll make an excellent agent. You're physically fit. Curious. Smart. You know you've got my blessing, as well as my recommendation. I'll write something today and send it off to The Eye."

"I can do the same, Jamey," Eddie promised. "It never hurts to have more than one agent on your side."

Jamey smiled as he enthusiastically pumped each of their hands in turn. "I've a bit saved. I'll need to turn in my resignation to Mr. Devinde, then I can pack my bags and make my way straight to New York." He thought a moment. "I believe I'll tell him now, as I take him and Miss Bradford to the station to make their train to Chicago." He smiled broadly. "I can't thank you enough, Mr. Callahan. Mr. McLeod. And who knows? We might work together on a case someday. After my training and all."

Rye kept a smile pasted on his face, even as hearing that Emma would soon be on a train leaving Denver shook him to his core. Like a candle suddenly extinguished, all his anger died. Emptiness replaced it. It seemed as if the very life had been sucked from him.

He had a choice to make.

He could let Emma walk out of his life and never look back. Cable New York for his next assignment once he finished up here. Go from case to case, year after year, with a heart that would grow as cold as stone over time.

Or he could swallow his pride and make a life with the most remarkable woman he had ever met.

If Renata Abetelli could forgive George, he was damned sure he should forgive Emma. Adele was right — the decision was his. Rye's heart told him what it should be.

He raced to the front door and threw it open. Luggage sat grouped next to the stairs. Inside the foyer, Walt embraced Adele. Rye looked into the eyes of the woman who'd given life to him. She might not have raised him— but her words would keep him from a wasted life. She nodded her encouragement to him.

Emma stood to the side, her back to him as she said goodbye to Renata. The diva wore a genuine smile on her face.

As he moved toward them, he heard, "You must come see me in Italy. Or France. Or Germany. Wherever I am, Emma, you are welcome. You can sing there, I know you can. You have the talent, *mia dolce amico.*"

"Thank you, Renata. I'm afraid I'm too broken. I don't think I'll ever sing again."

Rye winced at her words, knowing how deeply he'd hurt her. He reached for her hand and entwined his fingers with hers.

She turned, shock registering on her face. "Rye?"

Wordless, he enfolded her in his arms. He hungrily took her mouth with his, oblivious to those present. He had to show her as much as give her the words. He kissed her with all the longing and passion that he'd kept pent up for far too long. His lips claimed her. All was right in his world when this woman was in his arms.

She melted against him and Rye knew he was forgiven. He broke the kiss, breathing heavily.

"I can be a hard-headed fool, Emma. I'm not sure you want to be saddled with me for the rest of your life but I'm not giving you a choice in the matter."

The corners of her mouth turned up. "You're not?"

"You can choose where we go. Where we live. What we do. How many children we have. But you have to choose me, Emma. Because I choose you. I love you. I have since the first moment I saw you sitting in that train station. You were reading and you smiled at something on the page. I wanted to kiss you from that moment on."

Tears stung his eyes. "I'll always want to kiss you, Emma. And love you. Now and forever. You hold my heart in your hands, my love. Say you'll be mine."

A smile lit up her beautiful, angelic face. "For me, Rye, there's no choice at all. It's you. It's always been you." She pulled him down until his lips met hers.

It would be a good life. Because they would be together.

ALSO BY ALEXA ASTON

The Hollywood Name Game
Hollywood Heartbreaker
Hollywood Flirt
Hollywood Player
Hollywood Double
Hollywood Enigma

Lawmen of the West
Runaway Hearts
Blind Faith
Love and the Lawman
Ballad Beauty

DUKES OF DISTINCTION:
Duke of Renown
Duke of Charm
Duke of Disrepute
Duke of Arrogance
Duke of Honor

MEDIEVAL RUNAWAY WIVES:
Song of the Heart
A Promise of Tomorrow
Destined for Love

SOLDIERS AND SOULMATES:
To Heal an Earl

To Tame a Rogue
To Trust a Duke
To Save a Love
To Win a Widow

THE ST. CLAIRS:
Devoted to the Duke
Midnight with the Marquess
Embracing the Earl
Defending the Duke
Suddenly a St. Clair

THE KING'S COUSINS:
God of the Seas
The Pawn
The Heir
The Bastard

THE KNIGHTS OF HONOR:
Rise of de Wolfe
Word of Honor
Marked by Honor
Code of Honor
Journey to Honor
Heart of Honor
Bold in Honor
Love and Honor
Gift of Honor
Path to Honor
Return to Honor
Season of Honor

NOVELLAS:

Diana

Derek

Thea

The Lyon's Lady Love

ABOUT THE AUTHOR

A native Texan and former history teacher, award-winning and internationally bestselling author Alexa Aston lives with her husband in a Dallas suburb, where she eats her fair share of dark chocolate and plots out stories while she walks every morning. She enjoys travel, sports, and binge-watching—and never misses an episode of *Survivor*.

Alexa brings her characters to life in steamy historicals, contemporary romances, and romantic suspense novels that resonate with passion, intensity, and heart.

KEEP UP WITH ALEXA
Visit her website
Newsletter Sign-Up

MORE WAYS TO CONNECT WITH ALEXA